Stanley Morgan is fast becoming one of the world's bestselling authors. His string of successful Russ Tobin adventures have been compared to the invincible 007 and named him the 'un-put-downable' author.

The sexploits of this randy-man-about-town, Russ Tobin, have conquered the hearts of millions of readers throughout the world. Every story as amusing, amorous, outrageous and bestselling as the last.

Stanley M
lives in Ir
his four c

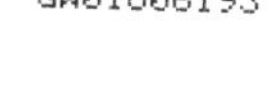

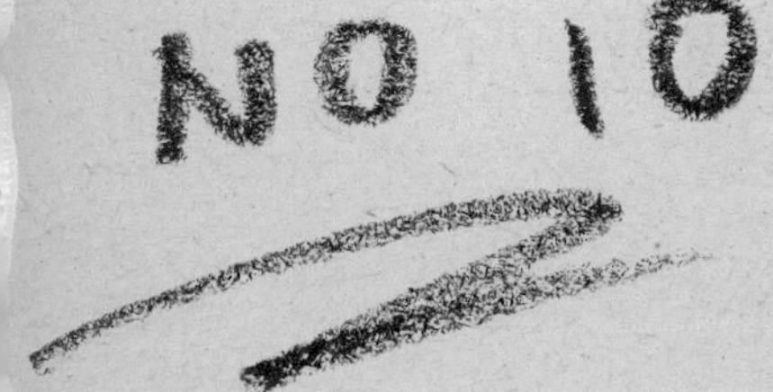

Stanley Morgan

Tobin in Tahiti

Futura Publications Limited
A Futura Book

A Futura Book

First published in Great Britain in 1976
by Futura Publications Limited

ISBN 0 8600 7284 3
Printed in Great Britain by
Richard Clay (The Chaucer Press) Ltd
Bungay, Suffolk

Futura Publications Limited
110 Warner Road, London SE5

CHAPTER ONE

I SURFACED in some confusion, wondering where the music was coming from and why it sounded so close and clear, as though the tape was playing right inside my head, then realized I'd fallen asleep with my earphones on and that the skipper must have just activated the in-flight entertainment programme.

'Ugh.'

I removed the phones, irritated by James Last's monotonous, piercing trumpet, and massaged my earholes, finding them quite raw. Hardly surprising after six hours continual listening.

'Mornin' . . .'

The rumbled mumble emanated from a mountain of crumpled, blond manhood on my left, the travel-bashed remains of once-handsome Buzz Malone, Australian tennis pro and dedicated bird chaser. I only hoped he wasn't feeling as blasted as he looked.

'*Good* morning, Buzz, and how are *you* this excruciatingly beautiful Pacific morning?'

He winced agonizedly and buried his face in his pillow. 'Tobin, shut up . . .'

'Now that's a fine way to start a new day . . .'

'How many bottles did we annihilate last night?'

'Three hundred and twenty-six.'

He groaned. 'Jeezus, I believe you. How come you're not hung over?'

'You're kidding. Even my nails hurt.'

He came out of the pillow, tasting his tongue and pulling a face of patent disenchantment, eyes like blood-streaked marbles and a complexion vaguely reminiscent of an undercooked bread pudding. Then he grinned, dispersing the illusion. 'A lovely night, though, hm?'

I returned the grin. 'Terrific.'

'What time is it?'

I consulted my watch. 'Nine.'

'Los Angeles time or Tahiti time?'

'L.A.'

'Christ, still four hours to go.'

He roused himself and looked about, across and down the endless length of the cavernous Qantas 747, finding succour, as did I, in the coming alive of its three hundred inmates. At last the long, dark night was over and the new, exciting day had begun. The thrill of expectation rippled through me.

'I'm going to hit the lav before the rush begins,' he announced, getting up. 'If I don't get my teeth brushed in the next two minutes I'll go berserk.'

'I'm ahead of you.'

I swung out into the aisle and headed towards the rear, amusing myself with the sights of yawning, stretching, scratching humanity in the intervening seats, victims of time-lag and jet-cramp, the penalties for speed.

Here, while we perform our private ablutions, a short pause for personal identification.

My name is Tobin – Russ Tobin, six foot tall, brown hair, blue/red eyes and a splitting headache. And the purpose of my imminent visit to Tahiti? Pleasure. Pure and, I hope, abundant, but for three days only. Then it's on to Sydney, Buzz's home town, and a spell of work to recharge the badly depleted Tobin coffers.

How I met up with this good-hearted, happy-go-likable nut has already been told, so suffice it to say here that it happened in New York, continued in Toronto and Las Vegas, and looks like continuing unabated for quite a while yet. And I am more than happy with the arrangement.

Travelling the world, working at odd jobs to keep body and soul intact, it's a lot more fun having a pal like Buzz along to share whatever comes. How much more poignant the sight of a good-looking girl when you can nudge a mate's arm and mutter, 'Cor, getta lodda that'. It's so much more rewarding than talking to yourself.

Locking the door of the claustrophobic loo, I stripped to the waist and had a thorough sluice, a miracle of achievement in a zinc bowl the size of a breakfast cup, then scrubbed the residue of six hours alcoholic self-indulgence from my teeth, combed my hair, climbed back into my crumpled clothes and inspected the result in the mirror. Yerk . . . but not so yerk as before.

Opening the door I came face to face with Buzz and hardly recognized him. He looked almost human.

'By God, that feels better,' he said, smacking his tongue. 'Now all I need is twelve cups of steaming coffee and a fag and I'll be ready for anything.'

We resumed our seats just in time for breakfast and I could tell that Buzz was operating normally by the way he ogled our airstew, a big, suntanned blonde with a blouseful of breasts men go to war for.

'Good morning,' grinned Buzz, his charm factor topping two hundred, hangover forgotten.

'Good morning, Mister Malone,' she smiled, sneakily, leaning across me to place a tray on his table and blinding me with desire in the process.

Buzz did a surprised double-take. 'You . . . you know my name?'

'Of course. You know Charlie Dwyer, I believe?'

Buzz laughed, still in shock. 'Charlie, yes, sure . . . I play with him a lot.'

She fed me with a tray and stood up, grinning down at Buzz. 'He's my brother.'

'Well, I'll be . . .'

'He has a photograph of the two of you in Brisbane last summer.'

'Sure, I remember. Well, I'll be . . .'

'Fame at last,' I muttered, but I don't think he heard. He was locked in that state of slavering concentration achieved by a dog when confronted by a fresh-cooked bone.

'And your name is . . .' his eyes momentarily left her left breast and flicked to the name badge pinned a little above it, '. . . Carol. Well, what a coincidence.'

'Are you returning to Sydney now?' she asked him.

'Yes, but we're stopping over in Tahiti for a night . . . a day or two.'

'Another coincidence,' she smiled. 'How're your breakfasts . . . anything else I can get you?'

'Mine's fine,' I said, but nobody was listening.

'In what way another coincidence?' pleaded Buzz.

She turned away, grinning. 'Anything else you need – just ring.'

Buzz sat nonplussed, then let out in an excited gasp. '*By* the cringe . . . !'

'Goodbye, Buzz.'

'Mate, did you . . . would you . . .'

'I certainly would. Malone, remind me to take up pro tennis some time, will you.' I shook my head disbelievingly. 'Would you mind telling me what it is about bashing balls over a net that drives 'em cuckoo?'

'The tanned animal muscularity of it . . . the brute force . . . the masterful power. It reaches out to their primeval desire to be beaten, subjugated, dragged off by the hair to the nearest cave for a good . . .'

'And thank you, Doctor Malone.'

'Tee hee,' he chuckled, slapping his great tanned animal hands together and slopping his coffee all over the tray. 'Russell, if that was not a thinly-veiled invitation to partake of carnal pleasure, I am Lew Hoad's mother-in-law. Oh, *boy*, oh, boy, what a start to the festivities. Hey . . .' his grin vanished, '. . . that *was* what she meant, wasn't it – that she was stopping over in Tahiti too?'

'Can I read the bird's mind? You'll have to ask her yourself.'

'I will, I will. Hey . . . you're not narked, are you . . . I mean, that I . . .'

'Cut to the quick,' I sniffed, pretending pique. 'Huh, fine thing . . . we haven't even landed and here you are already planning to leave me stranded solo on a strange island.'

His face was a study of indecision, perplexity. 'Aw, mate,' he slumped, 'yeh, you're right.'

I laughed. 'Yuh daft bugger, I'm only kidding. Go on, get in there, she's terrific. You can't pass up an opportunity like that. I tell you, if the situation was reversed, I'd be in that galley by now, making sure of her before somebody else sneaks in.'

A grin split his face. 'You're sure, now . . . I mean, you could end up on your tod.'

'You must be joking. Tobin in Tahiti on his own? Maybe for the first half hour but not a minute more. Go on, get moving.'

'Maybe she's got a pal!'

I shrugged. 'So – lovely. But don't worry about it – or me.

But, er, if she has, don't go committing me until you've inspected the goods, hm? I mean, not *all* the stews on board are raving beauties.'

He fingered the side of his nose. 'Leave it to Malone. I wouldn't land you with anything I wouldn't make a try for myself.'

'That's hardly reassuring, Malone. When the urge is upon you, the damned *cat* would do well to keep out of your way.'

'We-e-ll, some of us are blessed with a more potent libido than others . . .'

'You mean, some of us are just plain bloody randy. Go on, swallow your coffee and get down there. I see a tall, handsome bloke mooching around, as though he's waiting for her to come out . . .'

'The hell you do!' He flung the coffee into his mouth and quickly spat it back into the cup. 'Jeezus, that's scalding!'

'Oh, you and your hot lips.'

'Here, let me out . . . quick!'

'It's all right, he only wanted a glass of water. He's going back to his seat.'

'Bastard.'

I slipped out into the aisle and let him through, then sat down again. 'Best of luck, mate . . . happy landings.'

'Thanks. I'll see what I can find you . . . maybe a steward if I can't land a bird?'

I tutted and wiggled my lips. 'Cheeky.'

And then, with a bracing of his broad shoulders and a clearing of thc throat, he was gone, striding down the long aisle with a determination that would've frightened a Soho hooker.

I didn't see him again until we were coming in to land at Tahiti.

Not long after Buzz had departed, an announcement came over the tannoy that it was movie time, that splendid time-consuming innovation now available on most long distance jet flights. I welcomed it. Our departure from Las Vegas to Los Angeles had been so precipitate, to say nothing of downright panicky, that I hadn't given reading matter a thought, and with no one to talk to time was already beginning to drag heavily. So now a two-hour film would fill the bill nicely. For those of you who haven't experienced in-flight movies, the system is this: two screens are lowered from the roof of the cabin, one forward, one at the rear, and two different films are projected simultaneously, the sound being received by the viewer through earphones plugged into an outlet in the arm of each seat. The object of two movies will be obvious – they provide a choice. Being newly-released films the odds are fairly good that most passengers will not have seen both, but in the event that they have seen both – or wish to see neither – they simply refrain from listening in and are free to read, sleep, talk or listen to music on another channel. All very civilized.

However, the point I'm getting to is that with a choice of two films there is usually a bit of seat-changing among the passengers just prior to the start. Those, in this case, who had seen the latest Bond film could move forward and enjoy the latest Disney adventure, swapping seats with those up front who abhor Disney violence and enjoy a good lavish giggle.

Fine. So all this to-ing and fro-ing took place and when everyone had got themselves sorted out, all the window blinds were then drawn, plunging the cabin into a nice murky gloom.

The film began, the projected beam dispelling some of the darkness and leaving just enough light to enable passengers to find the loo in relative comfort.

Up came the titles. I'd settled back, relishing the prospect of seeing Bond in action again, when a figure standing in the aisle, to the left of the screen, distracted my attention, the sight of her instantly removing all thoughts of Bond's romantic conquests from my mind and replacing them with similar thoughts of my own.

Even in that uncertain light there was no mistaking her charms. She was gorgeous, a living doll, her summery, floral cotton dress, belted at the waist, revealing a full-breasted, perfectly undulating body and a breathtaking pair of suntanned legs. The face was pert, knowing, her mouth a miracle. Bright copper hair surrounded it in a cap of careless waves.

She stood there surveying the seating situation, quite at ease, almost cheeky, with an amused smile, as though she was contemplating something outrageous.

My heart tripped into triple time. I had to talk to her . . . sit by her. It was love at first sight. I was crazy about her. I came forward in my seat, stared at her, willing her to look at me.

Dammit, there were two empty seats right there next to me. She could have my seat . . . all three – I'd sit in the aisle if necessary. Cooee . . . hey, miss . . . angel face . . . over here . . . look at me . . . for Pete's sake look this way!

She looked. And passed on.

My heart sank.

Her eyes swept back . . . caught me up, held me. My heart exploded. Her eyes went to the two adjoining empty seats then quickly returned to me, sizing me up. For a small, pregnant eternity we were lost in each other's searching gaze while she fed me into her computer, ran me through, analysed all that was to be seen and awaited the result.

Its arrival was heralded by the smallest curving of her adorable mouth . . . and when she took her first step towards me I almost died of ecstasy.

As she drew close I stood up, forgetting I still had the earphones on and nearly lost my ears as the phones ripped off. It was an opening gambit of unprecedented success and one I shall use frequently from now on. She shrieked with laughter, then quickly stifled it with a hand over her mouth.

'Oh, I'm sorry . . . I shouldn't have laughed.'

'My pleasure,' I winced, rubbing my ears.

'Are they both free?' She indicated the seats.

'As air, be my guest. Here, you take the aisle seat, it's more comfortable.'

'Oh, no . . .'

'I insist.'

I did, too. That way I could watch her as well as the screen.

'Well, that's very nice . . .'

'No, it's very selfish. This way I can look at you as well as the screen.'

She looked at me, her smile undiminished, then acknowledged the candour with a nod. 'Honest . . . a trifle hasty, but honest.'

'You won't run away?'

'Not yet,' she laughed and took her seat.

I sat down next to her, the drift of her perfume making mincemeat of my mind.

'Have you . . . seen the latest Bond film?' I croaked.

She glanced up at the screen. 'Oh, is that what's showing, I didn't know. I just can't stand Disney.'

'As an American isn't that tantamount to treason?'

She laughed, delightedly it seemed. 'You have a good ear. My father would be appalled. With the schooling he's paid for you're hardly supposed to be able to tell.'

'Swiss finishing school?'

'Hey, you're good! What else do you know about me?'

'That you're extremely lovely . . . and I'm desperately in love with you.'

She abandoned all pretence of looking at the screen and turned to me, really looking at me, covering my face with a thoughtful appraisal. 'Who are you?'

'Russ Tobin. Who are you?'

'I'm Maggie . . . Maggie Kennedy . . .'

'Of . . . *the* Kennedy family?'

She grinned and shook her head. 'No, I'm afraid not. I was only born with a *silver* spoon in my mouth, not a platignum one. Are you Englsih?'

'Yup.'

Her big green eyes widened. 'Really?'

'Yes,' I laughed. 'Why the surprise?'

'Oh . . . nothing.' She turned momentarily back to the screen, as though needing time to digest the information, then spun round again. 'Where are you going?'

'Sydney.'

'Oh.'

My God, she was disappointed!

'But we're staying in Tahiti for a day or two . . . just a quick couple of . . .'

'We?' She glanced towards the third empty seat. 'Oh, you mean . . .'

'No. I'm travelling with a pal . . . he's up front seducing our airstew.'

She exploded a laugh. 'Heavens, what have I walked into! Well well . . .'

'And how about you? Who are you travelling with?'

She gave a little shrug. 'The one I always travel with . . . me.'

'And where to this time?'

A small pause. 'Tahiti.'

'On . . . vacation?'

'Mm, sort of. I call it "finishing my education" . . . the way *I* want to finish it – by seeing everything first hand.'

'The only way.'

'You approve!'

'Indubitably. I'm doing much the same thing – working my way around the world. I mean, I'm not suggesting you're working your way around . . .'

She laughed. 'No, I'm not. I'm just going around . . . in any direction that takes my fancy.'

'You're a lucky girl.'

'Yes, I am. So . . . you're English, hm?'

'Does it mean that much to you?'

'Yes.'

'Why?'

'I won't tell you.'

'Oh.'

'Not yet anyway.'

My heart did another backflip. 'You mean you may . . . later.'

'I might.'

'How much later?'

Her eyes crinkled in a teasing smile. 'Shall we watch the film?'

'If we must. Here . . . you can use Buzz's earphones.'

'Is Buzz your pal? What nationality is he?'

'Australian.'

'Oh.'

The revelation seemed to hold no excitement for her.

I plugged in her phones and handed them to her. She slipped them on and relaxed back in her chair, and gazed up at the screen.

I took my time fixing my own phones on, so I could have a good look at her. She was wonderful, so appealing it was all I could do to stop myself grabbing her. Her thin cotton dress hid nothing, indeed emphasized everything – the swell of her breasts, the flat plane of her stomach and the slender stretch of her partly opened thighs. Boy, I was in a mess.

Deafened by my heartbeat, I lay back in my seat and tried to concentrate on the film but it was impossible. Her closeness, her flesh, the excitement of her perfume washed over me, paralysed me, imbued me with a boldness I couldn't help.

'Maggie . . .' I croaked.

She turned her head and looked at me, very close, far too close, and knowing, by the expression in her eyes, precisely what she was doing to me.

'Yes?' she asked softly.

'I . . .' I couldn't get it out.

She laughed, knowing. 'What is it?'

'You . . . you've really knocked me for six, you know that?'

She nodded. 'I know it.'

'Can this be happening?'

'Don't you want it to be happening?'

'Of course. It's just that . . . it's all too good to be true. A man sitting alone on a plane has fantasies that an extravagantly beautiful girl will sit down beside him and say and do the things you're saying and doing . . .'

'Then you're in luck, aren't you?'

I shook my head. 'But it only happens in fantasies.'

She shrugged. 'Obviously not.'

'Yes, I know, but . . .'

'Does it frighten you?'

'*Frighten* me? I'm nearly sick with excitement.'

She laughed and turned back to the screen. 'Good.'

'Oh, my God . . . Maggie, talk to me.'

She turned again, sliding the phones from her head. 'All right.' Her face was so close, her eyes so warm, her mouth so excruciatingly tempting. My eyes flew to it and it parted in a wide smile. 'You want to kiss me, hm?'

I groaned miserably. 'Yes.'

'I'm very glad. But not here.'

'No. Can you feel my heart rocking the plane? Any minute now the captain will come rushing back and throw me off for endangering the flight.'

'I think you're awfully cute.'

'And I think I'm going out of my mind. How can it happen this quickly?'

'Why question it – it's happening.'

'But how can you like *me* this quickly? I mean, you're different. You're the sort of girl men fall head over heels for at two thousand yards!'

She chuckled sexily and wrinkled her nose. 'You're awfully good for a girl's ego. But you really do underestimate yourself. Don't you think girls fall head over heels for men at two thousand yards? Take a look around the cabin. You're by far the most dishy thing back here.'

'I am?'

'You are and you know it. What's worrying you is the speed with which we've got to like each other – right? Would it have been OK if it had happened over a period of a day or two, say in a hotel? . . . if we'd met in a group, danced, had a few drinks, talked? Would that have surprised you?'

'No, but I'd be just as sick with excitement. Heck, I'm not *worrying*, Maggie, I'm just overwhelmed.'

'Blame it on Women's Lib.,' she grinned. 'Or thank them for it, whichever. I'm a free soul. I don't see why men should always make the running or be called upon by tradition to make the running. I'm me. Call me fast, call me anything, but it's the way I choose to operate. Hell, we haven't got *time* to go the long traditional route. You've got two days – right? I've got one, then I'm off to Hawaii. I like what I saw and I'd like to spend that day in Tahiti with you. If you can't or won't, too bad. But if you can and will . . . well, I believe it could be quite a day.'

I released my pent-up breath. 'Wow! Now I know I'm dreaming.'

'What sort of an answer is that?' she laughed.

'An affirmative one. Maggie, I would be delighted and honoured to spend your day with you . . . and thank you very much for it.'

'Delighted and honoured,' she smiled. 'How perfectly English. I believe we're going to have a *lovely* day.'

'So do I,' I said, noticing she'd so far made no mention of the night. This train of thought led me to ask, 'Where are you staying in Tahiti? Have you been before?'

'Lots of times, I adore it. It's perfect. Yes, I've booked a room in the Hotel Tahiti. Haven't you and your friend booked in yet?'

'No, we left it kind of loose.'

'I can recommend the Hotel Tahiti,' she smiled. 'It has everything you could possibly need.'

'Is that right?' I grinned. 'Such as?'

'Well, it's very central – only three miles from the airport and a mile from Papeete. It's set on a *magnificent* lagoon with breathtaking views of Papeete harbour and the island of Moorea – the sunsets are out of this world! The food is superb – French, American and Polynesian ... and it offers accommodation either in rooms or in thatched bungalows, which means endless privacy ... *and* ...'

I held up my hand. 'Say no more, I shall convince Buzz that there is no other place to stay but the Tahiti.'

'Good, I'm going to enjoy having you for a neighbour.'

'You are, hm?'

The look she gave me started my motor again. 'Yes ... I am.'

I cleared my throat. 'Er ... tell me about Tahiti, Maggie.'

She lay back with a contented sigh and gazed at the roof, recalling the island in her mind's eye. 'How do you describe paradise? You must have seen it on films? Well it's exactly like that. The water is unbelievably clear, heaven to swim in. The air is warm and soft. The people are divinely uncomplicated, happy, full of fun. Did you know that tipping for service isn't allowed in the islands? – that it's actually contrary to the Tahitian idea of hospitality?'

'Really. What a refreshing change.'

She gave a cynical little laugh. 'After travelling the States, it's miraculous. But it'll give you an idea of the life-style of these lovely people. They really do *enjoy* being of service.'

'Shamefully I know very little about Tahiti. I ought to have read up on it. It's a French possession, isn't it?'

'Yes, but virtually self-governing. The official languages are French and Tahitian but almost everyone speaks English. Do you speak French?'

I laughed. 'I can order a vodka tonic and a hamburger. Yes, a little. Tell me about Papeete ... and the night life.'

'The night life ...' she smiled. 'A brochure I read described Tahiti nightlife as "tropical joie de vivre ... barefoot sophistication with a limitless capacity for fun", and I guess that sums it up beautifully.' She gave a shrug. 'How can I describe it better? Whatever you could possibly need for a gay romantic evening is there. Fabulous sunsets, warm scented air, dancing under the stars, exquisite food ...'

'And a beautiful girl.'

She laughed. 'And a handsome, fun man, yes. Oh, you're going to love it.'

'I know I am. But I'm beginning to feel desolate already that you're only going to be there one day. Must you go on to Hawaii so soon?'

She nodded. 'Yes. I'm . . . expected.'

'Oh.' She didn't explain and I didn't pry. I reckoned I was very fortunate to have one day with her. 'And the town of Papeete – what's that like?'

'Small but very lovely. Lots of superb resturants and quaint bars full of oddball characters. There really is no place like it on earth. Life is so casual it takes a state occasion to require anything more formal than a sport shirt, yet you'll not eat better food in Paris. You're going to fall in love with it, I know.'

'Yes,' I sighed, 'so do I. Will you show it to me, Maggie?'

She smiled. 'Of course. Tonight I'll take you to Quinn's bar overlooking the harbour on the Quai Bir-Hackheim, to see some of the whackiest characters that ever bummed around the South Pacific. Quinn's is famous for its characters – guys who keep coming back in their boats time after time and swear they can't find their way out of the islands.'

'Sounds like a Somerset Maugham setting.'

'What else? This is where he got his material.'

'I can't wait to see it. I feel as excited as a kid on his summer holidays.'

'Good, I hope you always stay that way. I can't stand world-weariness, it's a crime when there're so many beautiful places to see.'

I looked at her, caught by her earnestness. 'You really mean that, don't you.'

'Of course. It makes me sick to hear some of my rich friends say they're bored with travel when nine-tenths of the world would give their right arms for a glimpse of places like Tahiti. I adore travelling, seeing new places. And I know I'm very lucky to be able to do it.' She laughed suddenly. 'Heck, I'm getting serious, that's unforgivable. Come on, tell me about you, you haven't told me a thing.'

'Oh, there's not too much to tell, Maggie. I was born near Liverpool . . . you've, er, *heard* of Liverpool?'

'Of course – who hasn't? Thanks to the Beatles.'

'Well, I worked there for a while, then moved down to London, did a spell in commercial television and earned a bit of money, then decided to work in the sun – as a travel courier in Majorca. Since then I've moved around quite a bit . . . I worked in Africa, spent a bit of time in the Bahamas, Miami, New York. That's where I met Buzz – well, strictly speaking, I met him on the Miami–New York train.' I laughed. 'Some meeting – he actually saved my life.'

Her eyes widened. 'Really? How?'

Well, that was it, we talked right through the film and beyond. I told her about the jobs I'd done, making her laugh at things that had happened, the characters I'd met. And she told me about a very different kind of life, of a rich dream-filled childhood in Boston, South America, Switzerland and of de luxe travels around the world, with adoring parents.

In her lovely company time passed unbelievably quickly. And suddenly Buzz was standing there, regarding me with a grin of quizzical surprise, his eyes saying, 'Jeezus, Tobin, how did you pull this one?'

'Maggie ... meet my reprobate pal, Buzz Malone, professional tennis player and airstew seducer. Buzz . . . Miss Maggie Kennedy and I am glad you pushed off.'

Buzz beamed a grin at Maggie and shook her hand. 'I don't know where you came from, Maggie, but I'm certainly glad you're here. How did he manage it – hijack?'

'No, he looked so forlorn sitting here all alone, I just had to talk to him.'

'Yes, he's got a great forlorn expression – works every time.'

'Come and sit down, you bum,' I said, 'and tell us how the great romance went.'

Maggie and I moved into the aisle and let Buzz through, then resumed our seats. 'Well?' I said.

He winked and circled a thumb and finger. 'Unbelievably. She's got a two-night lay-over in Tahiti and *insists* on spending it with me. I fought hard but to no avail, she's a very determined bird.'

I turned to Maggie. 'This is one good-looking airstew we're talking about – a blonde named Carol Dwyer. Her brother plays tennis with Buzz.' I turned back to Buzz, slipping him a wink to let him know my own position. 'Well now, this all sounds very promising. Maggie also has a overnight lay-over, she's off to Hawaii tomorrow. Has Carol fixed up a room yet?'

'Yes, she's staying at the Royal Papeete in town.'

'Oh. Well . . . Maggie is booked into the Hotel Tahiti, just outside of town and I, er, well, I figured it sounded just about right for us and . . .'

He grinned. 'Sure, why not?'

'Oh . . . but I thought you might . . .'

He shook his head. 'Not a *town* hotel, mate. I want something with a view. I'll go along with the Hotel Tahiti if Maggie recommends it.'

'Well, fine . . .'

An announcement over the tannoy interrupted me. 'Ladies and gentlemen, we will be landing at Faaa Airport, Tahiti in a few minutes. Would passengers kindly return to their own seats and fasten their seat belts.'

'I must go and get my things together,' Maggie said. 'I'll meet you in the terminal, hm?'

'Yes, fine.'

She stood up, gave us a smile, and walked off down the aisle. Buzz let out a gasp. 'Holy *cow*, Tobin, how did you manage that?'

I turned, regarded him archly. 'Same as always, Malone – through sheer animal magnetism.'

'Aw, mate she is *fantastic*! How did you meet her?'

'I told you – I just sat here and exuded, didn't do a thing. She came back here to miss Disney, caught sight of me and that was it. Fought her way into the seat like a wildcat . . . made a terrible scene . . .'

'Aw, shut it,' he grinned. 'Is this for real, though – is she really available for tonight?'

'Absolutely. I still can't believe it, it just – happened. I saw her standing there, looking for a seat, and fell in love with her on sight. Incredibly, she doesn't seem to object too strongly to me, either.'

'Blinkin' miraculous,' he muttered.

'Up yours, Malone. Well, how did you really make out with the blonde goddess?'

'Oh, brother,' he groaned. 'Like a house on fire. I reckon

we're in for a bit of a time, mate.' He chuckled. 'Blimey, what a way to start – two absolute smashers. I couldn't have wished for anything better if I'd sent in an order form. She's American, hm?'

'Yes . . . and apparently not pushed for a bob or two. This is all she seems to do for a living – travelling the world enjoying herself.'

'Tough.'

'But a lovely bird – not at all spoilt. She's terrific. She's going to show me Papeete this afternoon and take me to a place called Quinn's Bar to meet some characters tonight.'

He laughed. 'No kidding? It must be quite a place, Carol suggested the same thing.'

'Well, fine, let's make it a foursome, I'm sure Maggie won't mind. Hey, are you sure about this hotel arrangement? You don't want to book in at Carol's place?'

'No, it's better this way. We can split up later on – without making it too obvious.'

'Good thinking, Malone. How I envy you your devious mind.'

The plane dipped noticeably and began to descend. Buzz turned to the window, emitted a gasp. 'There she is . . . come and have a look.'

I eased my seat belt and leaned across, peered out and down, and experienced a kick under the heart at the sight. Set in a sea bluer than I'd ever imagined lay the island of Tahiti, skirted by bands of pink coral and palm-fringed sands, its twin mountain peaks rising sheerly and majestically in its centre, the whole evoking disbelief that anything so breathtakingly beautiful could really be ours to enjoy.

'Oh, boy . . .' I murmured.

'Ain't she a beaut,' muttered Buzz. 'And would you believe that airstrip?'

Faaa Airport was a miracle of engineering, an incredibly long, thin ribbon of white and black tarmac laid right in the sea, looking as though it had just floated in and docked a few yards off-shore.

Around and down we came, the airstrip rushing to meet us. With that curious metamorphosis peculiar to flight, the surrounding vegetation, buildings, ocean waves grew alarmingly from unreal miniature toys into the real thing . . . then with a slight jarring bump we were down and racing along the ribbon, slowing rapidly under reverse thrust . . . to a final halt.

Buzz turned from the window, grinning like an idiot. 'Aloha, Tobin, and what do *you* intend doing during your brief sojourn in this tropical paradise?'

'Oh . . . visit a few museums, study the flora and fauna, investigate the immensely interesting history of the island . . . the usual things.'

'Yeah, same here,' he beamed, 'come on, let's get out of here.'

From the moment I stepped through the aircraft door I was a goner. One sniff of that warm, sea-humid, flower-scented tropical air and I went funny in the head, buckled at the knees, and felt twenty-six years of accumulated urban strain slip from my shoulders and dissolve in a puddle about my feet.

'Aw . . . Buzz!' I moaned, eyes closed against the onslaught of ecstasy. 'Did you ever smell air like it?'

'Tobin, you're holding up three hundred people who're also anxious to sniff it.'

'Don't care . . . don't care, let 'em wait.'

Nevertheless, I moved down the steps and was overjoyed to find Maggie at the bottom.

'He's sleep-walking,' explained Buzz. 'The air got to him.'

'So I see,' laughed Maggie. 'Come on, he needs help.'

They both took one of my arms and assisted me, staggering towards the terminal building. 'Wonderful . . . miraculous . . . people of Liverpool, London, New York, do you know what you're *missing*! You victims of the LA smog, come . . . breathe . . .. and re-discover your lungs.'

'I'll mention you to the Tahiti Tourist Board,' laughed Maggie. 'I reckon you could personally triple their business in a week. They can send you on a coughing tour of the States.'

'But seriously,' I said, disengaging my arm from Buzz's grasp but slipping my other arm around Maggie's waist, 'isn't it just . . .' I hauled in another gigantic breath . . . 'fabulous. You know, I'd forgotten how to enjoy breathing.'

'Beautiful,' said Buzz, also having a go. Then he stopped, bringing us to a halt, and had a good look round – out across the flat, calm, indescribably blue sea and then inland to the twin towering, densely foliaged mountain peaks.

'The taller one is Orohena – 7,337 feet,' explained Maggie. 'The other is Aorai – 6,786 feet.'

'Hey,' laughed Buzz with surprise. 'We have an expert on Tahiti with us. She is by no means just a pretty face.' As we continued towards the terminal he said, 'OK, Kennedy, we'll test your knowledge . . . how big is Tahiti?'

Maggie joined in the game, assuming a formal, academic posture. 'Tahiti island is in fact two islands, joined by a narrow neck, and is shaped somewhat like a . . . if you'll forgive the simile . . . like a spermatozoon . . .'

I pulled a face at Buzz. 'Is she with you?'

Maggie laughed and went on. 'The larger island is called Tahiti Nui and the smaller Tahiti Iti . . .'

'Sounds terribly rude,' I said.

'. . . the whole covering an area of 402 square miles. Papeete, its capital, is also the only town of any consequence and has a resident population of about twenty thousand. Throughout this group of islands there is a population of about 100,000, 77% of whom are Polynesians of the Maori race, 9% are Asians and 14% Europeans. Next question.'

'I do hate smart birds,' growled Buzz. 'All right, how many islands are there *in* the group and what are their names?'

She sneered at him but continued undeterred. 'In the whole of French Polynesia, which covers an ocean area as big as Europe, there are some 130 islands contained in 5 archipelagoes, namely the Society Islands – which includes Tahiti – the Marquesas, the Tuamotus, the Gambiers and the Australs. Apart from Tahiti, which is the biggest of all islands, the main islands in the Society group are Raiatea, Bora Bora, Huahine, Manihi, Rangiroa, Moorea . . .'

'Stop . . . stop!' cried Buzz. 'I give in! Blimey, I bet she could name the whole 130.'

'I was going to,' she said nonchalantly, then laughed. 'Well, not really. I was glad you stopped me right then, it was getting mighty close.'

'Nevertheless,' I said, 'you are undoubtedly a *very* knowledgeable girl and I shall be overjoyed if you know the bars and dives of Tahiti half as well as you know the other statistics.'

Her eyes twinkled mischievously. 'OK, we'll start with the bars . . . now, let's see, there's the Bounty, the Zizou, Quinn's,

Wisky a Gogo, the Puuoro Plage . . .'

'She does, she does!' whooped Buzz. 'Goodbye world . . . hello Tahiti!'

Fifteen minutes later, as we passed through Customs, we were descended upon by a group of laughing Tahitian females, dressed in vivid cotton pareus, their long, shining black hair plaited with scarlet flowers and their lovely faces wreathed in smiles. From their arms hung dozens of *leis*, garlands of sweet-smelling frangipani, and with cries of 'Iaorana' . . . Iaorana!' they approached each passenger, looped a *lei* around his neck, and offered a kiss to his cheek.

'Thank you, love,' laughed Buzz, winking at me. 'Now, that's what I call a welcome. Funny, I don't remember this happening in Vegas. All we got there was a cop with a ·38 on his hip.'

'And this isn't just a tourist gimmick,' explained Maggie. 'They really do mean you're very welcome. It'll take a bit of adjusting to after Vegas – or anywhere else for that matter – but you can forget Western cynicism here. This is for real.'

We moved out of the building into the brilliant sunshine to where our porter had already organized a taxi and was helping the driver load our baggage.

'Where are you going to meet Carol?' I asked Buzz.

'I'm picking her up and bringing her to our place at twelve. She has a few things to do first.'

'Twelve! But it's . . .' I looked at my watch. 'Oh . . .' My watch said one o'clock but I'd forgotten to allow for Tahiti time. 'Hey, it's only ten! We've got three extra hours!'

'And the way I feel,' he grinned, stretching luxuriously, 'I'm going to need every minute.'

The smiling Tahitian taxi driver, cool and relaxed in a wildly coloured red shirt, slammed the trunk lid and came round to open the rear door. 'All three for the Hotel Tahiti, yes?'

We told him yes and Maggie climbed in. It was all I could do finally to drag my eyes from her legs as she moved across the seat, parting them excitingly. She knew I'd been looking and gave me a censorious eye as I settled beside her.

'That . . . is rude,' she murmured under her breath.

'What is?'

'You know damn well what is.'

I gaped, innocently. 'Maggie, I . . .'

'Lovely performance, Tobin, but it won't wash. You were ogling my legs.'

'Who, *me*?'

She raised her eyes. 'Oh, brother . . .'

'Well, it's your own fault, you look so edible.'

She frowned. 'I've got edible legs?'

'Why not?'

She chuckled.

Buzz climbed in the front with the driver and we set off, eyes everywhere, trying to take in everything at once – the sparkling sea, the soaring mountain peaks, the buildings, the lush natural vegetation and the gardens a blaze of flowers too vivid to be real. It was all too much to absorb. I felt stunned by so much beauty, colour, sunlight, so I gave up, relaxed back into the seat and let it all wash over me, smiling to myself with the sheer pleasure of being alive and wondering if I'd ever felt happier than at that moment.

Buzz, I knew, was equally affected. With muttered 'wows' and 'gees' and shakes of his head, he covered the panorama from side to side, finally summing it all up with, 'Christ, it's magnificent.'

'That it is,' agreed Maggie.

'No wonder the Polynesians are such a happy race.'

The driver turned to grin at him, as though to prove the point. 'Your first visit here, sir?'

'Yes . . . but I've got a feeling it won't be my last.'

'You won't be alone. We've got visitors here who've been trying to tear themselves away for ten . . . twenty years. They just can't make it.'

'Like I said,' Maggie said to me. 'They make the excuse they can't find their way out of the islands.'

Buzz turned in his seat. 'Tell us some more about Tahiti, teacher.'

She laughed. 'Buzz, I'm no authority on it. Most of what I know I picked up from travel brochures. Our driver could tell you a lot more.'

'Oh, sure,' the driver said eagerly. 'Did you know the English discovered Tahiti before the French? Captain Samuel Wallis discovered it in 1767 and claimed it for England. A year later Bougainville landed here, not knowing about Wallis, and claimed it for France. Meantime, in London, they couldn't make up their minds whether to leave us to our simple life or move in and civilize us, and while they were arguing about it, the French moved in and took us over.'

I laughed. 'Typical.'

'Later on, in 1842,' the driver continued, 'the French and English fought over us, so our Queen, Pomare IV, asked for French protection. And in 1880, her son, Pomare V, turned Tahiti completely over to the French and we've been French ever since, though nowadays we virtually rule ourselves. It works very well. Will you be staying in Tahiti long?'

'Not this trip,' said Buzz. 'Just a couple of days, we have to get back to Sydney.'

'Aw, that's too bad, you won't have time to see very much. You ought to drive right round Tahiti Nui and Tahiti Iti, they're very beautiful ... and you ought to take a boat to Moorea or a little plane to Bora Bora. Such beauty defies description, you will have to see it.'

'And we will,' said Buzz. 'We'll come back and spend a couple of weeks here.'

The driver laughed. 'Then beware. Two weeks can easily stretch to twenty years.'

'And I wouldn't be difficult to conquer,' grinned Buzz. 'This place is getting to me already.'

Much sooner than I expected we turned off the broad, palm-lined boulevard and drove into the grounds of the Hotel Tahiti, into gardens of graceful royal palms and vivid tropical flowers, and pulled up at the reception entrance.

'In these grounds was once the residence of Princess Pomare, the daughter of the last King of Tahiti,' our driver explained as he unloaded the cases. 'Go on through and take a look at the view ... I'll bet you stay more than two days!'

Maggie led the way into the reception. Again we were greeted profusely, this time by the male receptionist, with warm handshakes and a heartfelt, 'Iaorana ... welcome to Tahiti. We can offer you a bungalow or a room in the plantation wings,' he told Buzz and me.

'I'd advise the room,' Maggie chipped in. 'They're two-storey wings and from the upper floor the view is fantastic. Do you have an upper floor room?'

'Indeed we have, yes,' said the receptionist.

We booked in, changed some travellers cheques into the local currency (the Coloniale Franc Pacifique at 88 francs to the dollar, 236 to the £), paid off our taxi driver with thanks for his help and followed a young Tahitian porter to our rooms.

The hotel was not one single building of eight million rooms such as you find in the tourist traps of Spain, but a complex of many separate buildings designed to blend wih their natural surroundings. Nestling in the lush gardens were single-storeyed, thatched bungalows, as quaint as any English rose-covered cottage, each comprising not merely a bedroom but a suite of rooms. The other accommodation was located in five two-storeyed plantation buildings – long elegant pink-roofed colonial-style structures, each comprising perhaps a dozen rooms and each room having a wide verandah, enclosed by a railing of white iron filigree.

Following the young porter through the gardens, we reached the first plantation building, climbed the flight of stairs and went along a corridor, stopping first at Maggie's room.

'Give me an hour to settle in and wash away the jet-lag, hm?' she said. 'Give me a knock when you're ready.'

'Fine.'

The porter emerged and continued on to the far end of the corridor, opened our door and bowed us through – into a room straight out of a Somerset Maugham novel.

The furniture was scant and tropically lightweight – two single beds covered with bright red floral counterpanes, two easy chairs, a desk and chair beneath a window on the right, and a colourful scatter rug on the polished wood floor.

The facing wall was all louvered sliding door, thrown wide open to the verandah, furnished with a low coffee table and two high-backed easy chairs made of cane. The window on the right was also louvered, open to the air and to the breathtaking view.

'Oh, boy,' gasped Buzz. 'I reckon that driver could be right ... this could be a twenty-year stop-over.'

We crossed the room and walked out on to the balcony ... and stared. Before us lay the endless sea, a flat, calm, carpet of crystal turquoise water. Over to our right, to the East and only a mile away – a spectacular view of Papeete harbour, busy with ships and boats of all kinds and size. And to our left – twelve miles distant – the fabled island of Moorea, rising mysteriously from the sea, its mountain peaks sharp against the cloudless sky.

Down below us the profuse and colour-drenched gardens extended some twenty or thirty yards, then terminated at the water's edge. Beyond this – a coral reef covered by shallow water, reaching out perhaps thirty yards, at which point the clear, deeper waters of the lagoon began.

To our left a wooden pier ran out across the coral reef to service small sailing boats and out-rigger canoes, many of which were out there plying the lagoon. And near the foot of the pier, landscaped into the gardens, a good-sized swimming pool played host to a dozen boisterous bathers.

'They ain't kidding, are they,' said Buzz in a quiet voice. 'It *is* a paradise.'

I nodded slowly. 'It certainly is. I can imagine how Blye and the crew of the *Bounty* felt when they first clapped eyes on it . . . all this *and* hundreds of lovely dusky *vahiné* birds waiting to welcome them with open arms.'

'Not only arms, either,' he grinned. 'Hey, d'you reckon they still do, mate?'

'What – believe in free love?'

'Yeh.'

I shrugged. 'Don't know. I would think the missionaries might have sorted them out by now, wouldn't you? Nah, I reckon they're too sophisticated for that nowadays. Oh, I should think they're still potty about doing it, but not necessarily with the first bloke ashore and behind the nearest bush.'

The porter was at the verandah door. 'You like your room, gentlemen?'

We turned to him, a strikingly handsome young lad in his late teens, glowing with health and joie de vivre.

'It's terrific,' I said. 'Thank you very much.'

Automatically my hand flew to my pocket but I stopped myself in time.

'Enjoy your stay,' he smiled. 'Anything you want – just ring.'

I looked at Buzz. 'How about a couple of beers here on the verandah to help us unwind?'

'Spot on.'

'Could you bring us two beers, please,' I asked the porter.

'I'll arrange it for you. You'd like to try our local beer – Hinano or Manuia? They're very good.'

'Certainly. We'll try one of each.'

'I will arrange it.'

He departed.

'How about a quick unpack?' I suggested. 'Get it out of the way.'

'Right.'

We went into the bedroom and began throwing things into drawers and wardrobes.

'Still can't believe I'm here,' said Buzz. 'That's jet travel for you – doesn't give you time to adjust. Las Vegas one minute, Tahiti the next, Sydney the minute after. Bloody mad, aren't we, charging around the world like this. Hardly get time to sniff the flowers.'

' "What is this life if, full of care, we have no time to stand and stare," ' I qutoed. 'Mate, I do believe the islands are getting to you. Well, you're right, it is bloody mad. But where I came from there wasn't much incentive to stand and stare, you'd wind up with double pneumonia or they'd have you inside for trespassing. The only time I stood and stared in Liverpool was at a demolition crane knocking down slum tenements. You know, that's what gets me – that nine-tenths of the world's population live in such chronic squalor when there are places like this they could be enjoying. And it isn't as though they don't know such beauty exists. Nowadays they go abroad for their holidays and enjoy clean air, warm sunshine and a healthy outdoor life, then can't wait to get back to the Manchester docks and the joys of Stepney. Pity our ancestors couldn't have had more foresight. Those Vikings must have been crazy – invading Britain instead of Tahiti.'

He laughed and slammed his drawer shut. 'That's me finished. Come on, let's sit on the verandah.'

We had hardly sat when the beers arrived, and again I had to restrain myself from tipping.

'Feels all wrong, doesn't it,' I said, pouring a Manuia.

'What – not tipping? Yeh, especially after the States. Jeezus, it's a menace over there. I remember the first time I stayed in

New York. I had to tip a porter at the airport to get my bags on to the bus. Then when the bus stopped at Grand Central, a negro kid asked me if I wanted a cab and, thinking he was the driver, I tipped him for carrying my bags to the cab. But he wasn't the driver, he was just touting. Then I had to tip the driver when I got to the hotel, tip the major domo for carrying the bags into the hall, tip another porter for carrying them up to the desk, tip another porter for taking them up to the room . . . then do the whole lot over again next day when I flew out. It's a bloody disgrace. Maybe you wouldn't mind so much if they all thanked you, but the surly bastards regard it as their absolute right and just stuff it in their pockets. I reckon the US Tourist Board ought to take a good look at this place, they could learn a thing or two.'

'Cheers,' I grinned, raising my glass. 'What you're asking, of course, is that the great American nation should exchange its fervour for money for the pride and graciousness of a simple people – in short, totally to reverse its nature.'

'Yeh,' he laughed, 'something like that. And I guess exactly the same thing applies to the great English and Australian nations.'

'Well, let's put it this way – don't hold your breath waiting for a London cabbie to be insulted by the offer of a tip. He'll manage to overcome his pride to the extent of tearing you limb from limb if you don't tip 20% !'

'Ah, well . . .' he sighed, sinking lower in his chair, 'all that's a billion miles away for a couple of days, hey? By God, I take to this, Tobin. Can't remember when I felt so relaxed.'

'Me neither.'

I gazed out over the lagoon and slowly inhaled the warm, scented air, experiencing again the tranquillity that had overpowered me at the airport. 'You know something, Buzz . . . I may have hit on the secret of eternal world peace. I reckon if all the major powers sent their military chiefs here for a fortnight's holiday, there wouldn't be any more wars. They'd all be too lethargic to fight. Come home this instant, Comradgeneral Mikhailovitch, and make plans for the invasion of China! Get stuffed, cables Mikhailovitch, who in his right mind needs China? Besides, my good old mateski General Hoi Paloi is right here with me, ogling the *vahinés*. Have another Hinano, Hoi, old boy, and take no bleeding notice of those degenerate war-mongers.'

'Reckon you're right,' laughed Buzz. 'Ever wonder where you'll settle down, Russ?'

'Oh, yes, I've given it a thought from time to time. A year or so ago I'd have bet Liverpool. Back in those days even London seemed an outlandish dream. But now . . .' I shrugged. 'Well, all I know is that it won't be any dirty, smogged-up city – not with all this to be had. But that's a long way off yet, mate. I intend sowing a few more wild oats before I send down any permanent roots. There's an awful lot of world to see yet. Ask me again when I'm forty.'

'Sure,' he laughed. 'Tell you one thing I can never get over – that's the way these lovely birds pop into your life when you're hoofing around the world. Take Maggie . . .'

'And wouldn't I like to.'

'. . . and Carol. Up to a few hours ago we didn't know they existed, now here we are all sharing a couple of beautiful days together on a tropical island. Doesn't it make you feel sorry for those poor mugs working in banks and insurance offices!'

'My heart bleeds for 'em,' I grinned. 'I used to be one of them. I wouldn't go back to that life for a million a year and lunch vouchers. Boy, if they could see us now.'

'That Maggie is really something. They don't come that good very often. She's got everything.'

'Yes, she has. That was a real turn-up for the book. I can't get over how easily it happened. One minute she was standing there, looking for a seat and turning me inside out, and the next she was sitting with me, talking and laughing as though we'd been mates for years. Quite miraculous.'

'What's she doing here? . . . and what's she going to Hawaii for?'

I shrugged. 'Much the same as I'm doing, she said – just seeing the world and tasting life, taking what comes and enjoying the enjoyable.'

'Terrific. I once met a little pigeon down in Acapulco doing the same thing. Boy was she enjoying life. What a wild, wild wing-ding of a week that was . . . then I got up one morning and she was gone, just like that. Said she hated goodbyes more than anything and had never said one in her life.'

'I share her view – especially at stations and airports.'

'Yeh, me too.'

He drained his beer and glanced at his watch. 'I must go and get Carol. Where shall we meet up?'

'Well, how about coming back here? I'll have a shower and change into something suitably Tahitian, then call Maggie. How about lunch here?'

'Spot on.'

'Right – see you.'

He entered the bedroom, did a lightning change into a blindingly garish sports shirt, and presented himself for inspection. 'How's this, cock?'

'A mite dowdy, but you'll do. Wait till you see the creation I picked up in Miami – even the Tahitians will wince.'

'We may not be brainy, but, by God we're loud!' he laughed and went out of the door.

I finished my beer slowly, feeling the need to do everything slowly, hung on the verandah rail for a while, sucking it all up like a hungry sponge, then went into the bedroom, tore off my clothes, and stood under a cool shower for five minutes, washing away the last vestiges of urban cloy. Then I dressed in clean, fresh linen slacks, my thin cotton Miami shirt, light blue socks and beach shoes, and inspected the result in the mirror. Hideous . . . but *very* Tahitian.

Whistling happily, I left the room, walked down the corridor to Maggie's room and knocked.

She opened the door . . . blowing my mind afresh in a blue floral cotton creation so thin there was little left to puzzle about.

She laughed at my stunned expression. 'What's the matter?'

'You are. I'd forgotten how *very* beautiful you were.'

She chuckled and raised her brows at my outfit. '*Very* chic . . . come in.'

I followed her into the room, smelling the lingering perfume of her bath.

'How do you two like your room?' she asked, heading for the verandah.

'It's perfect, Maggie. I'm sure we couldn't have done better.'

'I like this hotel. As I said, it's very private.'

I grinned at her. 'Yes, so you did.'

'Would you like a drink? I ordered a bottle of Cinzano and

ice, I thought you might like it.'

'I love it. Shall I make them?'

'No – you can sit right down there and enjoy the view.'

I watched her work at the drinks, finding my heart doing triple beats again at the sight of her, at the loveliness of her face, and flame hair, and the perfection of her lithe, tanned body.

'I said enjoy the view,' she grinned, without looking up.

'I am. What's an old seascape compared to you?'

She laughed and brought me my drink. 'You should still be a salesman, Tobin – to women. You have a knack of saying exactly the things they like to hear.' She took the other cane chair and blew my fuse by crossing her legs.

'Well, here's to your Tahitian baptism. I hope it's a lot of fun.'

'It already is. I'm only sorry you've only got one night. Sorry? I'm desolate.'

Her eyes crinkled. 'Well, we'll just have to make the most of the time we've got. What would you like to do this afternoon?'

'Just sit here and look at you.'

'Seriously . . .'

'I am serious. You've no idea what a desirable picture you make with that lagoon background. Does a fella need more?'

She laughed. 'Well, that's very nice but very impractical. Buzz and his girl will be here soon, we'll have to do more than just sit here.'

'What *is* there to do in Tahiti?'

'Not too much, really. We could rent a car and drive round the island . . . swim in the pool . . . or in the lagoon . . . go underwater or deep-sea fishing . . . sail an outrigger . . . play golf . . . ride horses . . . climb a mountain . . . visit an archaeological ruin . . . or the Gauguin Museum . . . or the Botanical Gardens . . . or skin dive . . .'

'OK, OK,' I laughed. 'Well, for me that lagoon looks very inviting. How about hiring one of those little outrigger sailboats and swimming off it?'

'Sounds perfect. We'll put it to the others.'

'Do you mind them joining us, Maggie?'

'Not in the least . . . just so long as I have you to myself *some* time before tomorrow afternoon.'

My heart gave a thud. 'I'll make sure of that. What . . . sort of time did you have in mind?'

She repressed a smile. 'Oh ... some time between tonight and tomorrow morning. Perhaps a stroll through the grounds under the moon?'

I cleared my stricken throat. 'You realize you're ruining my appetite for lunch, don't you ... and for dinner. I wish it was night now.'

She laughed. 'Down, boy.' She sipped her drink and went on, 'Have you ... had many girlfriends, Russ? No don't answer that, it was a silly question, of course you have. That will never be one of *your* problems.'

'Yours neither,' I grinned.

'Maybe, but don't confuse the availability of men with the availability of the right *kind* of man. There are plenty of muscle-bound apes around – and I mean mentally muscle-bound as well as physically. Bumping into a guy like you is a rare and reassuring occasion.'

'Well, thank *you*. Hey, you'd better stop, I could get insufferably big-headed.'

'No ... you couldn't.' She regarded me earnestly over the rim of her glass, half-smiling yet serious, preoccupied with her private thoughts. I found the appraisal immensely exciting, knowing a big thing was happening, had already happened between us, the outcome of which would be volcanic, to say the least.

'Penny for 'em,' I grinned, heart pounding, hardly able to speak.

'I think you know,' she said quietly.

Held hypnotized by her gaze, I nodded. 'Yes.'

'It's beautiful ... all the more beautiful for happening so fast.'

'Yes. I'm not so sure about Buzz and Carol being so welcome now ...'

She shook her head. 'They won't change anything, it'll still be you and me.' She laughed, breaking the spell. 'Probably a good thing. You may not get to see anything of Tahiti – at least not until after I've gone.'

'Who needs Tahiti? And please stop talking about going. Maggie, do you really *have* to go? Sorry ... I won't ask again. Come on, let me pour us another drink.'

'I'll be sloshed before lunch,' she laughed, draining her glass.

'Well, it's holiday time. If we want to get sloshed, we'll get sloshed. We can always sleep it off on the beach. By the way, I noticed there's no beach here. What do we do for sand? Not that I need it, but I just thought I'd ask.'

'Oh, there're plenty of beaches all round the island, but mostly it's black sand.'

'What a pity.'

'But there's a white beach at the Tahiti Village Beach Hotel in Punaauia, five miles west of the airport. If you're really adamant, you and Buzz could drive out there.'

'After you've gone, hm?'

She didn't reply.

I poured the drinks and handed one to her, changing the subject. 'Bet you water-ski up a storm, Maggie ... and swim like a fish?'

'I get by,' she smiled.

'And what else do you do supremely well – horse riding, snow ski, hunt, shoot and fish ...'

'I've had a *disgustingly* privileged childhood.'

'I, er, must be honest and admit a degree of impatience to see you in a bikini.'

She gave me the eyes again over her glass. 'How big a degree?'

'How big can they get?'

'I see. Well, what's good for the goose ... I also admit a certain curiosity along similar lines.'

'I don't wear a bikini, Maggie. Mummy told me to stop it, it might be misunderstood.'

'Idiot,' she laughed.

'I thought male bodies were of minor importance to women, that they only served as receptacles for the mind?'

'Ha! Who told you that?'

'Oh, I read it somewhere – in a sex magazine, I think.'

'Well, I pity the woman who wrote it, she must be having a real lousy time. Certainly a body without a mind means much less to a woman than it does to a man – a lot of you guys actually *prefer* dumb broads – but the man who can boast both biceps *and* brains has everything going for him. You really think we could cuddle up to a barrel of lard and a slim, hard guy and not know the difference?'

'I'm only repeating what I read, Maggie. *I* don't know what goes on in a bird's head.'

'Like heck, you don't. You mean to tell me not *one* of your thousands of conquests has sunk her nails into you and told you through gritted teeth how good and hard you feel?'

'Well . . .'

'Ah, so you have made thousands of conquests . . .'

'I didn't say that!'

'I see, well now I know where I stand . . . just one more dame in a line of thousands.'

'Hey . . .'

'Just one more gullible female to use and toss aside . . .'

'Maggie, will you . . .'

'It's all right, Tobin, I get the picture. And I thought I meant something extra special to you.'

I leaned forward, threateningly. 'Kennedy, if you don't stop . . .'

'You'll do what?'

'I shall come over there and kiss you to a stop.'

'Should have known the first time I laid eyes on you . . . it's there in your eyes, in your slick approach . . . in . . . whoops!'

She got rid of her glass as I lunged for her, plucked her out of the chair, held her head between my hands and kissed her hard . . . for about three seconds. Then it all changed. I stopped kissing her and looked at her. Her lagoon-blue eyes were warm and loving, searching mine, and slowly I drew her to me and went wild to the touch of her mouth. She murmured plaintively and drew me tightly to her, pressed her firm, supple body against me, lowered her hands from my neck to my shoulders and with a more urgent groan thrust into me.

'Oh . . .'

'Maggie . . .'

We parted a little, looked at each other and saw the need, the desire.

'Wow,' I breathed, my heart thudding.

'That's . . . as good a word as any,' she gasped.

'Oh, boy . . .'

'You're surprised?'

'No.'

'Me, neither.'

'It's going to be a long, painful afternoon.'

'An eternity. I . . . think we'd better sit down . . .'

I grinned. 'Or?'

'Or the "Don't disturb" sign is going on the outside of that door and . . . well, it wouldn't be fair . . . would it?'

'Wouldn't it? No, I . . . suppose not.' I heaved a disconsolate sigh and drew away from her. 'You've got me in a right old mess, you know that?'

She stifled a giggle, her eyes flicking down to Herc who was caught up in the most uncomfortable tangle and making his presence very noticeable. 'Tobin . . . *that* is disgusting.'

'Really. Well, the blame's on you.'

She did giggle this time. 'That's *awful*!'

I flopped down into the chair, risking fractured ribs, and she came to me, bent down and kissed me teasingly on the lips. 'Beautifully . . . excitingly . . . awful. Now, I *am* anxious to see you in swim trunks . . . just like that.'

'Maggie, you're a devil . . . a witch! Just for that I shall refuse to change.'

'Fine – so shall I.'

'Ah, no . . .'

'Tit for tat, Tobin.'

She pinched my nose and sat down, still chuckling to herself. 'My, I had no idea they bred such big boys in Liverpool. What is it – the air or something?'

'We were poor, we had no toys,' I grinned.

'Well, well, this *is* going to be an interesting afternoon. I particularly want to see you floating on your back . . . though you'll have to be careful, the French navy might shoot you, thinking you're a Russian submarine.'

'Very funny.'

'Periscope . . . up!' She laughed.

'Maggie, you're obscene. Ladies do not make jokes about gentlemen's . . .'

'Periscopes? Well, now it's all perfectly clear . . . and I've mentally increased your conquests from thousands to millions. My, *what* a busy time you must have had . . . London, Majorca, Africa, Miami, New York. You're stamina must be quite extraordinary . . .'

'Maggie, if you don't stop, I'll . . .'

She exploded with laughter. 'You'll kiss me to one? Come on, I dare you!'

A loud rap on the bedroom door halted the game.

'Lucky for you,' I scowled.

'Ha!'

'Go on, answer it.'

She shook her head. 'No, you answer it – give Carol the fright of her life or the thrill.' She leapt from the chair, swooped on me for a quick, succulent kiss, then was off to answer the door, humming delightedly to herself.

As she disappeared, I stood up and eased Herc into a more comfortable position, cursing this outward manifestation of male excitement, the nuisance of which no bird could conceivably understand, then sat down again and tried to think of something unconducive to sex, like ... I couldn't think of anything. And Carol was upon me.

'Hi, there ...'

'Hello, Carol,' I said exuberantly, half-rising, then realized there were only two chairs and stood up fully, though with a curious stoop, as though my braces were fastened to my socks.

Buzz came through with Maggie, took one look at me and grimaced. 'What's up with you, you got stomach-ache?'

The bastard.

I laughed humourlessly. 'Good heavens no ... here, let's get you two chairs from the bedroom.'

I stooped past them, pretending to scratch my knee. 'Think I've been bitten.'

'Anybody interesting?' murmured Maggie, killing herself laughing.

Buzz said, 'Maggie, you haven't met Carol, have you?'

While they said hello I collected a chair and used it as a shield, plonked it down on the verandah and returned to collect the other, breathing a sigh of relief that things were abating.

'Here you are, *love* ...' I sneered at Maggie.

'How's the ... bite, *love*?' she chuckled. 'Not too painful? Is there any swelling?'

'I didn't think there were any poisonous things on Tahiti,' offered Carol, blissfully ignorant of the issue. 'Buzz was telling me you've both fallen in love with it on sight.'

'So we have,' I replied, flopping down. 'Carol, I would never have recognized you, you look so different out of uniform.' So she did, and very dishy, too, in a loose blue cotton shift, her blonde hair tumbling around her tanned shoulders. I glanced at Buzz, his wink telling me he thought so, too..

'How different?' asked Carol. 'Better or worse?'

'Ah, there's no qualifying perfection, Carol, you're unbeatable either way.'

I got a smiling bow from Carol and a filthy, narrow-eyed glower from Maggie.

'Very pretty, thank you,' said Carol.

'Cinzano, everyone?' said Maggie sweetly, crossing to the table. 'Russ, *do* continue telling me about your experience with the submarine.'

'Oh, what was that?' Carol asked eagerly. 'My father was in the navy, were you in it, too?'

'Heavens, no ... no, Maggie was, er, referring to the time a submarine docked in Liverpool and the public were allowed on board to inspect it. I was only a kid at the time, I went with my father ... and managed to get my hand stuck in the periscope mechanism.'

'He was telling me he's had trouble with it ever since,' smiled Maggie, avoiding my eye.

'With your periscope?' asked Buzz and roared with laughter at his own joke.

'No, my hand,' I said, balling a fist. 'Sometimes the only way I can relieve the ache is to hit something ... very hard.'

Carol realizing it was a joke between Maggie and me, changed the subject. 'Oh, what a heavenly day ... it's so good to be out of uniform and off that damned plane. Have you two made any plans for this afternoon?'

'Well, Buzz and I tentatively suggested lunch here,' I said, 'and Maggie and I did discuss swimming off an outrigger in the lagoon later on ... but let's hear it from you two.'

'You must be mind readers,' said Carol, accepting a drink from Maggie. 'We came up with the same idea. Wonderful day for swimming.'

'Fine – then let's do it.'

Maggie handed Buzz his drink, then brought mine, stood in front and smiled down at me, wickedly. 'Yes ... let's do it,' she cooed, and I damn-near dropped the drink.

CHAPTER TWO

We ate sparingly under the welcome shade of swaying palms and in the heady embrace of a thousand tropical flowers. It was perhaps the most delightful meal I've ever experienced, excellent food enjoyed in the company of a beautiful, sexy girl and two attractive friends.

'Oh, boy . . .' I sighed, for the umpteenth time, shaking my head and gazing out through the gardens to the sparkling lagoon, alive with little white sail boats playing in the fragrant breeze.

'I think he's caught island fever,' mocked Carol to Maggie. 'He's got that "leave-me-here-to-die" expression, I've seen it before on aircrew just before they desert the ship and go native.'

'How about it, Tobin, you thinking of going wild?' asked Maggie, continuing her tease.

'Aloha, vahiné,' I winked, 'you wanna come walk-about with me?'

'Jeezus, he's speaking the lingo already,' grinned Buzz. 'I'd better get him out of here fast.'

'You try and I'll have your whatsit broiled in an *ahimaa*,' I threatened.

'What the hell's an . . . *ahimaa*?' he gaped.

I shrugged. 'It's a Tahitian underground oven, everybody knows that.'

'Hey, that's very good,' remarked Maggie. 'Where did you pick that up?'

I reached into my shirt pocket. 'From this brochure, it was in the room.'

They all groaned.

'We-ell, you've got to learn it from somewhere. Listen to this, chaps. "Tahitian *tamaaraa*, or feasts, can be arranged through the local tour operators. These *tamaaraas* feature pork, breadfruit and a host of other native foods cooked in the *ahimaa* or underground earth oven. A dance group usually performs at these *tamaaraas*, often by torchlight. Buzz, I reckon we've got to see one of those.'

'What I wanna know is – are the girl dancers bare-breasted or . . . ouch!'

Carol had kicked him on the shin. 'No,' she scowled, 'they wear bikini tops.'

Buzz and I moaned and I had to duck to avoid Maggie's right hook.

'Seriously,' I said, 'how about a *tamaaraa* tonight, girls? Will it be abysmally touristy?'

'Not painfully,' replied Maggie. 'You'll have to sit at table with blue-rinsed American matrons wearing their *leis* and *pareos* with hilarious un-self-consciousness, but they provide half the fun.'

'Well, what do we say?'

They all said fine.

'Can you organize it, Maggie?'

'Sure, I'll speak to the receptionist . . . they might have one at the Tahiti Village Beach hotel tonight. It's a sister hotel to this one, and the only one with a white beach.'

'Er . . . What's a *pareo*?' asked Buzz.

Maggie smiled. 'It's a crown of flowers – everyone wears one. I reckon you guys will look just ducky in them.'

'Well, so long as they don't ask me to wear a grass skirt,' I said, and Maggie exploded with laughter. 'Now, that *would* be interesting.'

We finished the meal and prepared to depart.

Maggie said, 'You fellas go and change into your swim togs, Carol can use my room, but we'll book for the *tamaaraa* and hire an outrigger at the reception on the way up. Knock when you're ready.'

Buzz and I took off at a slow stroll, already gearing down to the leisurely pace of the island, actually pausing here and there to sniff a flower or inspect a plant.

'Russ,' he said, inhaling extravagantly, 'do me a favour?'

'Sure, what?'

'Pinch me hard, make sure I'm not dreaming.'

'Yeah, it's difficult to believe, isn't it. I never took to a place this quickly before. I reckon I could spend a long time here, Buzz.'

He nodded. 'Me, too. I've got to come back for a longer spell. Just a couple of nights is ridiculous.'

I grinned. 'But what a couple of nights!'

'You reckon, hm?'

'Don't you?'

He returned the grin. 'Guess so. Things were getting a bit warm over at her hotel when I picked her up. That's why we were so long getting here.'

'Oh, were you long, I didn't notice. Things were, er, developing rather nicely this end, too.'

He gave a chuckle. 'I reckon it's the island. This atmosphere has a gratifyingly basic effect on women – brings out their natural animal passions.'

'Oh, I had hoped I'd something to do with it.'

'Same on a cruise ship . . . two days out of Southampton and they start ripping their clothes off. Thought about being a deck steward one time, those guys really get their share.'

'Oh, you feel inadequately blessed now, Malone?'

He chuckled. 'Not exactly . . . but there's *always* room for more, son.'

We entered our room and quickly changed into swim trunks, wrapping a spare pair in a towel and throwing sun-oil, cigarettes, comb and all the other paraphernalia of the beach into an airline bag.

'This *tamaaraa* thing should be fun,' he said. 'Though I bet we get a bigger kick out of the tourists than the dancing. Was there ever a more ridiculous sight than tourists going native.'

'They may be saying that about us before the night's through. I can just see you with flowers in your hair trying to do a *tamuré*.'

'There you go again, Tobin . . . what the heck's a *tamuré*?'

'A frenzied Tahitian dance, old son, the great local leveller. Well, if they haul me out for an exhibition, you'll see a cloud of dust disappearing very fast over Mount Thing and I won't stop until I hit Tahiti Iti.'

'Same here,' he grinned. 'I've got another exhausting exercise in mind for tonight.'

We collected the girls, now dressed in bikinis under cotton shifts, and made our way through the gardens to the pier which extended out over the coral plateau to the deeper water of the lagoon. Entranced by the colour, the curious formation and the fishy activity of the coral, we took a long time to reach the pier end, stopping often to look at something or other – a shoal of brilliantly coloured fish, one of perculiar shape or strange expression, a dozen things.

'We'd better get on,' I said eventually, indicating a young, half-naked Tahitian boy, sitting watching us at the end of the pier. 'He's waiting for us with the boat.'

Maggie smiled and shook her head. 'One thing you haven't learned about the islands yet, and it'll take a lot of getting used to – for these people there's no such thing as time or impatience. Right now he's enjoying himself, as he always enjoys himself, every minute of every day. He wouldn't mind a bit if we sat down right here and talked for an hour, he's in no hurry to go anywhere. Which leads me to another reminder – don't go hairless if you think the service is bad in any hotel or wherever. When we booked in we were lucky the receptionist wasn't out taking a swim – otherwise we might have had to wait an hour.'

I laughed. 'Beautiful. Actually, it's not all that different from home. Have you ever tried to pay for anything on a Woolworth's counter on Oxford Street?'

We strolled on, reached the end of the pier. The young Tahitian lad beamed a smile and got to his feet.

'You can sail it OK,' he enquired, looking at Buzz and me.

Buzz nodded. 'I think so.'

'I sail it for you, if you want.'

'No, I guess we can manage, thanks.'

'OK, have a nice time.'

It was a simple craft, slim and white with a single white sail and an outrigger boom running amidships, the float on the portside. I jumped down into it, helped Maggie and Carol in, and Buzz followed.

'You care to take it out, Tobin?'

'Sure – if you want to end up in New Guinea. Strangely, we didn't get much chance to learn the art of sailing in the backstreets of Liverpool, the puddles were too shallow.'

'Ladies, how about you?' he offered.

'Sure,' said Maggie, winking at Carol. 'I'll take it out.'

'Oh,' said Buzz, crestfallen.

'Go on,' laughed Maggie, 'I know you're dying to impress us.'

'Well, if you insist . . .'

In a couple of minutes we were creaming across the unbelievably clear water, Maggie standing on the starboard gunwale boom, Carol seated in the stern with Buzz, and me standing in the bow, relishing the warmth of the sun and wind and marvelling yet again how beautiful the world could be.

'Ain't this the life!' whooped Buzz, scooping up a handful of water and throwing it in the air. 'What price the five o'clock traffic jam now, Tobin?'

I turned and frowned. 'What is "traffic jam", massa?'

'Aw, we're all crazy . . . *insane*, I tell you! You know what my father's doing right now? – he's sitting at a desk, in a jacket and tie, in a sweltering office that faces the building next door, getting all knotted up because a guy in Waverley sent in his life insurance premium three cents short! At five o'clock he'll fizz and fume in a traffic crawl all the way home and my ma will say, "Had a good day, Jack?" "Lousy, Phyl . . . some silly bugger sent in his premium three cents short, couldn't balance my books. Took me all day to find it." God, what a life.'

We all laughed, but I, perhaps better than the girls, understood the poignancy of Buzz's point. I'd been through it myself. They creep up on you, these miserable little matters of tremendous importance, reproducing like germ cells until life beyond them ceases to exist, insidiously transforming a healthy, robust male animal into a wizened adding machine, as far removed from his anthropological ancestors as a mouse from a mammoth.

Trouble is, it's such a gradual metamorphosis you don't notice it – not until you visit a place like Tahiti, then the full extent of your natural dehydration comes home with a bang.

I thought of my own father, drudging his life away in the office of the local council for . . . nearly thirty years! Never had a real holiday . . . never been further than Chester, fifteen miles from his home. And if he was here right now, he'd be on the nearest beach, paddling in the shallows with his trousers turned up to the knee, bless him. You'd certainly never get him in for a swim or a sail in a boat . . . and after three days I reckon he'd be pining for his office. Ah, well.

'Penny for yours,' said a voice in my ear. Maggie had come

up behind me. She looked marvellous at that moment, the wind ruffling her soft flame hair and plastering the cotton shift against her full-breasted body.

'Hello, *vahiné* girl, enjoying yourself?'

'I'm ecstatic. I find myself smiling all the time and bubbling with pleasure.'

I laughed. 'Me, too. I'm grinning so much my face is aching.'

She moved up beside me and slipped her arm round my waist. 'Did you ever see such water?'

'Never. You can see every grain of sand down there. How deep will it be now?'

'Oh, about eight . . . ten feet.'

'Never. It doesn't look more than three.'

'Shall I prove it to you?'

'Yes, I demand proof.'

She released me. There was a blur of colour as the shift flew from her head and dropped behind her, then another blur of tanned flesh clad in the tiniest yellow bikini as she arched into the air and cut the water like a knife.

'Haul in!' I shouted to Buzz, watching her arrow to the bottom, then curl to touch it with her foot, holding one arm high aloft, her hand still several feet below the surface.

Buzz swung the sail boom inboard and dropped the sail with a rush. 'Playtime?'

'Playtime.'

I discarded my shirt, kicked off my beach shoes and took a header, disbelieving the warmth of the water as it enfolded me. Down . . . down . . . down . . . straight between Maggie's open legs. She caught me, held me, so I turned and hooked my fingers into her little bikini knicks, threatening to pull them down.

With a playful smack she released me and shot to the surface. I followed, tickling her feet all the way. We broke surface, laughing breathlessly.

'You wouldn't have dared,' she gasped.

'Wanna bet?'

'No, you devil.'

'Isn't this water fabulous?'

'Fabulous. Come on – race you to the boat.'

As we struck out, Buzz executed a superlative jack-knife off the boat, followed by Carol. I would like to be able to say I let

Maggie win, but she beat me all ends up, streaking through the water like a female Mark Spitz.

'That's a thousand dollars you owe me,' she gasped clinging to the boat. 'Oh didn't I tell you there was a bet on it? I took it for granted you knew. It's an old Tahitian custom.'

'So is this,' I laughed, making a dive for her.

But she was off again in a supersonic crawl, round the boat, blinding me with her splashing wake. Cunning was called for. I took a breath and dived, cut under the shallow boat and came up the other side, right in front of her.

'Ohh!'

'Gotcha! You owe me a kiss. Oh, didn't I tell you, that's also an old Tahitian custom.'

She laughed. 'Well, who am I to deny an old Tahitian custom?'

I caught her head and gave her a nice, soft wet one, all warm and salty, the feel of her near-naked body on mine tripping my switch instantly.

Her eyes went funny, languid and dreamy and she murmured, 'Don't do that, I think I like it.'

'You feel wonderful, Maggie . . . all warm and squashy.'

'And you do not,' she said sternly. 'Doesn't take you long, does it, Tobin . . . even in water. I reckon you missed your vocation . . . you should be a standard-bearer for the Salvation Army. Put it away, for heaven's sake, or you'll have the navy gunboats out.'

With a whoosh she left me, dived deep to inspect a small coral formation on the bottom, and I went after her, marvelling at the perfection of her body, her grace of movement.

For perhaps fifteen minutes we kibbitzed around, dived for stones, chased each other, caught each other, kissed each other, then finally she headed for the boat and hauled herself inboard.

I didn't immediately follow her but skirted the boat, treading water and occasionally floating face-up to the sun.

Her laughter brought me out of one of these floats into vertical position. 'What's funny?'

'You are.'

'Really.'

'I wish I had a camera, you'd hoot, too. You look like U-boat

47 in camouflage out there.'

'You shouldn't be looking.'

'How can I help it when you fill the horizon?'

'How you exaggerate.'

'You think so? You're not sitting where I'm sitting. Come on in for some sun.'

I climbed aboard and towelled off, watching Buzz and Carol performing circus acrobatics a hundred yards off.

'Isn't it nice to see people enjoying themselves?' she said. 'What enormous, simple fun you can have in a place like this.'

She lay on a towel in the bottom of the boat and closed her eyes against the sun. I sat on the side of the boat and ogled her, finding delicious pleasure in the nearness of her near-naked body, its texture and contours, the flatness of naked belly and the rise of her breasts.

'Tobin,' she murmured, 'you're staring.'

'How do you know, you've got your eyes closed.'

'What are you looking at?'

'You.'

'What part of me?'

'All of you.'

'You're a fibber, you haven't looked at my feet once.'

I laughed.

'And what do you see?'

'An immensely beautiful and exciting woman ... glowing with health and sexuality.'

'You *are* in holiday mood.'

'Right. Strange, isn't it, how the sun and sea gives us licence to do things that are tabu in another time and place. Imagine us walking down Fifth Avenue dressed like this. And if you caught a chap sneaking a peep at your panties in a train, you'd blush like a beetroot and haul your dress down to your ankles.'

Her mouth spread in a teasing smile. 'Maybe not ... depends on the guy. Now, if it was you ...'

'Yes?'

'I'd scream blue murder and call the guard ... have you arrested for visual rape.'

'Do I really look that determined?'

'Worse.'

'Well, you're right.'

I moved, spread my towel alongside her and lay down on my stomach.

'Now, Tobin . . .'

'I'm only lying down.'

'You're only lying.'

'You know you look totally irresistible right now . . .?'

'Yes.'

I leaned towards her and planted a gossamer kiss on her soft lips.

'You mustn't . . . do that.'

'Why not?'

'Because . . .'

I kissed her again . . . and again, light, fleeting love-notes of tender affection.

She opened her eyes and smiled up at me, touched my cheek with her finger tips, her voice drowsy and bed-warm. 'You're making Tahiti all it can possibly be.'

'That's as nice a thing as a man could wish to hear, Maggie. That's the ultimate compliment.'

'Well, it's so. There's so much beauty here . . . so much idyllic, fairy-tale beauty, but without the right person to share it . . . without a handsome, funny, lovely lover to share it, it would be just another place, another island. You are making it . . . magical.'

I frowned at her, very touched. 'Maggie, I . . .'

She reached up and kissed me, laughed at me. 'You don't have to agree. I don't care if you're having a terrible time, I'm ecstatically happy.'

'So am I,' I grinned. 'And you're absolutely right – if I didn't have you to share it with, I'd be miserable as sin.'

'Ha!' she scoffed. 'You wouldn't be without a girl for five minutes. You'd have driven straight into Papeete and mesmerized the first good-looker you set eyes on.'

'You're wrong,' I lied. 'I'd have been lying on my bed right now, pining with thoughts of you.'

She gasped, appalled. 'Oh!'

I grinned. 'So, you see what you saved me from – death by inate grief . . . OW!'

A shock of cold water sprayed over the side of the boat, drenching us.

'Caught you!' laughed Buzz, elbowing himself up.

Carol appeared at his side. 'What were they up to?'

'I couldn't possibly describe it . . . unimaginable abandon.'

'Chance would be a fine thing,' I muttered.

They climbed aboard and towelled off, spraying us with water, Carol performing an intriguing display of voluptuous callisthentics in a blue floral bikini as brief as convention would allow.

'Fabulous . . . fabulous . . . fabulous,' she panted, shaking out her blonde tresses. 'I may decide to quit Qantas in the next hour and go native.'

'You can't, you're wearing too many clothes,' remarked Buzz.

'*That* can soon be rectified,' she retorted, and reached for the fastener on her bra.

Buzz and I laughed at the gesture, knowing she wouldn't go through with it, but our laughter was short-lived.

Snick!

My mouth dropped open, Buzz's followed.

She slid the strings from her arms, threw the bra away and presented herself to us with a smile of proud challenge. 'There . . . see if I care. It's all ridiculous bloody nonsense anyhow.'

I didn't know where to look. I gaped at Buzz . . . back to Carol . . . God, she was beautiful, an Amazon, stacked to perfection, her nipples standing out like deep pink bullets.

'Ha . . . *ha*!' laughed Maggie, sitting up. 'Well, good for you, girl! Just *look* at their faces!'

'What's good for St Trop is good for Tahiti,' Carol said defiantly. 'And I'm fed up with snow-white boobs and a tanned everything else. I look like a damn patch-work quilt.'

'Oh, I'm not complaining,' protested Buzz, grinning like a loon. 'I mean, I'm all for getting back to nature.'

'Then take your trunks off,' challenged Carol.

'Eh? Oh, now, wait a minute . . .'

'Marvellous aren't they?' she appealed to Maggie. 'They'd love us to walk around in the nude, but when it's their turn, they suddenly turn Victorian.'

'We-e-ll,' complained Buzz, 'we've got more to . . . protect than you birds.'

'Prove it,' said Carol, winking at Maggie.

'No,' said Buzz.

'Chicken!'

'I'm not!'

'Well, go on, get 'em off.'

'No.'

'Then you're chicken.'

Suddenly he was gone, backwards over the side, hitting the water with a hell of a splash. For a good ten seconds he was lost in the maelstrom, then suddenly bobbed up, his arm aloft, holding his swim trunks. 'There!'

'Come out, come out, wherever you are!' called Carol.

'Like hell . . .'

'Then I shall come in!'

Then she was over the side, reappearing a moment later close to the boat, her hand raised for the throw. Splot! Into the boat flew her panties. She was starkers!

'Christ . . .' howled Buzz.

'Come here, Malone!' she called. 'Give me those trunks!'

'You're crazy! You're a sex fiend!'

'Bullseye! Come here you gorgeous hunk of man!'

He was off in a flurry of strokes, his trunks gripped in his teeth, and she was after him, catching up fast.

Maggie and I watched them for a while then, laughing, lay down again on the towels.

'She's quite a character,' I chuckled. 'I reckon Buzz has got his hands full for the next couple of days.'

'Of anything in particular?' she grinned.

'Hm, very beautiful.'

'Were you disappointed I didn't follow suit?'

I shook my head. 'No.'

'Any particular reason?'

I nodded. 'Yep.'

'What was it?'

'Oh, I . . . happen to believe in things happening in the right time and the right place.'

She smiled softly. 'Yes, I know . . . that's why I didn't do it.'

I looked at her, excitement and deep fondness welling within me. 'You know something, Maggie . . . I think I rather like you.'

She didn't say anything, just turned away with a contented smile and closed her eyes to the benevolent sun.

CHAPTER THREE

It was almost five o'clock when we docked the outrigger and made our way back through the gardens to our rooms, arm in arm, saturated with sun and sea and salt and aglow with a sense of buoyant well-being, agreeing it had been a fabulous afternoon. Personally speaking, I hadn't felt so damn good in a long time, so filled with the kind of exhilaration that makes you want to leap in the air and shout out loud, just for the hell of it.

The girls, naturally complained about the condition of their hair and begged at least three hours to do something about it. So, refusing Buzz's offer to escort her back to her hotel, Carol quickly changed in Maggie's room and took a cab there by herself, Buzz and I retiring to our own room, arranging to meet them at eight o'clock.

'Yeeee ... owwww!' he exploded, flinging himself on his bed and almost snapping off the legs. 'What a day ... what a bird ... what a flamin' marvellous holiday! Ain't she the livin' limit? Whoosh! – just like that ... starkers! I'm glad to see you had the decency to keep your gaze averted, Tobin.'

'It's the very least a gentleman could do, Buzz. I mean, you don't go ogling your mate's bra-less bird, now, do you?'

'Pity you missed 'em, though ... wonderful. Hee hee ...' he sat up, rubbing his hands lasciviously. 'Oh, what a night it was, it really w-a-a-s such a night ...' he warbled, and sat up to light a fag. 'Well, so far old Tahiti is living up to its reputation. And I reckon a couple of weeks here some time in the very near future is an absolute must, what d'you say?'

'Have you ever known me to disagree with you on matters of real importance?'

'Never, you're a stout man, Here, have a fag.'

'My God, the spirit of the islands is really getting to you.'

I sat on the edge of my bed and lit up, then reclined against the headboard with a contented sigh.

'Ah, Buzz, Buzz . . . is this the life or isn't it? I reckon those guys who opt out of the rat-race and spend their days beachcombing a place like this are really on to something. Reckon you could do it?'

He laughed. 'I'd give it a bloody good try.'

'Heck of a far cry from what we've been brought up to, though, isn't it?' I said 'We'd really have to work hard at learning to relax the way these people relax. One thing we'd have to stifle is a thumping great conscience because we're not slaving away at something we detest from nine till five. Mind you, you're not so bad, you *are* doing what you like doing, playing tennis.'

'Well, so are you, aren't you?'

'At the moment, yes, but I'm beginning to squirm because I haven't done a job for a few weeks.'

He grinned. 'You worked in Toronto, didn't you?'

'Ha! That was work? – doing a few repairs for a couple of sex-starved housewives?'

'Well, we'll get you working in Sydney, son. If your conscience is crying out for good honest labour, I can fix you up digging holes for the Highways Department.'

'Now, don't let's get ridiculous. Anyway – back to the question, do you reckon you could chuck up civilization and bum around in the sun in a place like this?'

He shook his head. 'Not exactly bum around . . . not do nothing. But I reckon I could be happy running a little business here – maybe a boatyard or an inter-island flying service, something like that. Yes, I reckon I could do that.'

I nodded. 'Me, too.'

I got off the bed and strolled out on to the verandah, Buzz following.

'Oh, boy,' he murmured and I nodded, smitten to speechlessness by the indescribable stillness and beauty of the evening, by the turquoise luminescence of the lagoon and the vivid pink sun-fire that pervaded the darkening sky.

Out to our left the mountainous loom of magical Moorea was fading, blending into the blur of night, contrasting with the harbour, a mile to our right, now beginning to pinpoint its existence with a scattering of lights.

'Not much like Bootle,' I sighed.

'Oh! What's Bootle?'

I frowned at him. 'You call yourself a travelled man and you've never been to Bootle – gateway to the Liverpool docks? Now, there's a place for *real* sunsets. To stand on Miller's Bridge and look out over Brocklebank Dock on a summer's evening is an experience not to be repeated, I can tell you. Come on, let's get changed, I'm getting homesick.'

He looked at me, startled. 'Are you kidding?'

'Yes!' I laughed, and beat him into the shower.

The girls had surpassed themselves – Carol in a Grecian-cut, knee-length dress of red and white cotton, her blonde hair shimmering around her shoulders, and Maggie looking radiantly lovely in an off-the-shoulder pale green creation of sensuous silk that left no doubt whatsoever as to her sex.

We met them in the reception, gladly.

As for Buzz and me, we were relaxed and comfortable in slacks and sports shirts, the blessed custom of the island, and as for me, no evening can possibly fail when it begins in this gear. I was running full throttle on all six cylinders.

As we approached the girls I went into a feined stagger, shielding my eyes and groping for the wall. 'Buzz, I . . . I'm stricken . . . remove this blinding beauty from my sight!'

He pouted. 'Well, I knew I looked pretty sharp, Russ, but I didn't think I was *that* terrific. OK, I'll go and change . . . hang on.'

'Idiots,' laughed Maggie.

We went to them, gave them a hug, told them how good they looked.

'Ready?' asked Maggie.

'Ready.'

'Then – let's go.'

We piled into a waiting cab and barely had time to settle back before we were at Quinn's Club, situated on the Quay Bir-Hackeim and overlooking the wharf at the west end of the harbour.

We paid off the cab and let Maggie lead the way into bedlam, into a happy raucous confusion of laughter and music emanating from the big, smoky room with a huge round bar. There must have been twelve thousand people in there, many of them in French navy whites.

'Try over there!' Maggie shouted, pointing to the right, and I took the lead, easing a passage between the tight-pressed bodies.

I turned to her and grinned. 'Quiet tonight, hm . . .?'

'The fleet's in!'

'No kidding!' I laughed, squeezing passed a forty-stone stoker with a Polynesian dolly on each arm.

Making like an ice-breaker, I forged a passage through the dense throng and came out into a small clearing against the far wall, turning to relay the good news to the others.

'We got a table!'

They struggled through and flopped down gratefully, phewing at the crush.

'Is it always like this?' asked Buzz.

Maggie grinned. 'No – sometimes it closes. This is one of *the* places on Tahiti. Sit in Quinn's long enough and eventually you'll meet everyone in the world.'

A young Polynesian waiter approached, grinning happily despite the crush.

'Let's try something Tahitian for a change,' suggested Buzz. 'How about a rum punch or something – in a coconut shell?'

'Four Quinn's specials,' nodded the waiter, and departed.

I looked around the room and found myself grinning at the high spirits of the patrons, dancing and jigging to the rowdy Tahitian band or standing around in groups, shouting to one another against the deafening noise. Everyone – tourist, resident and uniformed man alike – having a great old time.

I leaned towards Maggie who winced, smilingly, at the racket. 'What a place to be stationed! I shouldn't think many of these navy guys ask for a transfer!'

She laughed. 'Only for recuperation leave – give them time to recover!'

'Hmm . . . when I get to Sydney I might just make a few enquiries about joining the French navy. Could be I've hit on the one career I was really cut out for!'

'Oh, is that so . . . well, I hope they post you to the South Pole to count penguins!'

I cast an eye across the room, only now getting my first close-up view of Polynesian girls in any number and finding them, with the odd exception, just as attractive as the travel brochures pictured them – gay, vivacious creatures with beautiful skin and dazzling smiles.

My reverie was interrupted by a kick on the shin. 'I know what's going through that scurrilous mind, Tobin, but you can forget about black-haired *vahinés* until I'm off the island.'

I gasped. 'Maggie . . . honestly, I . . . it was a study of purely anthropological interest.'

'Really . . . and I could say precisely the same about that tall, dark, handsome French sailor over there with the cute moustache.'

I swung round. 'Which . . . who . . . where?'

As I detected the pint-sized squirt and turned back to her with a glower, she burst out laughing. 'Well, he *might* have been tall, dark and handsome.'

'Yes . . . well . . . you just keep your eyes pointing in this direction.'

'Truce?'

I grinned. 'Truce.'

Our drinks arrived – piquant rum concoctions served in lopped green coconut shells.

'Aloha!' toasted Buzz, sucking up a goodly draught and choking. 'By the heck, eighteen of these and I won't know me *tamaaraa* from me *ahimaa* – nor care.'

We all took a gulp and got fags going, adding another three degrees of obscurity to the already dense fug. And then . . .

'Well, hel*lo*, there . . . !'

The voice came from my right, as through a 5,000-watt stereo speaker. I turned – and was blinded by the shirt. My eyes travelled up, over the proud mound of a beer-vat belly to cherubic cheeks and a Santa Claus smile, overtly distorted by at least six too many.

'*Say*, now, I'll bet you folks are from the good ole US of A – right?'

Maggie lowered her drink and threw me a wince, murmured, 'Here we go, folks,' and turned a smile of facetious welcome on our new-found friend.

'Only one of us – that's me. My friends here are Australian . . . and this gentleman is from England.'

'No kiddin'!' beamed Santa, thrusting a hand like an inflated rubber glove at Maggie. 'Maxwell F. Woolberry of Oklahoma City an' I'm mighty glad t'make your acquaintance, ma'm. May I ask where you hail from?'

'From Boston,' smiled Maggie, removing her hand.

'Well, I'll be . . . Boston, fancy that. You bin in Tahiti long?' He turned on me. 'Maxwell F. Woolberry, sir, delighted to make your acquaintance.'

'Russ Tobin, how d'you do.'

He stretched across the table, flattening my straw with his belly, and shook Buzz by the hand. 'Maxwell F. Woolberry, sir, sure is good t'meet you . . .'

'Hi,' grinned Buzz. 'Buzz Malone . . . Sydney.'

'Hey, now, which is it – Buzz or Sydney?'

Buzz laughed. 'No, it's Buzz Malone . . . from Sydney . . . Australia.'

'My mistake, I beg your pardon. Hi, there Miss . . Maxwell F. Woolberry, Oklahoma City, how gracious you look.'

Carol shook his hand. 'Carol Dwyer . . also of Sydney.'

'Well, now, ain't that just dandy.' He eased off the table, taking the menu and Maggie's evening bag with him, to the floor, without noticing.

In the next three minutes he back-stepped into a passing waiter, sending a tray and four glasses crashing to the floor, trod on my foot, punched a French sailor in the ear with an outflung hand, and sent a German tourist teetering into the crowd with an unconscious buttock-buffet.

Maxwell F. Woolberry, it was quickly transpiring, was not merely a cheerful, chatty, three-hundred-pound retired baby-wear salesman from Oklahoma City, he was also a living and breathing myth-shatterer – the myth that all fat men are light on their feet and always innately graceful. Graceful? Max in full stride made a rampaging bull elephant look like Dame Margot Fontaine on one of her better nights, and if we hadn't finally got him sat down I reckon he'd have cleared the bleeding bar before nine.

'There, that's better!' he chuckled, quite unaware of the devastation he'd caused and misconstruing our invitation to be seated as a gesture of spontaneous friendship. 'When folks invite Max Woolberry t'take the weight off of his feet, they really mean it!'

He exploded into bubbling laughter, his belly shaking the table and slopping our drinks. 'Say, this is mighty kinda you young people, askin' me to join yuh. An' old Max is gonna buy you 'nuther drink to show he's grateful . . .'

On that he swung round, flinging out an arm preparatory to calling a waiter, and knocked the flower pareo clean off the head of a guy behind.

'Er . . . garçon! . . . senhor! . . . could we have a coupla drinks over here, s'il vouz please!'

He turned back to us, grinning proudly. 'Kinda helps a bit if yuh speak the lingo around here. A fella told me t'learn a phrase or two of Française before I came out an', by golly, it sure has come in handy. You kids all on vacation here? Whatya think of it, ain't it just fantastic? I tell yuh, I've never seen anythin' so beautiful in my life. An' interestin'! Heck, I've met some real interestin' characters right here in this bar that just stop yuh breath with their stories. I wus talking to a guy last night who usta run a pearl schooner outta Papeete harbour . . . boy, the stories he had t'tell about the goin's on in these islands in the good old days, beggin' your pardon, ladies, but I reckon if I'd known what I know now, I never woulda bin a baby-wear salesman in Oke City! Ha ha, I'da bin right here in these islands manufacturin' new customers!' He erupted into volcanic laughter, earthquaking the table off its legs and finally dissolving into a coughing, choking fit that drowned out the band.

A flurry of grins and grimaces flashed between the four of us, the general consensus being that we had to get rid of Merry Max as quickly as possible, before he wrecked the table and split somebody's head open; but easier said than done. Max looked settled for the night.

The drinks arrived.

'Ah, merci, garçon . . .' said Max expansively, reaching for his wallet. 'Er . . . combi-yan . . . is this lot?'

The waiter grinned . . . and replied in perfect English. 'That will be five hundred francs, sir.'

'Oh . . . yeh . . .'

When the waiter had gone, Max shrugged and said, 'Well, how did I know?' He raised his coconut. 'Well, here's to as nice a buncha young folk as I could ever wish t'meet. A votre health, as the French say . . . have a real bien temps.' And with that he threw back his drink and spilled it all down his shirt.

'Oh, Jeezus . . . say, what you kids doin' tonight? Got a party lined up?'

'Yes, a native *tamaaraa*,' replied Maggie. 'As a matter of fact, we really ought to be making a move now.'

'Aw, that's too bad. Got far to go, have you?'

'To the Tahiti Village Beach Hotel, it's quite a way.'

'Aw, that's too bad. What kind of a wing-ding would that be, now?'

'It's an outdoor dinner,' explained Maggie. 'Polynesian food . . . an exhibition of dancing . . .'

'No kiddin'! Say, that sounds like real fun! Can anybody go? I mean, can they just run up on spec an get in?'

Three warning glances flashed in Maggie's direction but she was way ahead of us. 'No, I'm sure you have to book, Mister Woolberry. We booked through our hotel this afternoon.'

'Gee, that's too bad. Well, maybe another time. I sure would like to catch one of those . . . whatchacall' em?'

'*Tamaaraa*.'

He gave a chuckle, prelude, we sensed, to another destructive eruption.

'Well . . . if I don't catch one today . . . maybe I'll catch one *tamaaraa* . . . hee heee . . . ho . . . ho . . . ha ha ha ha ha . . . !'

We all lunged to save our drinks but he fooled us – this time toppling backwards in his chair and smashing into the guy behind. 'Oh, Christ . . . !'

We got out – quick, collapsing with laughter outside, and we were still laughing when we reached the Tahiti Village Beach Hotel.

Disembarking from the cab on the coast road, we entered the hotel reception area and passed through it, emerging into a palm and flower garden, the sounds of music and festive gaiety drawing us quickly towards the main body of the hotel a hundred yards further on. Built in traditional Tahitian style, the main body comprised four high-peaking, thatched-roofed sections converging on a central breezeway, this area containing an open-air terrace bar overlooking the gently sloping white sand beach and the fabulous lagoon.

Here, in this romantic tropical setting, the entire area illuminated by concealed artificial lighting and a perimeter of natural flame torches, perhaps two hundred guests, resplendent in colourful sports shirts and dresses and adorned with flower leis and pareos, sat at rustic tables watching the symmetrical contortions of a group of eight female Polynesian dancers, attired in gay red pareos and tops, and twirling flaming torches.

At our entrance, a beaming Tahitian maiden, a right nubile cracker in a scanty red-flowered skirt and a minimal bra, flowers in her hair and around her neck, approached us and bade us welcome, placed pareos of red and white hibiscus on our heads and leis over them, and led us to a table already occupied by four other guests.

As we took the bench seats, a waiter arrived with exotic drinks in green coçonuts, and with a sip of these we settled down and gave our attention to the dancers.

They were beautiful, the epitome of sensual grace, writhing and turning, undulating and swaying to the langorous yet joyful native music, their flaming torches describing golden cometlike arcs against the blackness of the sky and lighting their happy, radiant faces with flickering fire.

Maggie's hand on mine brought me out of my trance. 'You like it?' she asked softly.

I smiled and nodded, answer enough, then took her hand and held it as we returned to watch the dancing.

Suddenly a change of rhythm. The drums broke out in a wild, though as yet subdued beat, harbinger of the tempest to come. The dancers became transformed, from languid ballerinas into quivering, shuffling pagans, their hips vibrating like twanged tuning-forks, their pelvic contortions blatantly sexual.

Then into the arena, from the darkness beyond, leaped eight Polynesian males, similarly attired in brief red skirts and crowns of leaves and flowers (though without bras) and the gymnastics really began.

Jumping, wriggling, trembling and vibrating, they advanced on the maidens, skirted them, danced through and around them, getting them worked up into a right old state. The drum beat increased, became loud, wild, hysterical, deafening, driving the dancers into paroxysms of pelvic contortion . . . on and on . . . the intensity of the rhythm and the skill and endurance of the dancers drawing at first gasps of amazement, then a smattering of spontaneous applause from the crowd . . . now wholehearted applause, the reaction of a thrilled and excited audience. The beat increased yet again, the volume rose, building, soaring to a tremendous, exploding climax . . . and at the very pinnacle the dancers released a wild, exuberant yell and ran triumphant from the arena into the dark shadows of the garden.

Applause burst from the crowd. They yelled, whooped, cheered, bringing the dancers back for a well-deserved curtain call, and as the applause and excitement died, the music continued, once again, dreamy and romantic.

As the arena resounded to the buzz of comment, an army of Polynesian waiters and waitresses in native costume swarmed to the tables bearing trays of steaming food – wooden bowls and huge platters laden with a great assortment of dishes . . . fish, meat, vegetables, fruit, some recognizable, others not.

'Now, what have we got here?' I asked Maggie.

'Oh, all kinds of things . . . that's called *poisson mariné* – it's fish cut into cubes, marinated in lemon juice and cooked in coconut milk, quite beautiful. And that is . . .' she smiled, '. . . that's *rousette*, though I'm not sure I should tell you what it's made of.'

'Oh, why not?'

'Well, Englishmen are not notoriously adventurous about such things.'

I gulped. 'I see . . . well, go on, tell me. I can always miss it.'

She laughed. 'Well, it's – flying fox cooked in wine.'

I gulped again and she laughed again. 'It really is very good.'

'Really. Er . . . and what's that over there?'

'Coward. That is *lap-lap* – tapioca garnished with coconut milk and baked in banana leaves.'

'Sounds more like my style . . . go on.'

She pointed out pawpaw, mango, mangrove oysters, and for myself I could see lobster, prawns, pineapple, a dozen lovely things.

'Like to start with the *rousette*?' she teased.

'No thank you, Maggie, I think I'll stick to fish.'

Well, we'd just got started and we were thoroughly enjoying

ourselves, trying a bit of this and a bit of that, chattering among ourselves and to the other four people at the table (nice, quiet, middle-aged Americans), soaking up the balmy Tahitian night and the romance of a gentle love-chant now being sung by the dancers, when suddenly it happened . . .

'Well, *hi*, there, my friends . . . !'

The greeting came from behind me and at its sound my blood ran cold. Buzz, sitting opposite me, looked up, gaped and groaned. 'Oh, no . . .'

Maggie and I turned, our spirits plummeting at the sight of Maxwell F. Woolberry bearing down on us fast, a coconut cocktail clutched in one hand, a cigar in the other, a lei strung round his neck and a pareo of flowers, four sizes too small, stuck on top of his bald head like a napkin ring on an ostrich egg.

'Ha *ha* . . . surprise, surprise . . . guess yuh didn't expect old Max t'turn up, did yuh?'

He loomed over us, shoving the cigar between his teeth to free a hand in order to thump me a beaut on the shoulder. 'Russ, old buddy, how're you doin' there . . . looks like you kids are eatin' mighty high on the hog, quite a feast you got goin' here. Well, I just *had* t'take a gander at a Tahitian *tamaaraa*, you made it sound so temptin', Maggie, so after you'd gone I got right on the phone an' booked me a place. Sure hope you kids don't mind me joinin' you . . .'

With my face averted, I grimaced at Buzz and Carol and touched Maggie on the knee. What could we say or do? The guy had paid his money. We had no choice in the matter.

But one thing we were determined about – he wasn't going to sit with us. Fortunately, when we'd sat down, we'd bunched fairly close together at one end of the table, leaving a bit of a gap between us and the people already sitting there, so there was no chance of him squeezing in between us.

And now, the Americans, hearing and seeing him approach and quickly putting two and two together, were subtly closing ranks, edging towards us, obviously annoyed at the prospect of a noisy, three-hundred-pound intruder – and they didn't know the half of him!

'Well . . . no,' I said, hesitantly, 'but I'm afraid there's no room . . .'

'Aw, don't you worry about that . . . Max'll get himself fixed up somehow . . .'

His glance went down the table to the other four people who were head-down to their food, hoping he'd drop dead or disappear through a hole. 'Well, hi there, folks . . . dare I make a guess that you're all fellow-Americans?'

He moved off to a gush of relief from us and a groan from the others.

'Yeh, that's right,' one of the men answered shortly.

'By golly, I *knew* it . . .' He leaned across the table, stretching out a hand, forcing one of the ladies to bend so low her nose was all but buried in a bowl of prawns.

'Maxwell F. Woolberry from Oklahoma City . . . mighty glad t'make your acquaintance, sir.'

'Frank Dell . . . Dallas,' retorted the grey-haired man tartly. 'An' that's my wife Emily you're crowdin' a bit there.'

'Oh, my profound apologies, ma'm . . . this barrel a mine tends t'get in the way sometimes. Well, whadyaknow – Dallas, Texas, we're practically neighbours. I know Dallas well – usta cover that territory in babywear . . . sellin' it, not wearin' it, . . . ha ha ha ha . . .' he exploded into jiggling laughter, slopping his drink and dropping an inch of cigar ash on to the terrace of his belly.

'Ouch . . . wow, that's *hot* . . . !' he swiped at it, sending a cloud of ash in the direction of the other American man.

'Hey, careful there, buddy . . .'

'Oh, I'm sorry . . . Maxwell F. Woolberry, sir, an' do I detect anuther Texan?'

'Bill Moran,' scowled the Texan. 'Dallas . . . my wife, Jean.'

'A great pleasure, ma'am . . . my, just look at all that won'erful food. These folk certainly do you proud at these *tamaaraas*. 'Fraid I was a little late gettin' here . . . in fact, if it hadn'a been for my good friends down the table, there, I wouldn't be here at all!'

Frank Dell shot us a glance, got the picture from our expressions and returned to his food, dismissing Woolberry with, 'That so . . .'

'Yes, sir, indeedee . . . never gave it a thought until Miss Maggie there started telling me about it an' made it sound so goldarned enticin' I . . .'

At that moment the young vahiné who had met us and escorted us to our table came up, full of concern that Woolberry wasn't seated. 'Ah, you have no seat, sir . . . you would like to sit with your friends? So . . .' she turned and clapped her hands at a distant waiter who spotted the dilemma and came over at a run with a short rustic bench.

'There you are, sir . . . please be comfortable and enjoy your meal.'

'Well, merci, boocoo, mad'maselle . . . eel ay tray bonne of yuh.'

The faces of the four Americans were portraits of dismay.

'Sure, hope you folks don't mind me joinin' you,' chuckled Woolberry, 'but darn it, it's just like home. Ah, thank yuh, sonny . . .' the waiter quickly spread a selection of cutlery, added a plate, then departed. '. . . merci, boocoo, garçon . . . !' Woolberry called after him, turning in a shroud of cigar smoke to accept the plaudits of the assembly.

'Always like t'throw in a little local lingo, reckon they appreciate it.'

'Woolberry, would ya mind killin' that cigar,' growled Frank Dell. 'It's lousin' up my lobster.'

'Sure thing, no trouble at all . . .'

He dropped the offending stogey to the ground, pressed on it with his foot, grinned at Dell and let out a 'Jeezuschrist . . .'

'What the hell's the matter now?' rapped Dell.

'My sneakers . . . Jeezus, that burned . . . beggin' your pardon, ladies.' He recovered quickly. 'Say, I wonder if you'd mind passin' that fine looking dish of lobster . . . just so happens it's my favourite food.' To prove the point he cleared the dish. 'And a touch of that whateveritis . . . looks mighty appetisin'.'

Dell passed the dish and watched with ill-concealed distaste as Woolberry piled his plate.

'Well, reckon that's enough to be goin' on with,' chortled Woolberry, 'though it sure looks like there's gonna be plenty of seconds.' He drove his fork into the food and shovelled in a huge mouthful, the residue seeping out and clinging to his fat lips. 'Shay . . . thish is dee-lishus . . . what is it?'

'Flying fox,' said Dell quietly.

Like a run-down mechanical toy, Woolberry's jaws stopped grinding. He looked at Dell, in disbelief, his eyes searching for, praying for the joke. 'You're kidding . . .'

Dell emitted a short laugh and shook his head. 'No . . . it's flyin' fox, all right . . . you know, those bat-like creatures that fly through the air from tree to tree . . . like monkeys . . .'

All round the table we were locked in stifled laughter, in pleats at Woolberry's bug-eyed expression.

With a gasped, 'Oh, my God . . .' he lowered his fork and stared at the offending food as though it was crawling. Slowly, almost unconsciously, his jaws began to work again, then with a mighty, sickened gulp he swallowed the huge mouthful, grabbed for his drink, hurled away the straw and threw back his head, swallowing the lot.

'They . . .' he choked, slavering rum punch down his shirt, 'they got no right servin' Western folk that . . . Flyin' *fox*, ye gods, how terrible . . . ugh . . .' he shuddered.

'Would you care for some more lobster, Mister Woolberry?' Mrs Dell asked sweetly, gesturing towards another dish.

Woolberry shook his head violently. 'No, ma'm . . . no, thank you, nothin' else . . . I . . . I think I'll just go an' freshen up abit, if you'll excuse me.'

'Sure,' said Bill Moran. 'You go right ahead, Mister Woolberry.'

Max scraped back his bench and stood up, gave the flying fox one last withering glare, and lumbered off towards the bar.

As he disappeared, the table erupted in laughter, Frank Dell signalled a waiter to remove Max's plate, and we all resumed our dinner, each group retiring to its own conversation.

'Boy, you meet 'em,' said Buzz, shaking his head. 'Anywhere you go, you'll meet a Max Woolberry . . . loud, crude, pushy . . .'

'Well, I feel sorry for him,' dissented Maggie quietly.

Buzz and I looked at each other, then at her.

'You do?' frowned Buzz.

'So do I,' added Carol. 'I think he's a sad, pathetic man.'

Buzz gave a sigh and shrugged at me. 'Women.'

'He's obviously terribly lonely,' Maggie continued. 'And he must have a gigantic complex about his size.'

'Gigantic,' grinned Buzz. 'But, Maggie, you must admit he's a pain in the . . . neck. I mean . . .'

'Yes, he is, but I still feel sorry for him. He only wanted to have a good time on his vacation. He's probably worked hard all year, and he's looked forward to this trip so much . . . and now he's probably sitting in the bar all sad and lonely.'

'Maggie, stop, you'll have me crying,' said Buzz, helping himself to another lobster tail. 'Well, if he's sitting in there all sad and lonely, he'll have to ask himself why and change his approach. He must know he's his own worst enemy.'

'Easily said when you're you,' chipped in Carol, pinching a juicy piece of lobster off his fork. 'Different matter when you're born obnoxious.'

'Well, what do you want us to do,' asked Buzz, 'follow him and buy him a drink?'

'Over my dead body,' said Carol.

'How about you, Maggie . . . shall we join him?'

'Don't be ridiculous,' she cracked. 'I said I was sorry for him – not in love with him.'

Buzz repeated the shrug. 'Women. Don't worry about him, the Max F. Woolberrys of the world can take care of themselves. He'll be back.'

And he was.

But by that time dinner was over, thank God, and honestly speaking he entertained us more than the dancers.

One of the highlights of the evening was an invitation to the dinner guests to try their hand at doing the *tamuré*, the frenzied Tahitian dance we'd witnessed soon after sitting down, and as everybody was half-smashed on rum punch by this time, the volunteers were plentiful.

Primed by the demon rum into a hideously fallacious belief in their own sinuous grace and terpsichorean ability, a cluster of tourists, both young and middle-aged, accepted the challenge and took the floor, allowing themselves to be draped in grass-skirts which, worn solo, would on them have looked quite preposterous, but when worn over their Western clothes, presented a tableau of rib-cracking hilarity.

Still seated at the table, we watched the preparations in high glee, falling about as stately matrons with blue-rinsed bouffants abandoned themselves to the costumes and emerged looking like burst sofas and withered aspidistras.

Then it happened. Across the arena charged a gargantuan figure, arms waving his application to be accepted as a volunteer, the sight and size of him raising a roar of hilarity from the crowd and a thunder of approval at his sporting gesture.

It was, of course, Maxwell F. Woolberry, now obviously fully recovered from his flying-fox trauma and game for anything.

'Oh, no . . .' gasped Maggie.

Buzz laughed. 'I told you he'd bounce back.'

'What an unfortunate choice of verb,' drawled Maggie.

At Max's approach, the Tahitian dancers, sensing a plethora of fun in this rotund sport, made a big show of welcoming him, some emulating him by walking around in showy circles with their bellies extended, others taking his girth measurement with wide-stretched arms and exhibiting its extent to the crowd, yet others calling for an extra large grass skirt while their compatriots ringed his shoulders with *lei* after *lei* of flowers until his face had completely disappeared from view.

A skirt of incredible length was rushed on (probably three normal skirts quickly tied together), the sight of it inducing fresh outroars of laughter from the crowd, and, after fully displaying it to them, the dancers then rushed back to Max and made a big effort of wrapping it around his belly, wiping sweat from their foreheads as though exhausted.

At last the deed was done.

The drums thrummed into life, the Tahitian dancers jerked into action, each one gathering around him or her a small group of tourists for instruction, goading them into activity, demonstrating with preposterously superior style and grace how it should be done.

The arena became a madhouse of hip-swelling, bottom-twitching, pelvis-thrusting lunacy, at once screamingly funny yet hurtful to the senses, so gauche, clumsy, uncoordinated and downright ugly were the antics of the Westerners.

Then from the midst of this pantomime of ludicrous, twitching idiots, preceded by three gracefully vibrating vahiné, there emerged a figure of monumental grossness, his shirt abandoned and trousers rolled to the knee, the tyres of superfluous white fat encircling his body jiggling up and down to the beat of the drums and the side-to-side swing of his enormous arse reminiscent of a performing elephant.

'Oh, *no* . . . !' groaned Maggie.

'GO, BABY!' someone shouted. 'SHOW 'EM HOW THEY DO IT BACK HOME!'

Max, rising to the challenge, stepped up his exertions, thrust his bottom to far left and right, turned in circles, clicked his fingers, wiggled his non-existent hips and thrust his pelvis in a riotous combination of movements that had nothing whatsoever to do with the Tahitian *tamuré*, and more closely resembled the death-throes of a dying hippo.

Led by the back-peddling vahiné, he circuited the arena, drawing loud applause and a storm of catcalls and wisecracks from the audience as he passed, but looking from his ear-to-ear grin, as though he'd never been happier in his life.

And why shouldn't he be – he was the star of the show, the centre of attraction, applauded, fêted, accepted.

He drew close to our table, roared with laughter, waved, shouted, 'Look, ma, I'm dancin'!' and continued on, heading back towards the band.

'He recovered fast,' said Maggie, in a tone of admission.

'But you still feel sorry for him,' I ventured.

She nodded. 'Yes.'

I smiled at her. 'You've got a lovely soft heart. I bet you collected stray pups when you were a kid.'

She laughed. 'I still do . . . oh, my God, what's happened?'

At that moment an unholy noise rose from the direction of the band . . . a clattering, twanging, zinging rumpus. For a moment it was difficult to see what had happened, then the group of dancers and musicians parted and out staggered Max, one foot trapped like a snowshoe in the shattered remains of a guitar, the neck of the instrument trailing behind on its strings as though he was towing a toy train.

Carol shrieked with laughter. 'He fell into the band!'

Round in circles staggered Max, stunned, bewildered, then out of the band ran another musician, offering Max another guitar, presumably for the other foot.

With a laugh Max accepted it, placed it on the ground and made as though to drive his foot through it, but, having drawn an appalled gasp from the crowd, he stooped and picked it up, strummed it, then marched out of the arena, taking all the other would-be *tamuré* virtuosos with him like the Pied Piper of Hamlin, bringing the evening entertainment to a fittingly hilarious close.

Again Maggie's hand on mine drew me from the other world. 'Did you enjoy it?'

'I had a wonderful time, Maggie . . . just wonderful. But I'd give my right arm right now for a nice quiet drink just with you.'

'Save the arm, you may need it.'

'Oh?'

And the way she was looking at me put all thoughts of the drink clean out of my mind.

CHAPTER FOUR

'THE perfect, romantic, tropical setting,' she sighed, her voice low and contented. 'So perfect it's almost a cliché . . . palm trees whispering against a star-studded sky and a huge moon making love to the lagoon.'

I laughed and hugged her to me. 'Hey, that's very good – did you make that up?'

'Scout's honour.'

'You ought to put that down on paper, you'd make a fortune as a romantic novelist.'

But she was right, it was the perfect, idyllic setting. Having said goodnight to Buzz and Carol, who had departed by cab for her hotel, we'd taken a leisurely stroll through the deserted gardens of our own hotel, wandered aimlessly around the swimming pool and on to the pier, and had come to a final halt at its end.

Before us stretched an endless mirror of glittering, black moonlight, rippling and twinkling in the stir of a warm trade breeze, and only the lights of Papeete harbour, one mile to our right, intruded on the impression that we had the whole world to ourselves.

'Tired?' I asked her.

She shrugged. 'So so . . .'

'Want to go in?'

She smile and nodded. 'Slowly.'

We about-turned and wandered back, our arms around each other. I said, 'You know, I still can't believe I'm here. Tahiti . . . it was always one of those far-off dream places I never thought I'd get to.'

'Did you dream a lot about getting away?'

'Constantly. Real, crazy dreams of punching cattle in Texas, sheep farming in Australia or being a lumber-jack in Canada – anywhere and anything but working in Wainwright's office in

Liverpool.'

'It was that bad, hm?'

'Worse. Living death.'

'I guess I've been very lucky, missing all that. I've really had a wonderful time . . . money, travel, fun. I've never known what it's like to be cornered.'

'But you wear it well, Maggie. You couldn't act spoilt if you tried. You're what you Americans call "a reel hooman being".'

She laughed. 'I'm glad you think so.'

We entered our plantation wing, and climbed the stairs to her room. Maggie took the key from her purse, opened the door and entered, leaving no doubt that I was to follow.

Closing the door, I turned, finding her standing at the verandah door, gazing out over the gardens and the lagoon.

'Did you ever see such moonlight? It's like day.'

I joined her, slid my arms around her from behind and hugged her close, relishing the perfume of her hair and the warmth of her body.

'You know something . . .' she said quickly, covering my hands with hers, 'I've never had a nicer day in my life.'

'Well, considering the oodles of lovely days you must have had, I take that as a great compliment.'

'I mean it.'

She turned then, still encircled by my arms, and brought hers up around my neck. And then I kissed her.

It started slowly, very gently, and tenderly, each touch and taste savoured for itself, knowing we had all the time in the world.

'That's nice,' she murmured, her eyes sleepy, tone almost plaintive. 'I knew they'd be wrong . . .'

'Who . . . ?' kiss '. . . and about what?'

'People . . . about Englishmen. I reckon Eartha Kitt must have got hold of the wrong fella . . . you don't need any time at *all*.'

She eased away, gazing down and smiling censoriously. 'No, time at all!' I made to follow her but she halted me with a hand. 'Go see the moonlight for a while, hm?'

I nodded. 'All right.'

And as I walked out on to the verandah, she was heading for the bathroom.

Five minutes later her call brought me out of the lagoon and visions of Blye's *Bounty* dropping anchor for the first time.

'Russ . . .'

I turned and entered the room, my heart erupting at the sight of her lying naked on the moonlit bed, one knee raised to prolong the mystery and her hand extended towards me.

I shed my clothes where I stood and went to her, sat on the side of her bed and looked down at her, marvelling at the real perfection of her body and the sweet anticipation of its warmth.

Her hand reached out for mine. Wordlessly and slowly I lowered my face and took her right nipple in my mouth.

She gasped, fingers riding through my hair.

I kept right on, lips and tongue, now reaching out to take her other nipple between finger and thumb, the sensation drawing from her a fervent gasp and a yearning, arching of her thighs.

'Oh, my God, that's beautiful . . . Russ, I love it . . . love it. Don't stop . . . ohh . . . ohhh . . .'

She was coming, so incredibly quickly. She writhed, groaned, tossed her head and drove her fingers into my hair . . . then, with a sudden jerking spasm that brought up her knees with a snap, she was into it, stifling a cry with her hand and pressing my head to her breast as she shuddered to completion.

Slowly, panting for breath, she uncoiled her legs and relaxed, one arm flopping from my shoulder to the bed and the other to her stomach with a slap.

'That . . . was downright sneaky,' she croaked.

I chuckled and sat upright, grinning at her exhaustion.

She rolled her head towards me and opened one eye. 'That was sneaky, Tobin . . . that was taking gross advantage of a person's personal weakness.'

'Yes, ma'm.'

'And I want to know how you knew!' She patted the bed at her side. 'Come and lie down . . .'

I lay down and she snuggled under my arm, crossed one knee over mine and wriggled herself comfortable.

'You . . . don't hang about too long, do you, Maggie? How come you're such an exception to the American rule? I heard everyone had thundering great sexual hang-ups over there.'

'Probably because I'm not there – I'm here,' she explained. 'With you.'

'Ah, nice, that . . . good, quick thinking.'

She raised her head and rained a burst of quick, capricious kisses all over my chest, then settled back again, though not entirely back . . . for one hand remained behind, suspiciously indolent, resting on my thigh.

Sensing the tease, I waited for her first move with tingling anticipation, knowing she was geared for long, inventive play. It started a moment later, with a trickle of fingers, as she conducted a line of innocent chatter intended to fool nobody.

'What I'd like to know is . . . how come you know so much about a girl's anatomy? Where did you learn it, Tobin . . . hm?'

'Oh, in . . .' I shuddered as her fingers found a sensational nerve-end.

'Maggie, don't do that . . .'

'In what . . . where?'

'In books . . . magazine articles.'

'I see.'

'Wow . . .'

'What's the matter?'

'Nothing . . .'

'I'm only touching,' she protested.

'I know what you're doing, Maggie . . . ugh! . . . be*lieve* me.'

'Ticklish?'

'There, yes.'

'How about here?'

I jumped. 'Maggie . . . oh, that *is* nice.'

'Here?'

'Right there.'

'You were saying . . . about the books.'

'Yes – that's where I read it.'

'And you've had no . . . practical experience before?'

'None . . . I swear it.'

'I believe you.'

On that, she raised her cheek from my arm and brought it to rest against my stomach, her face averted, her head obscuring her finger movements from my view.

'Oh, my . . .' she whispered, pleasurably. 'What lovely . . .

knees you have.'

I chuckled, jiggling her head.

Her finger tracings continued, round and round in slow pre-occupation, skirting minutely that which cried out to be touched, teasing the hell out of me.

'Magg . . . *ie* . . .!'

'Yes, Russell . . .'

'You are driving me . . . nuts!'

'How, Russell . . .'

'You devil.'

'You mean by doing this . . .?'

'Maggie . . . please! . . . ohhh . . . boy . . .'

Now a slight forward movement of her head and suddenly my loins were engulfed in an all-pervading warmth, the glorious, unmistakable moist-heat of her sensational mouth.

'Oh . . . Maggie . . . Maggie . . . that is *good*! I'll give you exactly nine weeks to stop.'

She toyed, she played, she tickled and stroked, bringing every nerve-end in my body to fever-pitch.

'Maggie, stop . . . stop . . .'

'Sure,' she chuckled. 'My work is done.'

She rounded on me, knelt at my side and presented her handiwork with a flourish. 'There, what d'you think of that?'

I groaned.

'No answer, huh? . . . well, I'll tell you what I think – I think he's so terrifying . . . he needs to be hidden from public view!'

And then she threw one leg across me . . . and consumed him to the limit.

'Oh, my God . . .'

Sucking her breath between gritted teeth, she eased off a touch, then slowly, cautiously, returned her weight to my hips, wincing dramatically, her face a mask of pretended agony.

'Ohh . . . Tobin . . . how can you lie there so uncaring of my misery?'

I chuckled at her, evoking another wince.

'Don't laugh! Aren't things bad enough?' Then she stopped acting and relaxed, looked down at me with a smile and shook her head. 'It's like coming home.'

'I'm very glad.'

'Why don't I feel any embarrassment with you, we only met today. It's like I've known you all my life.' She sighed a little and looked down at my body, touched my stomach gently, a smile of realization dawning on her mouth.

'You're right inside me . . . you know that? You are *in* me. Isn't that wonderful?'

'Yes, it is.'

'Do you think most lovers stop to think about the wonder of that fact . . . that the man is truly *inside* his woman's body . . . as truly as if she'd swallowed him?'

'No, I don't think so.'

'Nor do I.' She sighed again, a frown of wonderment touching her brow. 'God, this is . . .' she shook her head, unable to express it fully, so left it. 'How appropriate . . .'

'What is, Maggie?'

'That I should have met you here, of all places.'

'Why here particularly?'

'Because Tahiti is the Mecca of joyous, uncomplicated, uninhibited love-making . . .' with a smile she came down and kissed me, '. . . and now I want *you* to joyously, uncomplicatedly, uninhibitedly make wild, passionate love to me. Let's give these Tahitians something to think about . . . What makes them so terrific anyway?'

I took her head between my hands and bruised her mouth with mine, the passion of the kiss causing her to gasp, and igniting the fuse of love.

'Oh, yes . . . yes,' she whispered breathlessly.

Eagerly she sat erect, received me with a stifled gasp, then commenced to rock and sway, hungry for every vestige of me, using me, thrilling to me, her body and senses zinging, captive to a pending . . . now exploding climax.

'Ohhhhhh . . . OHHHHHHHHHH!'

She blew . . . and how she blew – bellowing her joy to the four corners of the earth. She convulsed, spasmed, jerked . . . gasped small, dry, anguished sobs as sensitivity ran riot through her body, then, with a final, 'OhhhhHHHH!' fell dead-weight upon me and lay panting on my chest.

The end, perhaps one might suppose.

No – barely the beginning.

Caught up in the spell, the intrigue of our Polynesian challenge, we rose to heights of endurance and fulfilment bewildering to both of us, utter exhaustion only calling a final halt to our burning passions as the sun rose on another peerless Tahitian day.

'I'm dead . . . dead,' she moaned pitiously, strewn in boneless abandon across my chest.

I managed a brave, hard-come-by chuckle and brought her beneath my arm.

'Sleep . . . sleep,' I whispered, slurred.

And there we lay till noon.

CHAPTER FIVE

Buzz finally turned up at four, just in time for tea.

I was sitting on the verandah, sipping a cup and enjoying the late afternoon sun, when the door opened, with difficulty, and in he fell. On such occasions he is accustomed to demonstrating the degree of his sexual exhaustion with a display of grossly-exaggerated enervation, but this time I somehow detected a fair slice of genuine weakness in his performance and gathered his evening had not been entirely fruitless.

'Oh, God . . .' he cried, collapsing to the floor on his hands and knees, then falling on to his face and crawling, like a dehydrated Tureg in the pitiless Sahara, towards me, arm outstretched, begging assistance. 'Help me, Tobin . . . in Pity's name, help me!'

'One lump or two, Malone?'

'Tea! I need dexedrin . . . blood!'

'Are you getting up or shall I serve it down there?'

'You heartless swine!' He staggered to his feet and faltered the rest of the way, making wild lunges from pillar to post, finally collapsing into the wicker chair and burying his face in his hands. 'Aaaawwwwww . . .!'

'Malone, perhaps I'm being over-sensitive, but I have the sneakiest feeling you're trying to tell me something. Could it . . . could it *possibly* have anything to do with your evening with Miss Carol Dwyer? Here, you randy wretch, here's your tea.'

He crawled out of his hands, took the cup, looked at me and exploded into self-congratulatory laughter. 'Wey . . . hey!'

'Which, loosely interpreted, I take to mean you are screwed to a standstill.'

'Woa . . hoa!' he repeated. 'Well, not exactly a *standstill*, son . . . I reckon there's a drop of juice left in the old tank yet. But, by the cringe . . . oh, I forgot, did Maggie leave?'

I nodded. 'She left – caught the two o'clock plane.'

'Shame.'

'I agree. She sent her love ... as though you haven't had enough in the past sixteen hours.'

He grinned. 'Always room for a drop more. No, but seriously, that's too bad. I really liked her – so did Carol. It was a marvellous night. Well ...' he sighed, 'what now?'

I shrugged. 'Haven't given anything a thought. I've just been sitting here drinking me tea.'

'Did you two do anything this morning?'

'Yes,' I grinned. 'Slept.'

'Oh.' His face split. 'Aah – hum-de-hum-de-hum ... so, you're not feeling particularly Samsonian yourself, lad?'

'I'll recover.'

'And I'm feeling stronger by the minute.' He drank some tea, lit a fag, propped his feet on the rail and said, 'Well, now what about tonight?'

'I take it you'll still be shepherding Carol ... that you haven't had too much of each other yet?'

'You take it right.'

'Which leaves me piggy-in-the-middle. You two made any plans for tonight?'

He turned and grinned, idiotically.

'I mean, Malone, to pass the time *before* you hit the sack again.'

The grin persisted. He was hiding something. 'Well, now it just so happens ... that Carol ... being a girl not without connections in these islands, has come up with a beaut. She did some telephoning earlier on, to some of her airline cronies, and has unearthed a party ...'

I came alive. 'No!'

'Now, hang on, Tobin, don't exert yourself too early ... has unearthed a party that sounds like it *might* conceivably be fun. I don't know where it is, on the coast road somewhere, and I don't know whose it is – precisely – but there'll be a couple of thousand people there and half of them, according to Carol, will be good-looking dollies ...'

'Fan-tastic!'

'Thought that might cheer you up.'

'What time does it start?'

'This chum of Carol's, a pilot in Qantas who knows the people who're throwing the party, is calling for her – and us – at her hotel at nine.'

I checked my watch. 'Marvellous . . . that gives us time to grab three hours sleep and . . .'

He was shaking his head. 'I'm ashamed of you. I told Carol you probably wouldn't want to go because you'd be pining for Maggie.'

I gaped at him.

'Heartsore . . . inconsolable,' he went on. 'I said you'd be grateful, sure, but that you'd probably prefer to retire early with a good book, and . . .'

'Buzz!'

He roared with laughter. 'When pigs whistle! Come on, let's get that shut-eye . . . by the sound of things, we're going to need it!'

Amazing what three hours sleep can do – plus the prospect of a hairy party. I came out of it feeling nine weeks old and ready for *every*thing.

'I've come to the conclusion, Tobin,' said Buzz, stifling a yawn, still a-bed, watching me do a few knee-bends at the verandah door in preparation for the coming challenge, 'that you are eminently cut out for a life of shiftless fornication.'

I frowned at him. 'You've only *just* realized it? I knew it when I was six. Come on – out of that pit, we're going to be late.'

A minute later he was singing in the shower, fully restored.

We arrived at the Royal Papeete dead on nine, dressed, according to Carol's instructions, for outdoor fun – in sports shirts and slacks, and I reckon I could live happily ever – after on Tahiti because of this sensible sartorial custom alone. I don't know about you, but the moment I put on a formal lounge suit, shirt and tie I become a banker, and the last place I'd want to be is on a tropical beach juggling a coconut drink and a plateful of barbecued spare ribs.

Buzz was attired in a flaming red creation reminiscent of a bombed paint-shop, and I was playing it cool in blue. Add a couple of handfuls of 'Black Whip' after-shave and you've got two *very* sexy creatures. Well, everybody's entitled to an opinion.

The Royal Papeete is a small, smart hotel situated right on the waterfront boulevard, and this being my first glimpse of the town, I did a bit of rubber-necking while Buzz was paying off the cab.

At first glance there isn't a great deal to Papeete. Perhaps two miles from end to end, the town is the harbour and its heart is right there on the waterfront. Unlike most harbour towns, Papeete is clean, spacious, modern and uncluttered, and all credit to the French for keeping it low-built and elegant.

Palm trees and flowering shrubs are plentiful along the broad, new waterfront boulevard, and the shops and government buildings are a melodious blend of modern and tropical-colonial.

I realized, of course, from the many streets leading inland from the harbour, that there was much more to Papeete than just the port, and I decided there and then that, time and other factors permitting, I'd take a look at it.

With Buzz in the lead, we entered the hotel and made for the cocktail bar, finding Carol already there, seated regally on a stool talking to a handsome, blond bloke with a Burt Reynold's moustache, shirt neck wide open exposing a muscular tan.

Carol looked devastating in a brown and yellow Tahitian-style dress, very low cut to expose her own muscular tan which at the moment of our arrival, appeared to be the object of Blondie's riveted attention. I heard Buzz grunt in disapproval and he quickened his pace before Blondie went the whole hog and plunged his head down her cleavage.

'Hi, there . . . !'

She turned, her eyes momentarily retaining the sexy amusement resulting from Blondie's attentions, then changed her expression to one of innocent conviviality at our arrival.

'Hi, Buzz . . hello, Russ, you fully recovered?'

'Try me.'

'You've recovered. Buzz . . . Russ . . . this is Paul Martin, he's a pilot with Qantas and the man who arranged our invitations.'

We shook hands and offered our thanks, Martin replying, in a distinct Australian accent, 'Nothin' to it, the more the merrier. It's all free-an'-easy, an outdoor do – barbecue, dancing, swimming . . . anythin' you damn-well feel like.'

'Who's our host?' I asked.

He grinned, displaying perfect teeth. 'Bloke by the name of D'Urville . . . quite a swinger hereabouts. Import/export, rich as Croesus and a collector of very beautiful women. You guys are gonna have your eyes knocked out.'

Buzz glanced at Carol, saying deliberately, 'I've had mine knocked out already. I'm more than happy.'

'Yeh . . . sure,' replied Martin, also glancing at Carol.

Carol said nothing, just smiled at him, and suddenly the situation was plain for all to see – she'd changed horses!

Buzz picked it up instantly, gave a cough, an embarrassed shuffle, and broke it by turning to find the barman. 'Well . . . let's have one for the road, shall we?'

'Sure,' said Martin, slipping a sly, conniving smile to Carol, 'we've got time for a quickie.'

I bloody bet, I thought . . . *and* a longie. My heart went out to Buzz, knowing how he must be feeling. She might have had the decency to hide it until after we'd got to the party. If she'd sloped off with Martin then, it wouldn't have been so bad – not with eight million other gorgeous creatures around to help salve his wounded pride, but to hit him under the belt with it at this stage . . . well, it just wasn't playing the game.

While Buzz ordered the drinks, they were at it again, sending each other subtle, smirking signals of sexual complicity which irritated me to a point of anger, so much so that I couldn't stand it any longer and went to join Buzz a little way down the bar, where he was watching the barman prepare the drinks.

'Well, well . . .' he said, with forced levity, the tone of hurt, 'looks like Malone will be free-lancing tonight.'

'Aw, mate, what a bloody rotten trick.'

He shrugged. 'Can't blame her, she's not my wife.'

'There are ways and ways though, Buzz.'

'Yes, well, maybe it's better this way. At least I won't be shattered when she disappears with him . . . and I won't have wasted half the night.'

'You really don't mind?'

He turned and grinned. 'To hell with it – life's too flamin' short. I'm buggered if she's going to ruin my party.'

'Good man.'

We collected the drinks and returned to Carol and Martin, lightness of heart restored, not caring now if they got down on the floor and had it away there and then.

And, perversely, in the strange ways of humans and perhaps because she detected Buzz's new-found indifference, Carol let up on her visual copulation with Martin and transferred her attention to Buzz. And it did me good to see him play it so cool.

With understanding having been reached as to how the evening would proceed, we all relaxed and chatted away, Martin, as sort of party authority, making most of the running with stories and rumours about our future host, Jean Pierre D'Urville – by the sound of things *quite* a lad.

'He's reputed to have made love to two thousand different women,' he explained. 'Though others say those are only the ones his wife knows about.'

I frowned. 'His wife? How does she take all this?'

'Alcoholically. Angelique's a lush . . . a beautiful, sexy lush.' He grinned at Buzz and me. 'Don't let her get her hooks in you, fellas, you may never get back to Sydney.'

'What's the party for?' I asked. 'Is D'Urville celebrating anything in particular?'

Martin laughed. 'Yeh – another million in the bank, I should think. The boy's loaded.'

'Boy?' I said.

'Figure of speech. He's thirty-five . . . thirty-six, I should think. Good-lookin' bloke . . . dark, suave, radiates Gallic charm like a lawn sprinkler. Even without his millions I reckon the birds would flip, but *with* them . . . Christ, he runs that place like a bunny club. I've seen thirty . . forty real good-lookers around his pool every time I've been, and he wasn't even throwing a party then! I don't know where he finds 'em all – maybe that's what he imports and exports!'

I got a glance off at Buzz, found his eyes glinting voraciously, and I had the feeling he was thinking maybe Martin had done him a big favour after all.

'Have you . . . actually been to one of his parties before?' I asked Martin.

His response was a grin of lecherous recollection. 'Oh, yeh . . . I sure have.'

'And . . .?' prompted Carol.

'Well . . . let's put it this way, Beauty . . . "wild" would be a grossly unfair description – a rank understatement that would probably get me banned for life if D'Urville heard me. So I'll put it *this* way . . . pinching the words of the great Captain Cook himself from his "Account of a Voyage round the World" written in 1773. "There is a scale in dissolute sensuality, which these people have ascended, wholly unknown to every other nation whose manners have been recorded from the beginning of the world to the present hour, and which no imagination could possibly conceive." ' Martin finished with an unwholesome grin. 'Cookie was, of course, talking about the Polynesians, but, Jeezus, he might just have well have bin describing one of D'Urville's parties. You fellas still keen on goin'?'

We broke into laughter, Buzz and I. Nice, very nice. Obviously Martin had learned Cook's quotation by heart and had used it many a time as a pre-party party piece, but that made it nonetheless effective.

'Thought you might be,' he grinned, swallowing his drink. 'Come on – let's get into all this "dissolute sensuality" and see how the rich half lives.'

CHAPTER SIX

You can probably guess the state of excited anticipation in which Buzz and I drove out to the house. Seated together in the back of Martin's Citroen, Carol up front with him, Buzz and I exchanged a flurry of winks, grimaces, grins and chuckles and could barely restrain ourselves from laughing out loud. I only prayed it wasn't going to be one thumping great let-down.

We drove west, passing our own hotel and, later, the Tahiti Village Beach Hotel, scene of the previous evening's festivities, and continued on, signs of civilization quickly diminishing, though the road stayed highway good.

To our left, the twin peaks of Orohena and Aorai loomed high and threatening, densely black against the lighter, star-speckled sky, while to our right, as though in defiance of the daunting mountain scenario, the moon-bathed lagoon lay in placid, puissant peace.

'Is the house remote?' Carol asked Martin.

'Just enough to afford the necessary privacy. It's very cleverly positioned . . . he's got a lovely stretch of beach in front and a mountain waterfall behind. Still, with his money, I reckon he could've bought Papeete if he'd wanted the site.'

'Is it a big house?'

Martin grinned. 'I don't think anybody knows – not even D'Urville. It isn't just *a* house, it's a complex – almost a small village. There are about twenty thatched guest bungalows, summer houses, boat houses, offices – he largely works from home – and God knows what all. He's got a private executive jet and a helicopter at Faaa . . . a motor yacht that sleeps fifty . . . half a dozen speed boats . . . as many cars . . . more clothes than Brooks Brothers . . . and, of course, all those beautiful sheilas.'

'Poor devil,' laughed Carol.

'You'll have to be careful – he might want to add you to the list.'

She shrugged fatalistically. 'Ah, well, if duty calls . . .'

I glanced at Buzz and got a grimace of comical indifference. He didn't give a stuff.

It was about twenty minutes later that Martin, without forewarning, suddenly slowed and swung sharp right on to a tarmaced secondary road that ran in twists and turns through land quite densely bushed. This continued for perhaps half a mile before suddenly opening out into clear palm-dotted parkland beyond which we could distantly glimpse the sea.

Another few hundred yards and the parkland became more formally landscaped, took on the appearance of a designed tropical garden, its formal beauty becoming more and more comprehensive as we neared the house, and then, as we took a decisive bend in the road the complex came into view.

'Oh, my God . . .' gasped Carol. 'That's a *house*! It's as big as the Beach Hotel!'

'Bigger,' corrected Martin. 'The Beach has only twelve acres of garden . . . this has two hundred.'

He drew to a halt in a vast, paved, palm-shaded car park set well to one side of the buildings, choosing a space between a British DBS and a Lamborghini, one of several on the lot, which boasted just about every type of expensive runabout you can put a name to.

It looked more like the Earls Court Motor Show than a parking place for a private party.

We got out and started for the complex, Martin and Carol in the lead, Buzz and I straggling behind, gawping around us like a couple of country bumpkins at Buckingham Palace.

'It ain't decent,' he complained. 'How can one guy afford all this?'

'He saves hard.' I said. 'Two quid goes into that piggybank every week, rain or shine.'

'Yeh,' he said, thoughtfully. 'Maybe I'll start saving mine, too.'

'Fancy a place like this, Buzz?'

He grinned. 'I wasn't only thinking of the place, mate.'

We had to hurry to catch up.

Now, as we neared the house, the gardens became exquisitely formal, and the pathway meandering through beds of blazing, scented flowers, shaded over by graceful palms and trellised by trailing vines.

Directed by the path, we skirted at quite a distance the immensely long, white, blue-shuttered Californian-style house, managing as yet not much of a view of it because of the trees and high bushes. Then we passed between two thatched bungalows and finally emerged into a park-like garden, alive with colour and lights and music and activity – the heart of the barbecue party.

Except for the fashions, it somewhat resembled a Sandringham garden party – tables and people everywhere, hundreds of them, dancing, milling, talking, laughing, drinking, drinking, drinking . . .

Then it struck me . . . or rather they struck me . . . the women. It was as though Hugh Heffner had just landed his private jet and disgorged the entire staff of his world-wide Bunny Clubs. There were dozens of 'em . . . all breathtakers, dark-haired vahinés, sleek Chinese, white Caucasians, brown Caucasians, blondes, brunettes, red-heads and all stations in between. Naturally, there were men there, too, but who the hell was interested in them?

Buzz came to a faltering, stiff-legged halt, mouth and eyes wide, gave a couple of gulps, and whispered breathlessly, 'I don't believe it . . .'

'Beli*eve* it, we're looking at 'em!'

He shook his head. 'No, this is but a cruel dream . . . they're going to disappear like a mirage as soon as we get within touching distance . . . pouff! in puffs of coloured smoke.'

'Even if we run?'

Martin turned back to us with a grin, knowing what we were thinking. 'Didn't I tell you? Come and meet the boss man, he's over here.'

Hesitantly, lest we break the spell, we followed, reached the outer perimeter of the bewildering bevvy of beauty, saw to our amazement that they were indeed flesh and blood and were not about to disappear in smoke at our approach, and finally came into the presence of the infamous Jean Pierre D'Urville himself.

He was everything that Martin had said, but much more – for there was no way in which Martin could have completely described the man who stood before us, wrestling good-humouredly with the cork of a champagne bottle. He was medium-tall, well-tanned and very good-looking – granted; he was well-built yet slim enough to wear his casual clothing to perfection – also granted. Yet one glance was sufficient to tell that these outward manifestations of attractiveness were only the iceberg tip of D'Urville's vast power over women, the remainder being contained in such a complexity of charm, urbanity, cleverness, suave sophistication and God-knows-what-else, as to defy detailed description.

Put simply, Jean Pierre D'Urville had 'it', and when you've got it, you've got it. He had it by the barrow-load. It dripped from him, radiated from him, hung around him like a shroud – but don't take my word for it, ask the dozen or so girls who were crowded round him, every one a breath-snatcher, each eyeing him anxiously as though she'd been waiting all day for as little as a casual half-smile.

'There!' he laughed, extending the bottle, 'she's coming!'

'Lucky old she,' cracked a flamboyant brunette with a ninety-seven inch bosom.

The cork exploded, sending a shower of champagne into the air, a few droplets landing on the shelf of the brunette's tits.

'Oh!' she cried, hand a-flutter.

'Ah, did I drench you, my poupi . . . here, I will remove it.'

He lowered his mouth to her shelf and licked it clean – all of it.

The girls were in hysterics . . . terrific fun.

Jean Pierre came out of her cleavage, ostentatiously licking his lips, then spotted Martin and gasped in surprise. 'Paul, my friend . . . so glad you could come.' He held out his hand to Martin. 'Forgive me – I had a little cleaning up operation to do.'

His calm, totally confident grey eyes flicked to Carol, then quickly to Buzz and me, then shot back to Carol, a smile of enchanted discovery forming on his lips. 'But who have we here . . .? Paul, you have been keeping things from me.'

'This is Carol Dwyer, Jean Pierre, she's with Qantas. We're old flying buddies.'

'How could Miss Dwyer possibly be an old anything, Paul, how ridiculous.' He reached for Carol's extending hand and raised it to his lips, his eyes boring into hers with fierce and fiery interest. 'Enchanté, mademoiselle ... you are most welcome.'

'Thank you,' she whispered, her voice weak and fluttery, and I reckoned right then she'd be number two thousand and one before the night was through.

'... and two friends, Jean Pierre ... Buzz Malone and Russ Tobin,' Martin was saying ... 'I did phone about them.'

Reluctantly, D'Urville released Carol from both his manual and visual captivity, and turned to us, his manner changing to brisk bonhomie, now every inch a man's man, though still charming.

'My friends, welcome ...' he shook our hands with a strong, earnest grip. 'My house and everything in it is yours to enjoy ...' a man-to-man smile, '... well, almost everything. Please – wander where you will ... eat, drink what you wish ... amuse yourselves as your fancy takes you. My only house rule is that on no account must you leave a D'Urville party having had a dull, boring, unamusing time – that I cannot allow. Now, where was I ... oh, yes, I was about to pour champagne for us all ... Carol, come – you shall help me. Glasses, everyone ... glasses ...'

And so the evening began.

You don't take a party like this in a headlong rush – not like the parties of my extreme youth when it was one crate of beer in someone's front room and if you didn't get there early and in quick, it was all over bar the groping.

No, this was a pageant of such broad scope and spectrum it had to be analysed, inspected, mulled over and thought about – much akin to choosing only one chocolate out of a twenty-pound box – if you made the wrong choice, you were done for, and kicked yourself for wasting the opportunity.

Fortunately, Buzz was of the same frame of mind, and so, having collected a couple of glasses of bubbly, we sidled quietly away from the group and came to rest at a picnic bench beneath a palm tree, lit a couple of ruminative fags and settled down to analyse the situation, his opening remark, accompanied by a bewildered shake of the head, being, 'Jeezus ...' and I couldn't have put it more succinctly myself.

'Quite the boy, our host, what?' I said. 'Caused Carol to rechange her recent change of heart in a hurry. Blimey, one place I would *not* bring a bird of mine to is a Jean Pierre D'Urville party – not unless I wanted to get rid of her. What puzzles me now about him is not *has* he made love to two thousand different women – but on which night did he *do* it!'

Buzz chortled and sipped his champers. 'By heck, mate, I have *never* seen such a proliferation of pulchritude at one time and in one place – not even in the Miss World contest. They're unbelievable!'

'Which brings us, does it not, to the problem at hand? God, what a dilemma ... and what a reversal from normal form. Fancy being faced with *too many*, it ain't natural.

'Don't worry – we'll make out somehow,' he said consolingly. 'The problem in my mind at the moment is – who's going to bury my remains? Because about a month from now, someone will be strolling through the gardens and will spot something under a bush ... a ragged piece of shirt ... he'll haul it out and attached to it will be the gaunt, emaciated skeletal remains of Buzz Malone ... fucked to death in the line of duty. Russ, I wonder if you ...? No, of course, you couldn't – you'll be lying dead under the next bush.'

'OK,' I laughed, 'well, if that's the plan, we'd better get cracking. Let's just sort of stroll around and see what happens, playing it cool, though, keeping each other out of unprofitable traps.'

'You're on ... by gum, that's lovely bubbly. Perhaps another small libation on our travels?'

'Why ever not?'

We started off.

I will skip the first hour of our adventures – because nothing adventurous happened. Like most parties, this one took some time to get warmed up and for the first hour or so everyone was very polite and well-behaved – at least the people we came across were polite and well-behaved.

Buzz and I took a turn round the park (it doesn't seem right calling it a garden), stopping here and there to watch the action, most of which was happening around the bar areas and the dance floor, though the native underground ovens, the *ahimaas*, in which all sorts of meat were being cooked were also attracting a fair sprinkling of interest.

Finally we gravitated back to the dance floor – a fifty-foot square of polished concrete set in the earth and surrounded on three sides by a backdrop of palms and flowering shrubs, forming a sort of natural amphitheatre.

The music came from a spirited group of Tahitians, dressed in matching red-floral shirts and white trousers, and at this stage of the evening they were playing Western-style music for modern dancing, and playing it very well.

Buzz and I stood at a table-bar watching twenty or thirty couples doing their stuff and at the same time kept a roving eye on the other spectators, sifting the attached from the availables and generally getting our bearings, and after we'd got them, decided it was about time to take the plunge.

'The little Tahitian filly in the green dress,' nodded Buzz, putting his drink down. 'Think I'll have a go.'

'Good fortune, son ... I'm going to ask the blonde with the knockers over there.'

'Right. If nothing happens, I'll meet you back here, hm?'

'Toosh – as the French say.'

He wandered off.

I peeled away to the right to where the blonde stood chatting to a Tahitian barman. She was a good-looking doll with a damn good figure and superb hair, and it puzzled me that she should be standing alone. As I drew near she saw me coming, did a double-take and half-smiled a greeting.

'Good evening,' I said, turning it on a bit. 'I wondered if you'd like to dance.'

Her big grey eyes widened. 'Eeee ... you're English! Well, fancy that!'

My heart sank like a stone. Can you believe it ... broad Lancashire! Voice like a rusty hinge. Now I knew why she was standing alone!

For a second or two I lost my wits, otherwise I might have come up with a fainting fit or a bad attack of cramp or something, and in that moment of nonplussedness I lost the initiative. Before you could say 'Coronation Street' her arm was linked in mine and we were heading for the floor.

'Well, *fancy* meeting you,' she gushed, swinging in front of me and breaking into a weird, graceless stomp, a cross between a frenetic Twist and a punchball exercise, and looking for all the world as though she was dying to go to the loo. 'Where d'you come from? . . . and watcha doin' here?'

'London,' I lied, dreading her reaction if I said from the North. 'I'm on my way to Sydney. And what are you doing here?'

'Oh, I'm on a cruise . . . we docked yesterday, leave again tomorra. I'll be sorry to get back on board, I can tell you.'

'Really? That surprises me. I thought cruises were supposed to be great fun . . . very romantic.'

'Ha! Not this one. The boat's full of old fuddy-duddies, they're all in bed by ten. You should see them in the lounge after dinner – all noddin' off over their coffee. Their idea of a wild time is doin' the *Telegraph* crossword!'

'Well . . . are you travelling alone? I mean . . .'

'No, I'm with a girlfriend . . . or rather I *was* with a girlfriend. She's gone queer on me. I tell you, the way people can change when they get on board a ship. You think you know them pretty well, then . . . boom! . . . they change completely.'

'How d'you mean – she's gone queer on you? You mean . . . lesbian?'

She dipped her head. 'With the ship's manicurist. I just can't believe it . . . I've known her for five years. Never the slightest sign at 'ome. She's *never* made a play for me or anything.'

'Is she married?'

'Yers! That's the daft thing about it! Her husband's on the council back 'ome! . . . with *my* husband! I mean, what am I goin' to *do*?'

'Nothing, obviously. Don't your husbands ever come on holiday with you?'

She grinned, mischievously. 'I reckon we see enough of them during the rest of the year. This is our . . . little treat. Usually we go to Italy or Spain, but this year we thought we'd try a cruise – hearin' so much about them. By gum, it's opened my eyes, I can tell you.'

'But . . . the other holidays you've taken with her – has she never . . .?'

She shook her head. 'God knows. Obviously, on dry land we sort of . . . well, go our own ways, so to speak. I find my fun and she finds hers – though I shudder to think what sort of fun she's bin *havin'* all these years! Ee, it's goin' to be so embarrissin' when I go back on board. I've a good mind to fly home.'

'And there's no fun at all for you on board?' I grinned, changing the subject. 'How about the crew – aren't there any young, dashing officers to . . . entertain you?'

'Ha! Not a damn one I'd fancy drunk. We must've picked the ugliest bloody crew on the high seas.'

'Well, I certainly sympathize with you.'

'Anyway,' she said, smiling bravely, 'enough about my troubles – what about you? Are you 'ere by yourself?'

'Er . . no, I'm here with a . . . friend.'

Her face fell. 'Oh . . . I thought it was too good to be true. – Why is it all the nice men are always spoken for?'

I laughed. 'Oh, come, now, the place is crawling with good-looking fellas . . . and a lot of them are Frenchmen, too.'

'Well, if they're anythin' like the creep that brought me, you can keep 'em! Customs officer off the docks an' does he fancy his chances. I mean, a little fun's what you come on holiday for – but he wanted it in the back of the car on the way here! I told him to get knotted and walked off as soon as we arrived. I'd rather not have it at all than in the back of a car.'

'Well, cheer up, I'm sure you'll have a lovely time. There are plenty of other men here . . .'

At that moment, thankfully, the band finished.

'. . . well, thank you very much, that was lovely. I, er, think I'd better find out what my friend's doing . . . I don't trust these Frenchmen.'

'Yes, well, thank you very much . . .'

I made a move back towards the bar. 'I'm sure you'll have a good time, it's only early yet, give it a chance to warm up . . . aye, aye, it looks as though you have another suitor homing in now . . .'

'Oh . . .'

She followed my gaze to a tall, dark-complexioned guy with a small moustache and a lecherous leer who was moving in to intercept us. We exchanged glances, male-to-male, and I cleared the runway for him with a friendly smile and a nod.

His lips split in a bleached smile and a nod.

'Would madam do me the honour of bestowing upon me the next dance?' he asked, in French.

Blondie blinked and glanced horror-stricken at me. 'Oo ... er.'

I grinned. 'He's asking you to dance.' I turned to Romeo. 'Do you speak English?'

He broke out the smile again. 'But of course, my sincere apologies – I should have known by the lady's exquisite complexion that she is English, it is quite incomparable.'

I raised a brow at Blondie whose mouth was slightly open with pleasurable astonishment. 'Well, now, how *about* that?' I laughed.

'That ... is just luvly! Thanks ever so much ...'

I wiggled my fingers. 'Have fun.'

As they took the floor, she was saying to him, 'I do think it's quite shameful that we can't speak French like you people speak English. I really will have to learn it ...'

His smile was the personification of lascivious charm. 'Perhaps I can teach madam one or two little things ... while we are dancing ... ?'

Away they went and away I went, lightheaded with relief, back to the bar and ordered another drink.

'Great party, huh?'

He was standing at the side of me, a portly, middle-aged soul of obvious American origin – American clothes, American rimless glasses and American accent – all nicely smashed.

'Wonderful,' I said, taking my drink from the barman.

He sidled up, hand extended. 'Harold Lichter ... Polynesian Imports Inc. Los Angeles ...'

I took the soft fleshy hand. 'Russ Tobin ... from London.'

'Yeh? What line you in, Russ?'

I laughed. 'Hard to say, I'm in between jobs right now.'

He frowned. 'That right? What's your connection with D'Urville, then – if you don't mind me askin'?'

'Not at all – there's no connection. I was invited here by a friend of a friend of a friend – you know.'

'Oh, sure ... thought you might have been doing business with him. I do quite a bit ... Polynesian artifacts, that kinda thing. Man, I'll tell yuh ...' he shook his jowls and chuckled, 'when this guy throws a shindig, he really throws one. Were you here last night?'

I frowned at him. 'Last night? Why, has this been going on

since last night?'

He gave another chuckle. 'For all I know, it's bin goin' on for a week! Fact is – I don't think it ever stops! Man, he really knows how ta look after his business associates. No expense spared with D'Urville. Hell, I was kinda bushed when I got here yesterday, with the flight an' all, so I turned in quite early – around eleven, I'm sleepin' in one of them bungalows in the grounds, there . . . Well, sir, I'd just got inta bed when there was a knock on the door and inta the room came two of the goldanged prettiest Tahitian babes you ever laid eyes on, an' I do mean real good-lookers. What in tarnation d'you two want, I said, thinkin' they musta mistaken the room or somethin', but I didn't get any sorta reply – not in words, that is. They just giggled and laughed like they were playin' some practical joke on me – then, before you could say snap, powee, they were stark naked and right there in bed with me! Hell, I nearly died . . . till I got used to th' idea, that is. After that . . .' he released another belly chuckle, downed his drink in one, thumped the glass on the counter and checked his watch. 'Well, nice talkin' to yuh, son . . . time for beddy byes. Hee hee . . . see yuh tomorrow – maybe.'

Off he waddled, shaking with laughter.

Well, there was a turn-up – an old fogey like him getting his oats and here was I . . .

The thought reminded me that Buzz had not returned and I wondered whether he was making any headway. I peered around the dance floor but couldn't see any sign of him, and I was just about to start off on a slow circuit of the floor when a female voice, light-hearted and tipsily provocative, said behind me, '*Bon* soir . . .!'

I turned, discovering, in a superbly-cut, knee-length, jade-green Dior dress, a dark-haired creature of exquisite though slightly dishevelled appearance, coquettishly appraising me through one half-closed jade-green eye.

'Hello,' I laughed, finding both her stance and her one-eyed expression highly comical.

'Aha!' she chuckled, 'he laughs! Sank God, I have found a man who laughs. What's your name, laughing man?'

'Tobin,' I grinned. 'Russ Tobin.'

'Roos Tobin . . . I like it. So – you have been elected.'

'To do what?'

She peered down at her dainty feet. 'To find my other shoe. I've lost it somewhere.'

'Oh, well, *about* where? Where have you just come from?'

She pointed behind her, towards a cluster of palm trees ringing a white garden seat, then shook her head. 'I don't know . . . never mind, I will abandon the other. There . . . now you are three inches taller, tall enough to buy me a drink.'

I grinned. 'What would you like?'

'Champagne, of course – and ask him for the bottle, I can't stand those silly glasses.'

'Well, I'll see what I can do,' I said doubtfully. 'But he may not give me a whole bottle.'

'Pouf! Of course he will give it to you, you are taller than he is.'

'All right,' I laughed, 'I'll try.'

I went to the bar, wondering who this beautiful nut was and *whose* she was, because she was wearing a wedding ring – as well as a diamond ring the size of a coconut. Was her old man around here somewhere, looking for her? She looked the type to have a very rich, possibly very jealous husband who might cause trouble, and with all the other good-looking women around here, I wasn't anxious to get lumbered with that!

The barman approached, glanced from me to her and back again to me, his smile broadening deferentially. 'Yes, sir, what would you like?'

'Well . . .' I faltered, unable to resist a backward glance at Lovely Face, 'we'd, er, like some champagne . . .'

'Certainly, sir – a bottle, I presume?'

'Hm? Well, yes, as a matter of fact, I . . .'

'Right away, sir.'

He shot under the table and brought up a dripping, iced bottle, deftly wiped it dry, wrapped the cloth around it and presented it to me with an unctuous smile. 'Madam's special brand, sir . . . and two glasses?'

'Er . . .' I nodded, thunderstruck.

'Here you are, sir.'

'Thank you . . .'

I wanted to ask him who she was but thought it might make me look a bit of a twit, so I didn't. I went back to her, flourishing the bottle victoriously.

'My hero . . .' she teased, accepting a glass.

'I'd like to take credit, but can't . . . you knew he'd part with a bottle all the time, didn't you? He said this was your special brand, so he had it waiting for you.' She smiled whimsically, enjoying her little secret while I popped the cork.

'May I ask your name?' I said filling her glass.

'You may call me . . .' she thought about it, '. . . Gigi! Yes, tonight I shall be Gigi.' She tipped the glass to her adorable lips then placed it on the bar, dangerously near the edge. 'Come . . . dance with me.'

I abandoned the bottle and my glass and took her proffered hand, excited at the prospect of holding her close.

Drunk or not, she was class all through. Perhaps thirty-four . . . thirty-five, she possessed that aura of mature sensuality, which, coupled with her abundant, classic beauty, the grace of high breeding and inate charm – to say nothing of a belting body – blinds men on sight to all but the prospect of her favours. In earlier times she might well have been a royal courtesan, the favourite mistress of a love-sick king for whom he finally abdicates his throne or has his missus done away with.

So thinking, I had no illusions about my role in this, her current dalliance. I doubted she'd even really seen me – particularly considering her condition. I was simply a man who had laughed and had made her laugh, a qualification sufficient, under the circumstances, to satisfy her momentary quirk, but if our liason lasted no more than the duration of one dance, it was good enough for me.

She turned to me, eyes closed, arms extended, swaying to the music, having already forgotten who it was she'd brought on to the floor. I slipped my arms around her, thrilling to the soft, silky sexiness of her body and the easy way she moulded herself against me, immediately at home.

Her cheek to mine, her perfume a regal aphrodisiac making meatballs of my mind, we shuffled round the floor, locked in sensuous limbo, lost to place, lost to people, lost to time.

After a while, as though suddenly realizing I was there, she raised her cheek and looked at me, with puzzled interest, as though uncertain of how she got to be there in my arms.

'You're new, aren't you?' she cooed softly, making it a statement. 'I don't remember seeing you before. That's nice. I like new faces. Do you like new faces?'

'Yes – especially when they're as beautiful as yours.'

'Oh . . . you think mine beautiful?'

'Ravishingly.'

She laughed, delightedly. 'Such extravagance. Where did you come from, my cavalier? Out of the sea in a golden boat?'

'No, from Los Angeles on a 747.'

'Shhh . . . ! she frowned, placing a fingertip against my lips. 'You mustn't break the spell. Mundanity will bring death to our romantic tryst.'

I smiled at her. 'Is that what we're having – a romantic tryst?'

'Don't you wish it?'

'Sounds terrific.'

'Then that is what we shall have . . . just you and I. We will adore each other . . . worship each other, body and soul. There will be no other. Is that a deal?'

'That's a deal,' I grinned, not for a moment thinking she was serious.

'I'm very glad you came,' she said wistfully, distantly, a little sadly, looking about her, 'These people . . .'

'What about them, Gigi?'

She didn't answer. 'You know what I would like to do?'

'What?'

'I would like to sail out into the lagoon . . . away from all these people . . . just you and I, would you like that?'

'Well, I . . .'

Oh, blimey.

'The moon will be beautiful . . . full and bright. Take me out there in your golden boat . . . and make love to me.'

I gulped.

Her long, elegant fingers crept to my neck and trickled tender trails through my hair and into my ear. Her smile was a lazy, taunting, challenge. 'Are you afraid, my cavalier . . . ?'

'Er, no . . . ! No, it's just that . . .'

'Just what? . . . that you don't like me?'

'No . . . ! Good heavens, no, I think you're . . . wonderful. It's just that I . . . don't know the lagoon, and I don't sail very well, and it might be dangerous for you . . .'

'Ssssh . . . !' she went, silencing me with her finger on my lips. 'There is no danger . . . . the water will be calm . . . beautiful. And there is no need to sail. Come, I will show you . . .'

She took my hand and made for the bar, gathered up the bottle and glasses and thrust them at me, then skirted the bar at speed and headed into the darker reaches of the garden.

With a grin I followed her, having to half-run to catch up, chuckling away to myself at the preposterousness of the situation and at her comical tipsiness. Away she went in fluid flight, arms flutteringly akimbo, picking her way through the stone-strewn garden with the grace of a well-bred colt, leaving me entirely to my own devices until we had completely cleared the garden and set foot on a shallow sloping beach.

'Come on, slow coach!' she turned and laughed.

'I'm . . . coming!' I gasped, clutching the bottle and glasses to my chest as though they were golden eggs. 'How much further?'

She turned and pointed along the beach, to our left. 'There.'

A hundred yards or so away I saw an inlet, the beach terminating at its near bank in a concrete wharf at which several motor boats and cruisers were moored.

Gigi started off again through the soft powdery sand at a fair old clip, eager to reach it, jokingly gesturing me to greater speed.

At last I reached the wharf and joined her, both of us panting from our exertions through the sand. Now I saw that the inlet was in fact an outlet, a broad stretch of deep water created by the outflow of the waterfall plunging down the face of a high-rising hill behind the estate.

What a site D'Urville had picked for himself – a mountain backdrop complete with waterfall, a natural, deep-water harbour for his boats, a magnificent stretch of palm-fringed beach and that incredible lagoon view with Moorea in the distance. Right then I couldn't think of anything else he could possibly need.

I turned to Gigi with a smile. 'Which boat, your Highness?'

She came to me with mischievous eyes, took a glass and proffered it for champagne. I filled both and raised mine. 'To the beautiful Gigi . . . Queen of Tahiti.'

She laughed gaily, enjoying this crazy fun, then spun round and levelled her glass at a substantial cabin cruiser moored at the far end of the wharf.

'That one!'

Before I could reply, she was off again.

'Hey, Gigi . . .! I've never driven one of those . . .!'

'Now is a marvellous time to learn – there's no traffic!'

No, I thought, but there's plenty of other things – like flaming great cobs of coral just underneath the surface.

By the time I'd caught up to her she was already in the rear well of the boat, seated at the raised pilot seat and jiggling the controls. 'Cast off fore and aft lines!' she commanded. 'Otherwise we won't get very far.'

With growing misgivings, engendered by her spirit of carefree abandonment – a state of mind hardly conducive to safe sailing – I slipped the rear rope from its bollard and threw it inboard, ran to the forward bollard and had barely cleared it when the mighty diesels roared into life.

'In!' she commanded.

I jumped down, misjudged the roll of the boat, teetered on one foot then went crashing into the deep cushioning of the banquette seats as she hit the throttle and stood the thing on its tail.

BBAAAAARRROOOOOOOMMM!!' The mighty engines cleared their throats and flew!

'YeeeeerrrHHOOOOOOOO!' she laughed, wild with the thrill of speed.

Away we tore, straight out over the flat, black, moon-flecked waters of the lagoon, kicking up a riotous, bubbling white wake, hitting thirty . . . forty knots in almost as many yards . . . the hull smacking down on the water with a leaping, exploding bafff . . . bafff . . . bafff . . . and throwing me around like a cork in a storm-tossed sea.

An appeal, I knew, was hopeless – she was gone, lost, drowned in a hurricane of rushing wind and sensual excitement. I managed a handhold round the leg of the banquette and there I lay and watched her.

She was a goddess, an avenging angel, charging into battle on a chariot of knives, legs braced hard against the roll and pitch of her thundering craft, the wind whipping her long dark hair into streams of fluttering silk and plastering her clothing flat to her lithe body.

Now she threw the boat into a long right curve . . . now back again. 'AHA!' the enjoyment of the sensation tickled her fancy, so she repeated the performance again. Left . . . and right . . . left . . . and right . . . Now she shortened the duration of the curves until they fitted three-four time and from then we smashed across the lagoon to a Viennese waltz.

'Dee *dum* . . . dee *dum* . . . dee *dum* . . . dum *dum*,' she sang, swinging the wheel hard over on each dum. 'Dee *dum* . . . dee *dum* . . . dee *dee* . . . di . . . *doe* . . . !'

'Oh, boy . . . 'cause while all this dee-di-doeing was going on, the bloody boat was still leaping up and down like a roller coaster, heeling far left and right and also shaking itself like a wet terrier – and I was floundering in the stern catching the lot.

'Gi . . . gi! *Gi* . . . gi! Gi . . . *gi*!' I bellowed, but she didn't hear me.

Coincidentally, however, at that moment she threw everything into neutral and stopped the boat on a dime.

'Ha ha!' she laughed, twisting out of her seat, then replaced the laugh with a pop-eyed gawp as she located me sprawled on the deck, clutching the banquette leg for dear life.

'What's the matter with you? Why aren't you sitting on the seat?'

'You were just a mite previous on the throttle back there, Gigi . . .' I nodded at the champagne bottle, skulking on its side under the seat. 'And I'm afraid we've lost our sea-rations.'

She dismissed the problem with a wave of her hand, about-turned and disappeared down into the main cabin.

She re-appeared a mooment later, cheerfully brandishing an exact replacement. 'Tra . . . laaaaa . . . !'

'Well, I'll be . . .' I caught the thrown bottle and regarded her suspiciously as I unwired the cork. 'Gigi . . .'

She went into a recline along the side banquette, chin propped on her hand, and regarded me playfully. 'Yes, beloved, what is it?'

'Who are you, Gigi?'

'Who do you think I am?'

'Well . . .' I popped the cork, filled the two glasses and

handed her one, '... from the reaction of the barman back there ... and the fact that you knew the gardens, the beach, the wharf and this boat so intimately ... I would say you are a *very* close friend of the D'Urville family, right?'

She nodded into her champagne glass. 'Hm hm ... would you have a cigarette?'

I gave her one, lit one myself, refilled our glasses.

'Are you quite comfortable down there?' she enquired. I was still sitting on the deck, my back to the banquette.

'I'm lovely – how about you?'

'Deliciously comfortable.'

I laughed. 'You look it. Erm, Gigi ... are you likely to be missed? I mean – by a husband or anything?'

'What an inappropriate question,' she teased huskily. 'No, mon amour, I am not likely to be missed by a husband ... or *any*thing.'

'But ... you are married,' I said, indicating her ring.

She looked at it, her expression almost surprised. 'Oh, yes ... does that bother you?'

'Not in the slightest.' I sipped my drink. 'So – you're not going to tell me who you are, hm?'

She rolled over on to her stomach and elbows, and regarded me through a veil of hair with a disturbingly sexy smile. 'Yes, I will tell you who I am ...' Now she lowered her head to the cushioning and curled into a impish ball, beckoning me to her with a finger. 'If you come here I will tell you who I am ...'

That did it. THUD! went my heart. I put down my glass, abandoned the cigarette over the side and went to kneel at her side, propped on my elbows, her face very close, resting on her arm.

She raised a finger and touched my nose, my mouth, then slowly traced the outline of my lips, her touch so delicate it caused me to shiver and this made her laugh.

'You are cold?' she asked.

'You know I'm not.'

'Then why do you shiver?'

'You know why.'

'Is it my touch?'

'Of course ... and you're doing it again.'

'Do you like it?'

'You know that too.'

'What do you think of me, Roos Tobin? Do you find me desirable?'

'Of course I do . . .'

'And do you know why I've brought you out here?'

I gulped. 'Well, I . . .'

She chuckled at me. 'The man is shy . . .'

'No . . . not really, I . . . well, not *normally*, that is . . .'

'So – why now? Do I make you nervous?'

I grinned. 'A bit.'

'But why? Have you not been alone with a woman like this before?'

'Yes, sure . . .'

'So why are you nervous with me?'

'Well, it's . . . it's not really nervousness . . .'

'No? Then what is it?'

'Excitement.'

Though her expression did not appear to change, her dark jade eyes nevertheless underwent a subtle transformation – their bright edge of jocularity supplanted by a glaze of alarming animalism. At its appearance my excitement soared, though hand-in-hand with an almost-fear, the heart-stopping panic of a youthful man suddenly confronted by a *very* experienced older woman.

Now her lips parted in a delightful smile, dispelling some of my forebodings, and at that moment I gave myself up completely to whatever was about to happen, knowing it would mark an important milestone in my experience.

'So . . . you are excited. That is good. Feed me some champagne, mon amour . . .'

I reached for my glass and gave it to her and she emptied it, so I refilled it and drank half myself.

'Tell me . . .' she cooed, her voice a velvet caress, her finger toying again with my lips, '. . . have you never desired to have a beautiful, desirable woman completely at your mercy . . . to do whatever you wished with her?'

I shrugged, laughed. 'Well, I . . . think it pops into most men's fantasies from time to time . . .'

'An evasive answer,' she chided. 'I asked about you, not

about most men.'

'Well . . . yes, I suppose so.'

'And what – in your wildest fantasy – would you like to *do* with this poor, helpless, beautiful, desirable woman?'

I laughed. 'Well, not play hopscotch.'

'No, somehow I didn't think it would be hopscotch. Perhaps you are too shy to *tell* me what you would do, hm? Perhaps it would be easier for you to *show* me?'

'Well, I . . .'

'Look around you,' she whispered. 'We are completely alone . . . just you and I . . . a man and a woman – in the perfect, romantic setting. And what a perfect opportunity to do what your innermost secret heart has always desired.'

'And . . . what will you be doing while I'm satisfying the cravings of my innermost secret heart?' I grinned.

'Satisfying my own,' she laughed. 'Come . . .' she swung her feet to the deck and took my hand, 'I will show you something very beautiful.'

Trembling inside, I followed her down into the main cabin – a miraculously designed compartment, luxuriously fitted out to provide all the comforts of home – D'Urville's home.

This, however, she quickly passed through to a door at the far end. With fingertip effort she slid it open and stepped through – into the bow compartment almost entirely comprising a vast, white, silk-covered double bed.

She turned and smiled archly, pleased by my surprise. 'You like it?'

'It looks wonderfully comfortable.'

'Try it.'

Gingerly, I sat on its lower edge and gave it a bounce.

'That . . . is *not* trying a bed,' she sighed, placing a hand against my forehead and pushing me backwards.

I went sprawling and she followed me down, dived on it, then quickly sprawled across me and looked down at me, her eyes jubilant.

'First fall to me . . . now you must do anything I say.'

I nodded, breathless. 'All right . . .'

'You really will?'

'Sure.'

'All right . . . then you must lie perfectly still while I undress you.'

Thud! Right under the heart.

She narrow-eyed me. 'You agree?'

I tried to grin but it came out more of a twitch. 'Sure . . .'

'Good.'

She started on my shirt buttons, no great barrier. Three . . . four . . . five . . . they were undone. Slowly, savouring every moment of the game, she peeled away the material and exposed my chest.

She nodded approvingly. 'Nice . . . I hate a lot of hair. Polynesian men have very little, their skin is quite beautiful. You may sit up and remove the shirt.'

I sat up and removed the shirt, then she pushed me gently back again.

Her fingers went to my belt and quickly slipped it loose, then she unfastened the top securing button and found the zipper tag. A thoughtful half-smiling, pause, then she drew it slowly down, her mouth pulling into a grim smile at what she saw beneath.

Now she got off the bed, took hold of each trouser leg and slowly drew them off, her expression reflecting a compressed inner jubilation as more and more of me was revealed.

A moment of quicker activity as she threw aside the trousers and discarded my socks, then a return to her languid attentions as she knelt back on the bed and came to rest at my side, her eyes glued to my bulging briefs.

'Oh,' she whispered, a small delighted sound, such as might be expressed on receipt of a child's gift. Then, with the utmost delicacy, as though removing a dressing from a tender wound, she hooked two forefingers in the band of my briefs and slowly drew then down . . . down . . . down.

For a long moment she held her rigid gaze, her face contorted in a fixed half-smile, her body quite still, then, with a sudden, rushing gasp she flung herself upon me and buried her face in my warmth.

'Oh . . .,' she murmured, covering him with quick, fleeting urgent kisses, as a mother would a son who had just been hauled out of the canal, then broke into a torrent of whispered French endearments . . . and took him into her mouth.

Well, there was no doubting *her* favourite occupation . . .

and, equally, there was no doubting she'd passed out of this school with the highest possible honours. Straight As – for Gigi. By gum, she put me through it . . . drove me bananas for two or three minutes then suddenly stopped and came up alongside, whispering in my ear. 'Undress me.'

She rolled on to her back, eyes closed, arms spread wide, legs parted. I knelt at her side and slipped one, two, three . . . four, five, six buttons. The jade silk dress fell wide open, revealing the skimpiest bra and an almost transparent pair of virtually inconsequential panties.

As I divested her of these minor encumbrances she lay totally inert, thoroughly enjoying the handling, and with its completion she raised her arms and beckoned me into them.

I lay on her, relishing her delicious, naked warmth. At first she seemed inclined simply to enjoy the same, my flesh hot against hers, but after a while she murmured a small, impatient moan and moved me down, spread her legs and guided me in.

Drawing a quick, ecstatic breath she released it in a sigh, arched her hips yearningly, embraced my lower back and drove me all the way home, then relaxed, seemingly content for the time being.

'My cavalier . . .' she smiled sleepily. 'You are perfection.'

'So are you, princess.'

'You have good control. Young men are very beautiful but they invariably come too quickly . . . and miss all the joys of dalliance.' She raised a languid hand and touched my hair, brushed it from my face, stroked it thoughtfully, totally at ease. 'Are you happy here?'

I laughed. 'Of course.'

'You wouldn't rather be at the party?'

'No, certainly not. How could I enjoy myself more than I am right now?'

'There are lots of very beautiful young girls there . . . readily available.'

'I repeat – how could I enjoy myself more than I am right now?'

'Perhaps this isn't quite . . . exciting enough for you?'

'How much more exciting can it get than this?'

She laughed wryly. 'It's obvious you haven't been to a

D'Urville party before.'

'Oh . . .? Tell me about them. What am I missing?'

She shook her head. 'No . . . I might lose you. Anyway, you will find out later for yourself. But in the meantime . . .'

'Yes?'

'I shall try to make this just as exciting . . . but in a different way.'

'Oh . . . how?'

She turned her head and glanced towards a cupboard fitment built into the bulkhead, 'I shall have to get up.'

Gently, she urged me down, wincing humourously as I withdrew, her eyes devouring me hungrily as I sat back on my heels. 'Don't move.'

'All right,' I laughed, wondering what she had in that cupboard.

She skipped off the bed, fantastically naked, her body as perfect upright as it had been in repose, her breasts firm and full, her skin taut, the muscles of her buttocks mounding hard.

'You like what you see?' she murmured playfully, sliding open the cupboard door.

'I love what I see. You have a body a man could never tire of.'

She gave a non-committal grunt.

'Perhaps I should have said *should* never tire of,' I said, and she turned her head and looked at me.

'You are wise for your years,' she smiled, then returned to the cupboard, bringing out a dark, labelless bottle and two small glasses.

Returning to kneel on the bed, she offered me the glasses and uncorked the bottle.

'What is it?' I asked.

She released a lop-sided smile – mystery well-laced with mischief. 'A love potion.'

My heart flipped. 'Really?'

She maintained the smile as she poured the milky liquid into the glasses and re-stoppered the bottle.

'What . . . sort of love potion?' I asked suspiciously. 'Native?'

She dipped her head, turning to replace the bottle in the cupboard. 'Yes, Polynesian.'

'What's it made from?'

'The leaf of a certain bush . . . I won't tell you which, it's a secret. If it ever became public knowledge the world population would treble in a year.'

'I see.'

She took her glass from me, raised her eyes to mine and laughed at my expression. 'You look terrified. There's no need to be, it's quite harmless.'

'Is it . . . a drug?'

She shrugged. 'Yes . . . but it's not habit-forming, I promise. You know I wouldn't do that to you . . . don't you?'

'Yes,' I said, with far more conviction than I felt. Well, I mean, I didn't know the woman, did I? For all I knew she might have been a local witch – the leader of a voodoo sect or something. Just because she didn't have a long, warty nose and a pointed hat didn't mean she couldn't be about to transform me into a zombie.

I tell you, prim though it may sound in this permissive day and age, the one thing I won't touch with a punt pole is drugs. I've seen too many mindless wretches staggering around Piccadilly to play that game. A vodka or two and a few fags – yes, I sink my share and thoroughly enjoy them, but I've never felt the need for any more lift than I can get from a couple of stiff shorts.

And now – for the first time on my travels – I was being confronted with the offer of an unknown mind-bender, knowing I didn't need it in order to have a marvellous time, and yet to be honest, secretly excited by its possible effect.

She read my doubt, my indecision, and smiled knowingly. 'It really *is* quite harmless . . . and I know you'll like what happens. It produces all the benefits of an alcoholic high and none of the drawbacks . . . no sickness, no hangover . . .' her smile deepened, '. . . *and* no depletion of your performance. In fact . . . quite the opposite.'

'Oh . . . really?'

'Are you . . . going to try it?'

I shrugged. 'Why not?' I raised the little glass to my nose, sniffed it, smelled nothing and threw the stuff into the back of my throat.

One gulp . . . and it was gone.

Her face fell. 'Oh, dear . . .'

'What's the matter?'

She laughed. 'Well . . . one doesn't normally swallow it like that. It's meant to be sipped . . . slowly.'

'Oh, my God . . .'

'No, don't worry,' she laughed, 'it's quite all right. It's just that . . . well, the effect will be a little quicker and more concentrated – as with alcohol.' She stifled a giggle. 'Oh, dear . . . I'm afraid you're going to be a little hard to hold . . .' She burst into laughter, realizing her *double entendre*. 'Well, there's only one thing for it . . . I shall have to catch up!'

And back went her head and down went the stuff.

'There . . . !' she laughed. 'And look out, Tobin.'

I handed her my empty glass. 'How . . . long does it take to work?'

She turned to replace the glasses in the cupboard. 'Oh . . . two or three minutes. Come – let's lie down and let it happen. The experience is quite delicious.'

We stretched out on the bed, on our backs, arms down by our sides, our bodies barely touching.

'Now, just relax,' she said softly. 'Gaze at the ceiling and concentrate on nothing but the rocking rhythm of the boat . . . let it take you up . . . and down . . . up . . . and down . . . are you completely relaxed?'

'Getting there.'

'Up . . . and down . . . up . . . and down . . . concentrate on your toes . . . relax them completely . . . they are asleep . . . no feeling in them at all .. now, your legs . . . your thighs . . . your fingers . . . hands . . . everything is heavy, dead-weight, relax . . . relax .. relax . . .'

It began as a small, comforting centre of warmth beneath my navel, a tiny surge of fire not unlike the glow of a brandy taken on a cold winter's day, bringing life to frozen blood and filling the mind with cheer.

At its arrival my heart-beat quickened and an uncertain excitement swept through me – fear and thrill combining in the face of the unknown. What would happen? . . . how would it take me? . . . would it do me harm? A dozen fears tumbled through my mind and yet the effect, so far, was so incredibly comforting I felt compelled to control my panic and simply let it happen.

Now the fire began to spread, billowing out in waves to the four corners of my body, flowing along arms and legs with the creeping insistence of hot water in a slowly filling bath. And with this glow came strength, an all-pervading power, an inundation of supreme well-being that annihilated all weakness and set me among the gods.

I was Samson, and Goliath, the strongest and the best. My right-hook was a mule kick and my left of concrete ... stressed!

Wow ... eeeeee! I felt good ... marvellous ... terrific! Stand back, world – Tobin is comin' through! I am all powerful! ... indestructible! I can stop bullets with my teeth ... tear down buildings with my bare hands! Anybody want a building torn down ... ?

Now, suddenly, the ceiling was eighty feet above me ... not frighteningly so, but simply up there. I looked down, at my legs, and they were a hundred yards long ... now normal size. I was floating ... weightless ... master of gravity ... master of all nature ... and STRONG!

'Has it worked for you?'

Her voice came to me across a valley, filling my head with its echo. I turned to her. She was smiling radiantly, aglow with her own well-being. Her jade green eyes were huge with happiness and her skin ... her skin ...

'I can see that it has,' she laughed.

'I am indefatigable,' I told her, feeling no conscience at the boast, no conscience about anything. I felt dramatic, theatrical, masterful, lordly ... powerful over all. 'I want you, princess ... now!'

'Thank God!' she gasped, and grabbed me by the hair.

In I went, strong as a steam piston, engorged with desire to wreak havoc on her feverish yearning, my prurient plunge unleashing from her a wild yell of ecstatic delight and triggering off a stupendous volcanic eruption.

'Oh, Roos ... Roos ... Roos ...!' she bellowed, throwing me up and down in a flurry of crazy jerks and bucks. 'Oh ... oh ... ohhhh!'

'Is that *good*, princess, is that *good* ... ?'

'My God, my God ... I'm coming ... I'm coming ...!'

'Atta, girl ...!'

'Oh . . . ah . . . eeeh . . aaaaaooooοUGGHHHHHHHHH ! !'

Arms and legs clamped round me like a koala bear's round its mum, she bucked, jumped, jerked and shuddered, yelled, gasped, hooted and hollered . . . right through her first climax and straight into another.

'Go . . . go ! Don't stop . . . don't stop . . . ! I'm on again !'

'Yours to command !'

'My hero . . . my hero ! Roos . . . ?'

'Yes, love?'

'I want it backwards !'

'Anyway you like, love.'

All change !

'I'm coming in . . . !'

'Quickly . . . quickly . . . OHHHHHHH ! !'

'All right?'

'Fan . . . TASTIC !'

And away she went again, face-down in the pillow, teeth clenched in an agony of ecstasy and fingers clawing hell out of the sheets.

'Oh . . . OHHH ! . . . OHHHHHHHH !'

'Anything happening . . . ?'

'Yes ! . . . Yes ! . . . *Yes!* . . . AAAAAUUUUUGGGGG-HHHHH !'

This one was a beaut . . . a, five-star, boat-jolter, heralded by a gasped bellow they must have heard in Hawaii.

'Oh . . . *GOD*, that was incredible . . . !' she howled.

'Care for a rest?' I enquired.

'No . . . no !'

'Care for a *change*?'

'Yes . . . yes ! On top of you !'

'Well, they do say it's as *good* as a rest . . '

I flipped out and over and she was on me in a flash, beaming down at me, pantingly, her eyes and body aglow with throbbing sexuality.

'How do you feel?' she gasped.

'Marvellous !' I gasped.

'So do I !' she proclaimed throwing her arms high and wide. 'I could go on all night . . . all week . . . all year ! He's wonderful ! *You're* wonderful ! Didn't I tell you it would be good?'

'You did, you did, and it is ! I feel . . . gigantic !'

'You are . . . you are!'

She fell forward and smothered me with breathless kisses. 'God, I love the *feel* of you . . . right up there, hard as iron . . .' her teeth came together with a snap. 'Hard as *iron*! I can't get enough of you . . . I want more and more and more! I want you to fill me . . . drench me . . . drown me! NOW!'

On this triumphant demand, she fell sideways, pulled me over her, threw her arms like encircling bands of steel around my waist and drove up into me with a force that shocked the breath from my body.

'NOW! . . . NOW!' she cried, desperate, feverish . . . and mad for it.

GERONIMO . . . !!

By heaven, we *really* went at it – tooth and claw, heart and mind, body and soul – as though we had thirteen seconds to Beat the Clock – first prize Fort Knox.

'Ohh . . . OHHHH . . . *OHHHHHHH*!!' she cried, tortured to ecstasy by every pounding plunge, screaming sweet obscenities in a language of her own.

And 'AAAUUUUGGGHHHHH!!' I bellowed as a great, tearing climax came thundering up from my boots.

'YYAAAARRRROOOOOOOOO!!' she howled.

'YYAAAARRRROOOOOOOOO!!' I wailed . . . and blew her apart with one gigantic, rip-roaring, tumultuous, devastating explosion.

'Ha ha! . . . ho . . . ho! . . . hee *hee*!!' she laughed – a crazy, delirious outburst of insane glee. 'You did it, my hero, you did it!'

Me . . . ? I was face-down in the pillow, my thundering heartbeat rocking my body, my senses swimming with exhaustion, fucked to the very brink of unconsciousness.

'Awwww . . . awwwww . . . awwwww,' I groaned, every vestige of strength gone, dissipated, sucked off like milk from a bottle.

'My hero . . . my hero,' she cooed maternally, patting my shoulder. 'It was superb . . . *quite* superb. Rest there awhile and I will caress you, this exhaustion is only temporary. In a few moments you will once again begin to feel the flow of power . . .' I groaned at the prospect and she laughed. 'No, I promise you – that is what is so wonderful about my little . . . cocktail. Under its influence every response is absolute . . . absolute power, then absolute repletion . . . then once again absolute power. But you needn't take my word for it – all you have to do is wait.'

I waited . . . knowing she couldn't possibly be right. Such was the bottomless depth of my exhaustion I had grave doubts *I'd* ever be able to sit upright again, never mind Herc.

I lay there upon her, totally inert, not a nerve, bone or muscle showing the slightest sign of life, strength or feeling. I was a zombie . . . dammit, I was a *zombie*! She's done it to me! I was now a fully-paid-up member of the living dead.

But who cared?

I was hers – totally. Do with me what you will, princess – break an arm, eat a leg, barbecue me slowly on an open spit, see if I care.

I suppose I drifted into a half-conscious doze then, a cosy floating euphoria, a condition of half-sleep in which, though dreaming, I was still aware of her presence beneath me.

And in the dream I was transported back to the beginning – to the drinking of her 'cocktail'.

Gulp . . it was gone.

Her face fell. 'Oh, dear . . .'

'What's the matter?'

She laughed. 'Well . . . one doesn't normally swallow it like that. It's meant to be sipped . . . slowly.'

'Oh, my God . . .'

We stretched out on the bed . . .

'Now, just relax . . . are you completely relaxed?'

'Getting there.'

'Up . . . and down . . . concentrate on your toes . . . everything is deadweight . . . heavy . . . relax . . . relax . . relax.'

Now it began again as a small, comforting centre of warmth beneath my navel . . . like brandy on a winter's day . . . now it spread . . . the glow . . . and with the glow came strength . . . an all-pervading power . . . an inundation of supreme well-being that annihilated all weakness and set me among the gods!

Once again I was Samson . . . Goliath . . . invincible . . . indestructible! I was . . . STRONG!

I opened my eyes, raised myself up on my arms and grinned down at her, discovering her own resurrected strength and joy.

'My God,' I gasped, 'it's happened!'

'You think I don't *know* it?' she laughed wryly. 'Must I

remind you I am harbouring the result?'

'Gigi . . this is *incredible*! How long does it go on re-working like this?'

She shrugged. 'That, of course, depends on the man. If he is young, fit, naturally virile . . .' she shrugged again, '. . . possibly for twenty-four hours. Then nature would put her foot down most positively and he would probably sleep as though dead.'

'Wow . . .' I gasped. 'Gigi . . . do you realize what a fortune you could make marketing this stuff? Any man with flagging virility would pay a fortune for a bottle of this . . . Cum-Cum Juice!'

She laughed, frowningly. 'Cum-Cum Juice?'

I shrugged. 'Well, you won't tell me its name, so I made one up.'

'I think it's very good – I shall call it that in future. But as far as making a fortune out of it . . .' she shook her head emphatically, '. . . no. A very dear Polynesian friend introduced me to its magic on the understanding I would never reveal the ingredients, and I would never abrogate his trust. As for making a fortune . . .' she smiled mysteriously, 'why should I want to make another when I have one already?'

'Oh. I see.' I sighed. 'Well, I *was* sort of hoping to take a bottle away with me . . .' I grinned at her. 'You know – for Australia. I hear the girls there tend to be a bit on the Amazonian side – rather demanding. I thought perhaps a thimbleful of Cum-Cum might help to even the odds a bit.'

She laughed. 'Do you honestly believe you *need* it?'

'Well, no, perhaps not *need*, but . . .'

She patted my cheek. 'All right, in the interests of scientific experiment, I shall give you the bottle to take with you . . .'

'You will!'

'. . . on one condition!'

'Oh.'

'That you write and tell me of your experience with it.'

I laughed. 'All right – it's a deal.'

'Faithful reportage, mind! I don't want any wildly exaggerated performances, I want the truth.'

'Scouts' honour – word for word.'

She released a sigh and did funny things with her insides,

making me jump. 'My God, I pity those Amazons in Sydney. They will certainly know it when Tobin enters their . . . territory.'

'You're too kind.'

Suddenly her expression and attitude changed. Prodding me on the nose, she said, in a tone of unarguable finality, 'And now you must go.'

I gaped at her. 'Go, go where, Gigi?'

'Back to the party. I've monopolized enough of your precious time.'

'I . . .' I stammered, nonplussed, but she silenced me with a finger on my lips. 'I know you are going to protest very beautifully – because you are a nice, kind, thoughtful man and do not wish to hurt my feelings, but I *want* you to go.'

I frowned. 'You do?'

'Yes. I wish to be alone for a while. I'm going to have a moonlight swim all by myself . . . the *other* great pleasure in my life. And you are going ashore to distribute your new-found virility among the many beautiful and wanton ladies at the party . . .'

'But . . .' I protested.

'Sssh!' she went. 'We're not very far from the wharf, you'll see the lights. You may take the painter, it has a little outboard motor. Just leave it tied to the wharf.'

'Oh . . .' I said, feeling suddenly deflated by this turn of events and yet . . . well, who wouldn't be excited by the possibilities ashore under the influence of Cum-Cum Juice?

'Come,' she smiled, easing me away, 'you will have a quick swim with me, it will refresh you. But only a quick one – then you must go.'

She skipped off the bed and led me out of the cabin, me feeling a right nana with Herc presenting arms like a well-trained palace guard.

Up on to the deck we went, into the stern, Gigi stepping quickly on to the banquette cushioning and taking an immediate header over the side into the dark sparkling water.

She surfaced instantly, gasping and laughing, waving to me. 'Come on – it's fabulous!'

Over I went, my mind blurring to the embracing coolness of the water.

I surfaced, receiving a splash in the eye from a laughing Gigi. 'Isn't it wonderful? You see – it will have the most *gratifying* effect on your staying power! Cold water plus the ... Cum-Cum Juice – how I love that name – will make you quite imperishable!'

'Gigi, I believe you! I don't think it's ever going to go down!'

She laughed. 'Love will find a way!'

She swam to me, placed her arms around my neck and embraced my waist with her legs. 'OHHHHH ...!'

I laughed. 'I did warn you ...'

In a rush of erupting passion, she slid home, took me whole, the fervour of her rampant desire evident in her contorted face, her clenched teeth and blazing eyes. This was no sweet, lingering dalliance; this was joyful, wanton, female rape!

The water around us thrashed and boiled. I kicked and splashed to stay afloat, the bobbing, sinking motion furthering her ecstasy, driving her to a delirious apex of sexuality that now burst in a wild, explosive cry that echoed and re-echoed across the bay.

'OHHHHHHH!' she gasped, her face to mine, her arms limp around my shoulders. A plaintive laugh. 'I think you'd better get out right now ... or we'll still be here a week from now ... waterlogged as sponges.'

'I don't mind, Gigi.'

She raised her head and looked at me softly. 'I know ... but I want you to go.' She kissed me wetly and slowly disengaged herself. 'Go and get dressed, I shall stay here and float.'

'Well ... if you insist.'

'I do.'

She moved away in a languid crawl and I struck out for the ladder.

While I dried myself and dressed, I chuckled and chortled to myself like a lunatic, unable to believe all this was happening. God, how dreamlike it all was ... how utterly fantastic. Here was I, me, Tobin ... aboard a cabin cruiser in a Tahitian bay, fixed to the gills with some crazy Polynesian aphrodisiac, making stupendous, endless love to a beautiful, wealthy woman who, for all I knew, might well be the French Ambassador's wife ... and now I was about to row ashore and ... and ...

The prospect of what might ensue on shore brought on another chuckle. I was mad, I decided – round the flaming twist. I was drunk or drugged or both or just plain loony and I didn't give a hoot. I felt ebullient, on top of the world, bursting with high spirits and general joie de vivre. Come one, come all, I'll take on the lot of you . . . and if you can't stand the pace, love, stand aside and let the next one through.

Wwhhhhhhheeeeeeee!

Floating weightlessly, I leapt across the bed and slid open the Juice cupboard. Surprise – there were *three* bottles in there, each the size of a half of Scotch.

What wouldn't I have given for all three!

But no – a deal was a deal. I withdrew one and closed the cupboard, kissed the bottle affectionately and climbed back to the well deck.

'Gigi!' I called, peering into the dark lagoon.

There was no reply.

My heart skipped a beat.

'Gigi!' I called louder.

Still nothing. Save for the quiet slap of water against the hull, the lagoon was as silent as the grave.

A premonition of terrible disaster swept over me. Had she been too drunk, too drugged to stay afloat? Had she drowned? Oh, my God . . .

I climbed on to the cushioning, hung on to the ladder rail and peered out over the side. 'GIGI . . .!'

Up she shot, in a great rush of water, directly under me, frightening the hell out of me.

'You called, my cavalier?' she laughed.

'God, I thought you'd drowned or something.'

'Would you have been sorry?'

'Not in the least – except it might have interrupted the party for a minute or two.'

'Brute,' she laughed. 'You are ready to go?'

'Yes. I . . . took a bottle, – just one.'

'I knew you would.'

'I don't like leaving you out here all alone like this. Are you sure you'll be all right?'

'Of course. I come out here to swim every night, it's perfectly safe. The little fish are my friends.'

'You're quite a girl, aren't you?'

She smiled a little inward smile. 'A girl, alas, no more.'

'No . . . something much more exciting – a wholly beautiful woman.'

She greeted the compliment with a thoughtful pause, then said earnestly, 'Please go . . . just turn that handle and the painter will drop.'

'I'd like to say goodbye a little more . . . demonstratively, Gigi.'

'I will kiss you down here.'

'All right.'

I turned my attention to the handle, released the rachet and lowered the little fibre-glass runabout to the water, and jumped into it. Unhooking the lines I threw them over the stern of the cruiser, then lowered the outboard motor into the water.

'A born seaman,' chaffed Gigi, coming to the side.

I sat down and took her face between my hands, kissed her salty mouth.

'I still don't like the idea of leaving you. Will I see you again before . . . well, before the party finishes?'

She shrugged. 'Perhaps. But if you don't – have a wonderful time in Australia . . .' she popped me on the nose, '. . . and don't forget to write.'

'I won't.'

'Go on – get that thing started.'

I kissed her fully now, a long tender thank you.

' 'Bye, Gigi . . . be careful now.'

'And you!' she laughed.

I turned in the seat, opened the fuel line, gave the cord one yank and the put-put coughed into life.

'Goodbye . . .' she waved, striking away from the boat.

'Goodbye, Gigi . . .'

I accelerated slowly, cutting between her and the cruiser, made perhaps twenty yards, then suddenly stopped, remembering.

'Gigi . . . I forgot! How can I write to you when I don't know your name?'

There was a small silence, then her reply came over the black water, teasing and jubilant. 'It's D'Urville, beloved. Angelique D'Urville. Bon soir, cheri . . .!'

And then she was gone.

CHAPTER SEVEN

I WAS still chuckling when I reached the wharf. Angelique D'Urville . . . the boss's wife! . . . and the woman Paul Martin had warned us not to tangle with. Ha! What Paul Martin had missed!

Or had he?

Ah, well, mine was not to reason if – or why. She and Jean Pierre were entitled to live life as they saw it and if this arrangement of do-as-you-please suited them, who was I to question it? They certainly didn't appear to be overly miserable.

Zinging with high spirits and humming to myself, I brought the put-put into the wharf and cut the engine, jumped up on to the pier and tied the fore and aft ropes to a couple of iron rings, then stood for a moment looking out over the water at the cabin cruiser, riding with lights perhaps a quarter of a mile out.

'RUSS . . .!'

The hoarse bellow close behind me startled me so much I damn-near dropped the bottle. I shot round, discovering Buzz loping towards me, having just come off the beach. Even in the poorish light I could tell he was nicely blitzed, he had that kind of grin.

He closed on me, panting, his brow crumpled in puzzlement as he took stock of me, the boat, the bottle and the fact that I was *on* the pier.

'Where in hell have *you* been?'

'Hello, mate,' I grinned. 'How's the party?'

'The party's out of this world . . . . but where've you *been*? I've been looking all over for you.'

I hooked a thumb over my shoulder. 'Out there.'

He peered past me, weaving a bit, narrowing his eyes. 'Out where? *There?* On that boat?'

'Yup.'

He grinned. 'No kidding? Whose is it? Is there another party going on there? A sort of splinter group?'

'Of one,' I laughed. 'Well, two until I left.'

His eyes widened. 'Just you and a bird? You crafty devil. Where is she now?'

'Still out there – swimming all by herself. She wanted it that way.'

'Weird,' he said, shaking his head. 'The whole bloody place is weird. Hey, what've you got there – a half of Scotch? How about a snort?'

I raised the bottle to eye-level, becoming dramatically solemn. 'Scotch? Oh, no, Buzz, this is not Scotch. This is . . .' my voice became a hushed whisper, '. . . nectar! . . . the Elixir of Life! Ho ho . . .' I kissed the bottle, 'Buzz, old buddy, I have stumbled across a *miracle*!'

'Yeh, sure. Tobin stop fucking about and give me a belt, I'm famished . . .'

'Buzz, I'm not kidding! It's the truth! *She* gave it to me . . .! We drunk it together! It's the most incredible aphrodisiac!'

'Eh?' he gawped.

'It's *true*! She had three bottles of it! One egg-cup full and you're away . . . master of the universe . . . horny as Harry Harris's horse . . .!'

'Who the hell's he?'

'Our milkman – back home. Randy devil. Buzz, I tell you no lie – next to this stuff, powdered rhino horn is as sexy as sherbert!'

'Get away! Well . . . what's it made of?'

I slumped. 'She wouldn't tell me, says it's a secret between her and a Polynesian witch doctor. I told her she could make a fortune flogging this stuff on the open market but she wasn't interested – says she's already got a fortune, what does she need with two. Besides, she's worried about a world population explosion if this stuff ever got loose.'

He gasped. 'Wow . . . it's that powerful, hm?'

'Unbelievable.'

'Well . . . how does it affect you?'

'At first it's like taking a nip of straight liquor – just warms your tum . . . then the glow begins to spread right through your body . . . then you begin to feel terrific – I mean really *fantastic* . . . strong, invincible!'

'Wow!'

'Then your eyes go a bit funny ... everything seems distorted – your legs seem fifty yards long, but that quickly passes ... and then ...!' I laughed. 'Then, son, you get so damned horny you could drill holes through sheet steel ...'

'Jesus Christ,' he gasped, eyes popping. 'And did you ...' he nodded towards the boat, '.... you know.'

'*Did* we? Oh, boy ... and what's more, I'm rarin' to start all over again! One belt of this keeps the old flag flying for twenty-four hours, she said.'

'Twen ... *holy* cow.' His face split in one hell of a grin. 'Hey ...'

'No,' I said, removing the bottle from his sight, behind my back.

'Eh? Aw, come *on* ...'

I shook my head. 'No, Buzz, definitely not.'

He gaped at me, perplexed. 'Aw, *Ru*-uss ...'

'It's for the good of the community, Malone. You're far too lethal as it is. My God, one belt of this and no woman on the island would be safe from rape. You'd probably start an international incident.'

'Aw, *mate* ...!' he wailed. 'Christ, I haven't had a crack at anything yet – I've spent most of my time looking for you!'

'For me? What for?'

'Because ...' he flung an arm out, towards the house, then paused, cunningly. 'No, I'm not going to tell you ...'

'Tell me what, Buzz?' I said, easing the bottle into view.

'Ho, no, you don't.' He shrugged. 'Pity ... you'd have enjoyed it.'

'Enjoyed *what*?'

He held out his hand. 'Snort.'

'I daren't – you'd go berserk.'

'OK – no snort, no ... whatever it is I was going to tell you.'

I grinned at him and brought the bottle out. 'You really think I wouldn't?' I uncapped the bottle, then looked round for a suitable place in which to dispense it. 'There – let's sit on the sand. I think it's better if you sit down, you might fall in the lagoon.'

Chuckling with anticipation, he quickly moved off and

plonked himself down, reaching for the bottle.

'Not too much, now,' I warned him. 'I had a small glassful and it hit me like a brick. She said I should have sipped it, but I took it in one gulp. I'd suggest the same for you – a couple of good swallows, no more.'

'OK,' he said excitedly, taking the bottle and sniffing it. 'Not much smell. Didn't she give you *any* idea what it's made of?'

'No – just said it was from the leaves of a certain bush. She didn't give it a name, so I christened it Cum-Cum Juice.'

He spluttered a laugh. 'Christ, it's that good, huh?'

'Better. You just have no idea.'

He held the bottle at arm's length, studied it for a moment with a compressed grin, sighed, 'Well, here goes . . . or comes,' then tipped the bottle to his lips.

Gulp . . . gulp . . .

'That's enough, Malone . . .'

Gulp . . .

'Buzz, for Chrissake . . . !'

My hand streaked out . . . gulp! . . . snatched the bottle from him.

'Buzz, you fucking idiot . . .'

He roared with laughter. 'Listen . . . you don't know what's going *on* back there! If you did, you'd take another couple of swigs to top-up your libido! Come to think of it, I'd advise it.'

'Yeh? Well, what *is* going on?'

'Ha! . . . Oh . . .'

'What's the matter?'

'Wow . . . I think it's started.'

'Warm glow?'

'A bloody furnace .. . right here in the gut.'

'That's it. Buzz, you'd better lie down.'

'You reckon?'

'*We* did. It helps when your eyes go funny.'

'OK.' He lay down, looked up at me. 'You going to take another swig?'

I looked at the bottle. 'Well . . .'

'Come on – join me. I'd feel better with company.'

'Well, maybe just a toothful.'

'Good man.'

I uncapped the bottle, swallowed one gulp and re-stoppered it, then lay on the sand. 'Feel anything?'

'Yeh – like you said . . . the glow . . . spreading right through my body. Jeezus, it's fantastic . . . like you'd been pumped full of proteins and vitamins . . . wow!' he laughed. 'By heck, I could do with a shot of this just before I go on court, son . . . I reckon I'd ace-serve the other bloke clean out of the grounds! POWEEEE! Hey . . .' he stretched out an arm, up towards the night sky, 'You want that moon, Tobin . . . I'll get it for you. Christ, my arm's a mile long! Ha ha . . .'

'Don't bother, I'll get it myself!'

'You there, too?'

'I'm there.'

'Blimey, look at my feet! They're in the sea!'

'This won't last long . . . just a minute or so – then watch out!'

'What happens next?'

'You'll see. I don't want to spoil the surprise.'

'How long?'

'Any second now.'

We lapsed into silence, each lost in his own suffusion of well-being . . . of burgeoning power, marvelling at the magnitude and magnificence of the overhanging universe . . . the stars, the moon, the mystery of its black and limitless space.

And then, from Buzz, a rumbling, exploding chortle of delight, the manifestation of overwhelming discovery, bursting from him in a joyful, shouted hallelujah. 'WWWWOOOO-OOOOOWWWWW!'

I roared with laughter. 'You got it, Malone!'

'I've got it . . . I've got it! YeeeeeOOOWWW! I feel *good*!'

He leapt to his feet, legs braced, fists furled, in the stance of a prize-fighter crouching triumphantly over a vanquished opponent. 'Tobin . . . I can lick the world!'

'I know it . . . I know it!' I laughed, jumping up beside him.

'KKEEEEE . . . RYST, I feel good!' he whooped, leaping in the air and right-hooking an imaginary ten-foot foe. 'POW . . .! SPLAT . . .! ZONK . . .! THWACK . . .! And how's *this* for an ace-service . . . ? KKEEEEEERRR . . . *POW*!'

He served so hard he over-balanced and fell on his knees in the sand, killing himself laughing. 'WWHHOOOOO . . .

PEEEEE!' he howled, hurling sand into the air.

'Huh, you think *that's* an ace-service, Malone . . . ?' I chortled. 'Then just watch *this* one!' Raising my left leg like a Dodger's pitcher, I went into ludicrously complex, arm-whirling wind-up, turned round in a hop three times and crashed down an imaginary racquet so hard I fell on my back, legs in the air.

Buzz was in pleats, pounding the sand with his fist. 'And the winner by murder . . . Russell Tobin!'

He leapt to his feet and gazed dramatically out to sea. 'I'm going to swim to Moorea . . . it's only twelve miles.'

'Oh, no you don't,' I said, getting up. 'You are going to tell me what the hell's going on at that house. Come on, Malone, what am I missing?'

He came to me, sobering outwardly though still bubbling inside, and threw an arm round my shoulder. 'You ever seen an orgy, son . . . ? I mean, not *an* orgy – but like twenty-seven going on at the same time?'

My eyes popped. 'No kidding?'

'God's honour. The things going on up there will drive you blind.'

'I'll risk it . . . I'll get a white stick.'

He shook his head. 'Nah, I think you're too young . . . this could mark you for life.'

'I'm already marked! I've danced with girls!'

'You have?' he tutted disgustedly. 'I had no idea you were so far gone. All right . . . follow me – but when I say shut your eyes – you shut 'em, see?'

'Yes, dad.'

With a laugh, he stopped acting the fool and went into a lascivious chortle. 'Mate, you're gonna get your *mind* blown . . .'

'Why, what's going on?'

'Everything! Every damn thing . . .'

'Where?'

'All over – in the bungalows . . . in the house.'

'You've been in the house?'

'I've been everywhere – looking for you, you twaddle. How did I know you were doodling a dolly in the middle of the lagoon? Eh, by the way – who was she?'

'Angelique D'Urville.'

He gaped at me, then snorted disdainfully. 'Aw, come on . . .'

I laughed. 'It's true.'

He stopped and stared at me. 'Aw, come *on* . . .'

'I mean it.'

'What, the . . . sex-crazed bird Martin warned us about? Jean Pierre's missus?'

I nodded. 'The same – though I don't go along with Martin's dirty description. She's a beautiful woman, Buzz . . . quite lovely.'

'Well, can you beat that?' he gasped. 'Up trolls Tobin, cool as you please, and lands the pick of the bunch – at least by reputation. How *do* you do it?'

'Well . . .' I frowned, 'it's damned difficult to explain, Buzz. I just have this certain *je ne sais quoi* that beautiful, rich, mature, sexy women find totally irresistible . . .'

'Ha!' he roared and slapped me on the shoulder. 'Good thing you're modest, Tobin, otherwise you'd be unbearable.'

'Thanks,' I winced. 'And watch that right-hook, Malone, you're under the Cum-Cum influence, you know.'

'And don't I know it,' he growled. 'I'm beginning to feel randier than a two-dicked dog in a poodle parlour.'

'Patience, Malone, your time will undoubtedly come.'

'It'd better,' he grinned. 'Otherwise there'll be so many holes in these palm trees, they'll think they're infested with woodpeckers!'

We broke through the denser vegetation that followed the shoreline and entered the 'park', finding it considerably less populated than before, although the band was still playing for a number of dancing couples and for the entertainment of those around the bars and food tables.

Ignoring all this, Buzz headed fast across the open space towards the lines of thatched bungalows, most of which were hidden in the shadow of densely clustered palm trees and other tall shrubbery.

As we approached the first bungalow, Buzz went into a 'see-if-anybody's watching us' act, glancing all around and peering into the undergrowth, then, deciding that the coast was clear, jerked his head at me, scuttled down the side of the bungalow and flattened himself to its wall like an escaping prisoner avoiding a searchlight beam.

'Come on!' he hissed.

Feeling compelled to copy him, I went in at a fast, furtive, scuttle, flattened myself against the wall and got a protruding sliver of bamboo straight between the shoulder blades.

'Coooorrrr . . .!' I gasped.

'SSSSHHHHHHH!!' he went, his ssh making more noise than my cor. 'What's up?'

I turned and snapped off the needle-sharp sliver. 'That!'

'Sssssshh,' he went again. 'Come on . . . this way!'

Like a shadow he slid along the wall, paused at the far end of the building, then waved me forward, disappearing round the corner as I reached him. I found him crouched beneath a window, smothered in vegetation.

I joined him, collecting a broken, rigid leaf-stem up the arse as I went into the crouch.

'Owwwwww . . .!!'

'Ssssshhhh . . .!' he whispered. 'Christ, what's the matter with you?'

'It's not my fault! I flunked my jungle survival course!'

'Ssssshhhh . . .!' he went again, jerking a thumb at the window.

'What's in there?'

He stifled a chuckle. 'Take a look!'

'Is it safe?'

'Sure! There's an insect gauze over all these windows . . . we can see in but they can't see out! Go on – take a look, I'll keep cavie.'

Bubbling with excitement, my heart thudding so hard I was sure whoever was in the room could hear it, I gradually raised myself up until my eyes cleared the sill.

The room was lit by a couple of lamps stationed either side of a big, bamboo-headed bed. It was a simply furnished room, done in Polynesian style – rattan walls, cane furniture, colourful woven rugs on the polished wood floor . . . very nice. I lowered myself down and told Buzz so.

'Ugh?' he gaped.

'I said it's a very nice room . . . terrific . . . very colourful. *Adore* the lamps.' I waited.

He mouthed silently. 'A . . . bu . . . it . . . *hm*? You mean . . . there's nothing going on in there?'

I gave it thought. 'Yes . . . there's an overhead lamp swinging in the breeze.'

He shot up, peered in and shot down again. 'Fuck it, they've gone! Well, stap me . . .'

'Did you *tell* them you'd be back with me?'

'Jeezus . . .' he shook his head sadly, 'and that was one of the best.'

'One of the best what?'

He looked up, past me, along the line of bungalows to the next one, then came up into a half-crouch. 'Follow me!'

I followed him . . . over to the next bungalow, and this time he left nothing to chance. He was straight up there, at the window, his eyes popping with delight. 'Aaahhhh!'

'What is it?' I whispered from below.

'Come up here . . . quick!'

I went.

Blimey O'Riley.

Similar room, similar bed . . . but there the similarity ceased.

Before our very eyes there unfolded a tableau of abandoned and joyous fornication, a right old catch-as-catch-can free-for-all.

There were four participants – two male and a pair of the gentler sex, all sharing the one large bed. One of the men was a strapping Tahitian lad, sveltly muscled and extremely handsome, the picture of health and strength. The other chap looked European, a distingusihed-looking cove with greying hair and a wealthy tan. One of the girls was Tahitian, the other a brunette Caucasian, and both built for distance – strong, well-padded birds with big boobs. All four, of course, were totally starkers.

In the opening round, the Tahitian lad was entwined with the brunette in a mystifying tangle of limbs, while the (presumably) French guy was tickling the Tahitian bird's fancy with his tongue, all four of them giggling and laughing like they'd been sprayed with itching powder.

These positions, however, did not pertain for long – the name of the game obviously being 'caprice'; for while the Tahitian lad was banging away at the brunette, she began playing 'let's peel a banana' with Frenchie, who in turn began tuning *her* left nipple into the right station while still bringing the Tahitian bird to the boil.

Then, suddenly ... all change! Frenchie tapped Tahitian Ted on the shoulder as in a Gentlemen's Excuse-Me, who immediately vacated the brunette with a farewell wave and slid into Tahitian Tessa neat as ninepence, sending her through the thatched roof with his first plunge, and while *they* were doing their best to wreck the bed, Frenchie was playing Vat 69 with the brunette who now patently resembled a sword-swallower I'd seen at Ormskirk fair.

'Hee hee ...!' chuckled Buzz, thumping me in the back with his fist.

'Steady, son, steady ... my God, what a party.'

'Ho, you've seen nothing yet.'

'It get's worse?'

'No, better ... follow me!'

Off he slunk through the undergrowth, me close behind, coming to a halt at the next bungalow window.

'Allez ... oop!' he whispered, and we rose like twin Chads above the sill.

Ah, refreshing normality here – one fella and two girls, one girl warming up in the pits while the other was tearing round the track. In she came, tyres smoking and engine screaming, for a quick cool-down and an oil change.

Flip! Over went our stalwart into the stand-by flier, a gorgeous little Chinese bird with a porcelain chassis. Baroom ... baroom ... and away she went, hitting ninety on the straight and squealing into the first bend.

'Think he needs any help?' I panted, sweat cascading off my brow. 'Terrible shame – leaving that poor kid out in the cold like that.'

'Save it,' panted Buzz. 'There's more and better to come.'

'Oh, Gawd ...'

'Come!'

Along we shot to the next bungalow, nestled in among the shrubbery and rose to our accustomed position.

Now, this *was* different! ... definitely *very* unusual – just one man and one woman.

But what a man! And what a woman! Tarzan and Jane ... Samson and Delilah ... two strapping specimens of beautiful humanity – he a muscular Polynesian Adonis, biceps like coconuts and thighs of steel, she a big-breasted blonde with a hungry eye and legs to match.

They were going at it heaven's hard, not on the bed but on the floor, on a pile of woven matting. By gum, the lad was really giving her what for and she was lapping it up like a thirsty camel, legs entwined round his waist like a couple of tug hawsers and fingers gouging great lumps out of his bulging shoulder muscles.

Buzz gasped so hard his hot breath clouded the window pane. 'It's all that hula dancing, you know ... builds pelvic muscles like laminated steel. Russ ... I've got to have a woman! We're the only blokes on the entire island not getting it!'

'*You* ... are telling *me*!'

'Come on!'

'Where to now?'

'To the pictures!'

'Eh?'

He was off.

God only knows how he knew about it, but in a couple of minutes we were at the back of the house and going through a rear door into a dimly lit corridor.

'Buzz ...!' I whispered, coming to a halt.

'Yes?'

'What ... ? How ... ? Where are we *going*, for Pete's sake?'

He grinned. 'I told you – to the pictures. It's all *right* – don't worry. Trust your Uncle Buzz! I've already been here ... come on!'

He went on, stopped at a door on the left, gave a quiet knock. It opened immediately, revealing the angelic face of the prettiest vahiné I'd seen so far.

As she recognized Buzz, her face lit up in a radiant smile and her eyes travelled to me. 'Ah, you found him! Good, come on in.'

We entered a large, dark room, so dark I stood rooted just inside the door, afraid to go any further. The door closed behind us, and the vahiné's gentle hand was on my arm.

'This way,' she whispered.

Like a blind man I followed her, peering into the blackness for a sign of what the hell was going on, beginning, as my pupils adjusted, to make out vague shapes ... couches ...

arranged in lines across the room . . . an occasional human head and shoulders silhouetted above them.

'Here is an empty one,' the vahiné whispered, guiding me into a seat. 'Your refreshment will be here in a moment.'

'Thank you.'

It was a second or two before I realized Buzz was not about to join me. I turned, looked for him, sensed his departure to the far side of the room and suffered a pang of unease. What was going on?

Now, as I turned to face the front, I could dimly make out the screen – a high, wide movie screen, perhaps fifteen feet by eight – very large for home movies.

I gazed about, vaguely discerning faces, all seemingly relaxed, smiling with anticipation . . . some men sitting alone, others, with women, nobody taking the slightest notice of me.

Ah, well . . .

I decided to relax and let it all happen. The couch was deeply upholstered, very comfortable, the room scented with the aroma of tropical flowers, a combination that banished tension and lulled one into a nice sexy euphoria.

My mind turned to the doll who had opened the door to us and a sudden yearning to have her there with me on the couch overcame me. I looked round, trying to find her, but before I could locate her, another vahiné also dressed in a red-flowered cotton *pareu* bearing a coconut drink, loomed out of the darkness and bent close.

'Your drink, sir.'

I looked up into strikingly beautiful eyes set above high cheek bones and a dainty nose. Another mind-blinder. How could there be so many devastating women in one place.

Emboldened by her smile – to say nothing of a double belt of Cum-Cum Juice – I took the drink and blurted out.

'Miss . . are you free?'

She raised an amused brow. 'Free? Everything here is free.'

'No . . . I mean . . . would you care to join me?'

Again the brow. '*Join* you?'

I laughed. 'I mean . . . would you like to sit with me . . . or are you on duty?'

She laughed quietly. 'Yes, I am on duty, I am serving the drinks.'

'Oh . . . all night?'

'No . . . not all night.'

'Oh, then do you think it's possible that . . .'

'I will see.'

My heart leapt. 'Would you? I'd . . . like that very much.'

'Yes!' she smiled.

At that moment a spear of white light split the darkness and struck the screen, capturing my attention, and when I turned to her again she was gone.

Oh, well . . .

I sipped the drink, found it pleasantly bitter-sweet and faintly aromatic, decided it was harmless and settled down to watch the film.

The title comes up, in French, 'Le Gymnase' – The Gymnasium. Aye aye, I thought . . .

The opening shots are of Paris on a beautiful spring day – sunlit scenes of the city, the Seine, and the chic mademoiselles going flirtatiously about their business of being chic, flirtatious mademoiselles.

Now the camera picks up one particular girl – a stunning blonde in a knee-length cotton dress and smart neck-scarf, her long pale hair wafting silkily in the soft morning breeze. She is carrying a small leather case.

She approaches camera, pauses at a doorway to check a sign which reads: 'Le Gymnase de Jacque Géant' and, with a tight mischievous smile, proceeds inside.

Cut to: the reception desk. A studious, bespectacled dark-haired girl greets Blondie with a knowing smile, hands her a key and directs her down a passage to a dressing room. Blondie takes off.

Cut to: the interior of the dressing room. Blondie enters, puts down her case, removes the scarf, shoes, unzips her dress and drops it to the floor. The camera follows. A moment later a bra and panties drop into frame. The camera then stays on her lower legs as she steps into a white leotard and in the next shot we see her ready for action.

By gum, she's got a right old handful, too, in that skin-tight costume – a pair of knockers that men leave hearth and home for. A final pat at her hair and out she goes.

Cut to: the gymnasium – a room fully equipped with wall

bars, vaulting horse, rowing machine, cycling machine and a vibro-massage machine.

Enter Blondie, an obvious stranger to the establishment by the way she wanders around, inspecting the equipment.

A close-up now reveals a door marked 'Jacques Géant – Privé'. It opens and out comes Jacques – and, by heck, he's rightly named. Jack the Giant is bloody enormous – six four in his sweat socks and built like an Angus bull . . . shoulders billowing out of his singlet and a chest like a coal bucket.

But a handsome lad for all that – good square jaw and ninety-seven sparkling choppers which he shows to Blondie in a welcoming smile while his lecherous eyes are running up and down her fabulous body like a couple of Olympic sprinters.

'Bonjour, mademoiselle . . .' he leers. 'You have come for a work-out?'

'Yes,' she smiles coyly, immediately aware of his overpowering maleness and loving every inch of it. 'A friend recommended I should come. . . she tells me she has received every satisfaction here.'

'And so shall you,' our Jacques assures her, in sexy French, of course. 'Now . . . shall we start with a few simple limbering up exercises on the wall bars?'

'As monsieur directs. You are the teacher, I the pupil. I will do precisely as you command.'

Close-up on Jack's eyes . . . and they are not nice to behold. Lascivious desire lurks behind that shallow smile and we know already what kind of limbering up exercises he has in mind!

'Step up here, ma chère,' he says, already getting a bit familiar. 'Hang suspended from the top bar and draw your knees up high.'

Up goes Blondie, her fantastic ass in glorious close-up as seen by Jacques. She turns, grips the top bar and hangs, then with enormous effort attempts to draw her knees up. Two . . . three . . . pathetic attempts, the camera slowly zooming in to fill the screen with her blatantly pubic mound, her heart-shape of black pussy-fluff plainly visible through the thin white material.

Close-up on Jacque's narrowed, gleaming eyes and passion-dry mouth. His tongue flicks out to moisten his lips . . . his voice breaks. 'A good effort, ma'mselle . . . but perhaps I should show you. Please step down.'

As she descends, up Jacques goes, nimble as a newt. He turns, hangs suspended, his white trousers of thin cotton stretching like a drum-skin over his bulging genitals. And, by gum, he *has* got a fistful . . . either that or he keeps his lunch in there.

'Now, ma'mselle . . . watch closely . . .'

Close-up on Blondie who is watching *very* closely – her eyes like ping-pong balls, rivetted on his lunch-box.

'Up . . . and down . . .' recites Jacques, closely watching her closely watching him. 'Up . . . and down . . .' He gives a wry laugh. 'You seem impressed . . . and yet it is not all that hard.'

Another close-up on him reveals he is not only a lecher but a goddam liar . . . because he's now got a hard-on the size of a baseball bat and growing by the minute.

Back to Blondie, open-mouthed with . . . horror? . . . surprise? . . . delight? . . . all three?

Jacques drops to the floor. 'Now you again – up you go.'

Up she goes.

He closes on her, his face in juxtaposition with her bulging short-and-curlies. 'Perhaps if I help you a little . . .'

Hooking his hands round her legs, he lifts . . . and lowers . . . his lips all but caressing her pubic mound on the downward sweep. 'Wonderful . . . and again? Up . . . and down . . .'

A swift cut to Blondie's face reveals her in a state of gasping ecstasy. She looks down. We take her eyeline, revealing the almost touching proximity of her cherry-orchard with Jacques's mouth as her legs drop . . . oh, God, those lips . . . that flicking tongue . . . if only . . . if only . . .

Back to Jacques's eyeline. 'Wonderful . . . you may come down now. I . . . think . . . a little vibro massage would help. Have you ever used one of these machines before?'

'No – never.'

'You will enjoy it, . . . it is so relaxing.'

He leads her to the machine. She stands on the platform and he fixes the wide canvas belt around her waist.

He smiles. 'Are you ready?'

'Ready.'

He switches on.

She loves it . . . adores it! She laughs . . . throws wide her arms . . . shakes out her hair . . . turns this way and that, revelling in its titillating, tickling tingle.

'Good?' enquires Jacques.

'Fan*tas*tic!'

'Try it a little lower, my dear.'

Hooking two fingers into the belt, he draws it down to her buttocks. At once the fleshy vibration sends her into pleats of delight.

'Now . . . turn slowly round,' he commands.

She does so.

Immediately the smile slips from her face, her eyes close, her mouth drops limply open. 'Ohh . . .'

'It is good?' enquires Jacques, knowing exactly what it's doing to her.

'Oh, . . . it's . . . incredible.'

'Perhaps . . . just a *fraction* lower?' he suggests, reaching for the belt, this time gripping the lower edge, his fingers sliding under and up.

Her eyes fly wide. 'What . . . what are you doing?'

'Relax . . .' he smiles. 'I am merely holding down the belt.'

A close-up, however, reveals precisely what our hero is doing – or at least what his huge, probing middle-finger is doing. Vibrating at nineteen thousand twitches to the minute, it is having her away before she can say zip . . . and before she *can* say it, she *is* away.

'OHHHHHHHH! . . . AAAHHHHHH! . . . EEEEEE-HHHHH! . . . OOOOOOHHHHH!'

And then she's all over him, hugging him, kissing him, sticking her tongue in his mouth, in his eye, in his ear . . . 'Oh, Jacques . . . Jacques . . . I want you . . . *want* you!'

Can a business man refuse a customer?

Jacques's brutal hands fly to the neck of her flimsy leotard and with one mighty wrench . . . rips it asunder! Bingo! Out pop two unbelievable suet puddings . . .

Rip . . . rip . . . our heroine stands naked.

Jacques's hands now fly to his own belt. Flick! Down shoot his trousers and out flies an enormous throbbing tool, twitching with impatience to be at it. Away goes his vest . . . leaving only his socks, but who cares about them?

'Beloved!' she cries, hurling herself into his brawny arms and wincing a bit as he drives his jack-hammer between her legs.

'Where . . . where?'

'Right here,' grins Jacques, eyes a-glint. 'Turn round, baby, you're about to be reborn!'

Mystified, she obeys – about-turns and drapes herself across the machine. Quick as a flash, Jacques grabs up the vibro belt, slings it round his athletic buttocks, takes a sighter on Blondie and plunges to the root.

'Banzai!' he cries . . . and flicks on the machine.

BBBBBRRRRRRRRRRRRRRRRRRRRRRRR!!

Big close-ups now of our hero's juddering buttocks . . . following through in a slight pan to the effect it is having on his fo'c'sle nine-inch gun which is vibrating in and out of Blondie at a firing rate of twelve million rounds a minute.

Close-up of Blondie's face . . . her eyes great staring pools of disbelief, her mouth a cavern of incredulity. She's in outer space . . . gone . . . blitzed . . . shocked . . . stunned . . . wild-eyed with delight. She claws the machine, thumps it, her face now contorted with the anguish of a great, galloping orgasm.

'YAAAAAAAAAAAAA!' she yells, rattling the windows, now bashing the machine with a fervour bordering on mania. 'OHHHHH . . .! OHHHHH! . . . OHHHHHH!'

But does our hero stop?

Does he heck. The boy keeps right on, bringing her up again, driving her right over the hill with another beaut . . . and now she's beginning to *like* it!

Suddenly she disengages herself, turns to him and feeds him in the front entrance, and away she goes again . . . clinging to him like a limpet, crashing kisses into his mouth, biting his ear, nose, neck . . . disengaging her mouth only to cry out as another climax bursts over her, through her, her head thrown back in a snarl of savage animal ecstasy.

And now to Jacques! Things are quickly coming to the boil for the lad himself. His great chest begins to heave chaotically . . . his eyes stare wildly . . . 'I'm coming . . . I'm coming . . .!'

'Bravo!' cheers Blondie . . . but this she's got to see!

As the first triumphant cry roars from his strained and pulsing throat, she leaps away, agog at the miracle exploding before her very eyes, his beloved essence too dear, too precious to waste . . . and with a yearning cry she drops to her knees, opens her mouth and . . .

'Another drink?'

I turned, stunned, and came face-to-face with Angel Eyes. 'Hm . . . ?' I let out my pent-up breath in a gasp. 'Er . . .'

She smiled nicely. 'Are you enjoying the film?'

'Er . . . *yes*, lovely . . .' I glanced at the screen. 'Oh, it's over . . .'

'There will be more. Would you care for another drink?'

I gulped. 'I'd love one. Are you . . . still on duty?'

'For a little while longer. I will come shortly.'

Much more of this, I thought, and so will I!

She disappeared with a little wave and a lot of promise.

Oh, boy.

I looked round the place, trying to find Buzz, but he was safely tucked away somewhere in the shadows. In the other direction the people were laughing and chattering, commenting on the film, some of the fellas who had previously been alone now sitting with girls, the realization doing nothing for my own composure.

Come on, Angel Eyes, get sat down. I've always hated going to the flicks by myself. Well, that's my story . . .

Again the shaft of light lit the screen. What this time, I wondered . . . The Burglar? The Driving Instructor? Raped by the Plumber? I hoped not – I'd seen all those.

No – something far more topical this time – and in living colour. The title: 'Le Naufragé' – The Castaway.

The setting: A South Seas Island – where else?

The opening shot is a wide expanse of sunlit turquoise sea, much like Papeete Lagoon, though without the island of Moorea.

The camera now closes on floating wreckage – bits of shattered wood, boxes, furniture and, finally, the inevitable life-belt bearing the doomed ship's name: SS *Wanderlust*.

Now the camera pans up, re-establishing the awesome extent of the sea, then moves in, on a long, slow zoom, to pinpoint a tiny wooden life-raft on which is sprawled, in an attitude of total exhaustion, a belting piece of blonde crumpet in a sexily tattered dress, legs akimbo, garment rent from neck to navel to expose a pair of top-weight melons.

She stirs, sits up, brushes her tangled blonde tresses from a lovely face and peers around her, hand shading her eyes from the blinding sun.

She gives a start! A smile of joyous relief! The camera whip-pans to her viewpoint and we see . . . an island! A South Seas tropical paradise, surprise, surprise . . . golden sands, waving palms and . . . safety!

Revitalized, she grabs her paddle and starts churning up the water like a rescue launch, her burgeoning boobs threatening to burst from her ragged dress with every stroke.

Fade to: the beach and in she comes, staggering through the shallows and up the sand to fall exhausted but overjoyed on to her back, face-up to the sun for a bit of heavy breathing which puts further strain on the remnants of her dress.

Smiling with relief and gratitude for her safe deliverance, she closes her eyes and relaxes, deciding to build up a little suntan before starting for home.

Ahh . . . the peace of it all . . . but not for long!

Suddenly the sun goes in. She opens her eyes with a start, wondering where that big black cloud came from. She looks up, her eyes becoming saucers of horror, mouth opening in a silent scream.

From her viewpoint we see – yes, a towering, terrifying savage, an ebony mastodon, hideously war-painted, grass-shirted and plumed, the epitome of animalistic evil.

Lasciviously his gleaming, animal eyes rake her lush body . . . her ballooning boobs and strong, tanned, widely parted legs – and decides this is just what the witch doctor ordered.

His cruel lips part in a sickly grin and in his own words (a series of pig-like grunts) tells her 'Baby, have *you* come to the right place'.

And what of our heroine? Does she scramble to her feet and get the hell out of there . . . make a run for the raft – a dash for the deep? No, of course she doesn't. She does what every red-blooded, lush-bodied, helpless blonde castaway does in these circumstances . . . she faints.

Lovely swoon, . . . all soft and limp and inviting.

Cut to Polynesian Pete, grinning like an idiot. He's having a ball. Hasn't had so much fun since he shrunk his mother-in-law's head.

Cut to: the village square and all hell breaking loose.

It's not every day a tasty blonde tit-bit like Castaway Clara gets washed up on the shore and the event has inspired something of an occasion. You can see their point – you can get fed up with nothing but dark meat all the time. It's nice to have a slice of white chicken breast for a change.

Poor old Clara is really in hot water – or nearly. At the moment she's tied to a post in the middle of the compound, struggling valiantly but fruitlessly against the bonds that bind her while staring bug-eyed at the huge iron pot warming up nicely over a roaring fire. And as if that wasn't enough torment, the entire tribe is dancing round her, hurling insults and abuse and making it perfectly plain that they love her not for her mind alone but also for her delectable body.

Poor kid, she's really in a stew.

But what's this . . . !

Enter, now the Chief, a chap of such majestic proportions he makes Polynesian Pete look emaciated. 'What's going on here?' he demands (or grunts to that effect), then suddenly espies the lush Clara pinned to the post like a Catherine Wheel. 'By gum, lads, and what have we got *here*?'

'Found it on the beach,' answers Pete, waving his spear in that direction. 'Honestly, the pollution down there is getting *awful*, Chief.'

The Chief advances on Clara, chortling at his good fortune, disgusting thoughts permeating an otherwise fine mind. Tee hee, he chuckles, pinching her arm, her thigh and finally her left boob, finds he likes that, so has a go at her right one.

'OK,' he says to Pete. 'What's the plan, lads?'

'Thought we'd have her boiled with a few dumplings, Chief. Five minutes to the pound and ten for luck.'

'What! Over my dead body!' thunders the Chief. 'How long is it since we had an orgy?'

Pete thinks. 'Three months this Saturday . . . no, I tell a lie – it was Sunday. I remember now, because I'd been to choir practice . . .'

'Right!' roars the Chief. 'Then tonight we'll do it up brown . . .'

'Cheeky,' grins Pete.

'These other old bags need a bit of a knees-up, anyway,' he says, pointing to their own women. 'So, we'll have a good old general rape and the highlight of the evening will be a spear-throwing contest for who gets the white bird – OK?'

A roar of approval from the lads.

Fade to: Same scene – night time.

Poor old Clara, still trussed up like a loin of pork, gapes horror-stricken at the spectacle of drunken debauchery around her.

The tribe has been on the wine gums for several hours and things are hotting up nicely – particularly the pot of water which is hardly helping Clara to relax. She knows she's on a hiding to nothing – a fate worse than being boiled alive to start with and then that! Poor cow.

The camera now commences a leisurely track around and through the tribal carryings-on, pausing here and there to capture a particularly choice titbit of sexual abandonment.

Here a warrior pours a pint of tiger juice over his bird's boobs and sucks it off without losing a drop . . . here a brown-skinned lovely suggestively peels a huge banana while languishing in her boyfriend's lap, prepares to take a bite, then hurls the banana away and dives in for the real thing . . . over here another muscular buck decides he's finishing stuffing himself with food and reckons it time to stuff his bird. Over she goes, dutifully compliant, and in he plunges, setting off a chain reaction around the group.

Now they're all at it . . . all shapes and sizes, positions and techniques, one great heaving mass of rising, falling, grunting, groaning humanity . . . a right old knees-up.

I felt a presence at my side . . . a chuckle . . . and turned, heart pounding. It was Angel Eyes, her face bright with laughter at the action on the screen. She settled gently on the couch, drawing her legs beneath her, glanced at me once and then returned her chuckling attention to the screen.

She settled close to me but not touching, as though just barely complying with my request to sit with me but making it plain there was to be no hanky-panky. For a moment I studied her, stirred by her young, fresh beauty, her skin and the perfection of her profile, the aquiline profile of an adorable kitten.

My eyes travelled over her, drinking in the shining softness of her raven hair, the slender smoothness of her naked shoulder and the sweep of her covered breast. And now her perfume hit me – the perfume of the scarlet hibiscus in her hair, perhaps no more than that, but it was enough to rouse a shivery tingle through my scalp.

Concentrating on the screen, she laughed again – the delightful chuckle of a happy child, and I turned to see what had caused it.

It was apparently the Chief, a preposterous figure in a knee-length grass skirt and a battered crown on his head, four sizes to small.

Angel Eyes flashed me a grin. 'He is funny – no?'

'I think he's hilarious.'

'You think the film is funny?'

I laughed. 'It's a riot.'

She turned again to the screen. 'Oh, look! They are going to throw the spears!'

'Ten to one the Chief wins.'

'Oh . . . you have seen the film before?'

'No – but the Chief always wins. Besides – he's the biggest bloke there . . . makes it more horrifying for the girl and more exciting for the audience.'

'Oh . . .' she said, as if the thought hadn't occurred to her.

We returned to the action.

A target had been set up on the far side of the compound – a white bullseye painted on a palm tree – and the males of the tribe were now lined up with spears, fifty yards from it.

Close-up on Clara, looking horror-stricken (her only expression throughout the entire film) at the preparations.

Close-up of the Chief looking lip-licking lascivious (*his* only expression throughout the entire film) at the prospect of possessing her body.

Close-up of Pete, determined he shall win Clara for himself.

Close-up of ten other blokes all thinking the same.

Back to the Chief . . . he raises his knobkerrie . . . then drops it for the off. 'GO!'

The first guy in the line hauls back his arm and lets fly. Lovely panning shot as the camera follows the spear through the air and . . . twang! It strikes home – two feet above the bullseye.

A chorus of boos greet the effort.

The Chief smirks.

Pete smirks.

Clara collapses against her bonds, though with relief or disappointment I wouldn't know.

Next bloke up ... swish! He misses the bleeding tree altogether. Hoots of derision.

Third bloke ... swish! He brings down a coconut, which convulses Angel Eyes so much I think she's going to fall off the couch.

Fourth bloke ... pow! He sticks his in another tree, three feet to the right. Angel Eyes explodes with laughter.

Fifth bloke ... zonk! His spear hits a rock and shatters in fourteen pieces. Angel Eyes is in desperate danger of splitting her pareu.

Sixth bloke ... zoing! Ooh, *very* close – no more than three inches away.

Seventh ... eighth ... ninth ... hopeless. I reckon they're all pissed.

And now the tenth fella ... left arm, good clean action. Dooiing! By gum, he's clipped the edge of the bull!

The Chief sneers.

Pete scowls.

Now it's Pete's turn.

A last lecherous leer at the doomed Clara and he's into it – and praying he soon will be! He draws back ... steadies his aim ... and let's fly. Whhiisshh! Booiing! Eureeka! Straight in the bull though an inch off dead centre.

Pete jumps up and down for joy – or, rather, for Clara. She's as good as his! The Chief, silly old fool, will never get in between those two spears and into the centre.

That's what you think, thinks Chiefie, hefting his spear. Take ... *that*!

Wwhhheeeeee ... clunk!

Has he done it?

Of course he has. Right on the nose – smack dead centre, to the nearest wormhole.

Ha ha, me beauty! he roars.

Close-up on Clara ... horror-stricken.

The Chief strides over to her, whips a cruel-looking knife from his belt and with one mighty swipe severs her bonds. She falls ... he catches her ... sweeps her up in his brawny arms and marches triumphantly through the cheering crowd to his hut.

I glanced at Angel Eyes, finding her agog, enjoying every frame.

Fade to: Inside of Chief's hut.

He enters, bearing Clara. He sets her on her feet, gloats down at her for a long, lascivious moment, then reaches out and rips her tattered rags asunder.

How she managed to lose her knickers on the raft has not been revealed, but lose them she did, for now she stands noddy-naked.

Meanwhile, a curious transformation is overtaking the Chief – or rather his grass skirt, for it is now rising in front like an inflated balloon.

Clara sees it and gasps – horror-stricken, of course.

The Chief looks down at himself and roars with laughter, reaches for the fastening at his waist, then ... *flings* the skirt wide open and drops it behind him, revealing the biggest hampton it has ever been Clara's (or anyone else's, for that matter) horror-stricken privilege to behold.

It is ee ... *normous*!

A gasp on my right brought my head smartly round. Angel Eyes had her hands to her mouth, her eyes protruding like gob-stoppers. 'Ohhh ...!'

My laugh snapped her attention from the screen. 'Is it ... real?' she gasped.

I shrugged. 'Why not – it's only average.'

Her eyes opened even wider. 'You mean ... you ...?

If I'd kept up the tease I'm sure she'd have leapt off the couch and run for her life. I laughed and shook my head and with obvious relief she returned to the screen, wide-eyed with wonderment, though not so wide-eyed as poor old Clara who looks positively horror-stricken.

'My God, no ... not *that*!' she wails.

'This!' insists Chiefie, grasping it with two hands but still leaving room for two more. 'Lie down on that mat!'

'No ... never!'

'How about kneeling up, then?'

'You *must* be joking!'

He advances upon her voraciously.

She retreats, horror-st . . . well, you know, reaches the mat and . . . trips! Down she goes . . . and down old Chiefie goes – straight in, no trouble at all, which leaves a sneaking suspicion that Clara has not been quite so horror-stricken as she's been making out.

There followed eight or ten quick shots of the most intimate nature, the wonder of them being not so much their artistic composition, the clarity of focus and steadiness of hand as how the hell the cameraman got in their at all!

The performance continued interminably, cheered to the echo by the audience, everyone hooting and jeering and whistling and stomping as Chiefie continued to drive and thrust and pummel and bellow. And then . . .

'You wish to see more?' she asked quietly.

I turned to her, wondering what lay behind the question. 'No.'

Her eyes went across the room to the door. 'You would like to walk outside?'

'Yes, I would.'

'Come,' she smiled, reaching for my hand.

Her touch was magical, exciting. Quickly we reached the door and went through into the corridor, ran down this and burst through the outer door into the fresh night air, laughing and deeply breathing as though we'd narrowly escaped from some kind of threat.

'Oh, that's better,' I panted, very aware that she was still holding my hand.

'Much better.'

We became still, collecting our thoughts, each adjusting to being suddenly alone with a stranger in a situation where it suddenly mattered.

'Hello,' I smiled, starting right from the beginning.

'Hello, you, too.'

'What's your name?'

'Leoni.'

'That's beautiful. Mine's Russ.'

'Russ,' she repeated. 'You are very nice.'

I chuckled at her forthrightness. 'And you are very beautiful. You're what we call in England "a sight for sore eyes".'

She laughed delightedly. ' "A sight for sore eyes." I would

make sore eyes better?'

'You'd do wonders for any complaint.' I looked around, then back to her. 'Well, now, what would you like to do?'

She thought about it, then shrugged. 'I would just like to walk . . . and talk with you.'

I nodded. 'Perfect . . let us walk and talk, I couldn't think of anything nicer. And in which direction shall we walk?'

She pointed. 'That way – to the beach. I would like to see the lagoon under the moon.'

'Perfect again.'

We started off, holding hands, in a slow stroll, getting used to each other and the feel of each other's flesh.

'And in which direction shall we *talk*?' I asked her.

'In all directions,' she smiled, covering the world with a wave of her hand. 'I *like* talking.'

'So do I. But tell me . . . how much time do we have to talk together? Do you have to return to that room?'

She shook her head. 'Oh, no. I do not work there. I please myself what I do. If I want to, I can talk to you all night until dawn and then all day tomorrow.'

I laughed. 'You'd be pretty hoarse, I'm afraid, but it's nice to know.'

'What is nice to know – that I do not work here or that I can talk to you as much as I please?'

'Both. I'm glad you don't work here.'

'Oh? Why?'

I shrugged. 'Didn't seem the place for you – that room.'

'You didn't like those films?'

'Oh, they're all right for a bit of a laugh, but . . .'

'You have seen many of them?'

'A few, not many. They're pretty much all the same – only the settings differ.' I grinned at her. 'The end result is *always* the same.'

'You do not like to see other people making love?'

I shrugged. 'Not particularly. Human beings are hardly at their most attractive when viewed from those angles – and at such close range. Especially members of my own sex!'

'Yes, I agree . . . but they make me laugh.'

'Oh, they're a hoot. The acting is terrible.'

We passed out of the shadows of the house and entered the

park-garden, some distance from the dance-floor and the bars.

'Would you like a drink?' I asked her, indicating the bars.

Her eyes went to the bottle under my arm. 'What is that?'

'This?' I grinned. 'This is not for lovely young ladies. It's for . . . well, for men.'

'Is it whisky? I have drunk whisky.'

'No, it's not whisky. It's . . . well, I don't really know what it is – I only know what it *does*. It was given to me tonight by a la . . . by a certain person – as an experiment, I guess. It's a local drink . . . made from the leaves of a certain bush, she sa . . . this person said.'

Her eyes twinkled. 'You said "she". A girl gave it to you?'

'She'd love you for that. Yes, a lady.'

'May I taste it?'

'No.'

She pouted. 'Why not?'

'Because . . .' I sighed, 'because it has a certain effect that . . . well, it wouldn't be fair to give it to you.'

'Fair? Why not fair?'

'Because . . . well, it's a sort of drug . . . makes you feel . . .'

She grinned wickedly. 'Sexy?'

I laughed. 'A whole lot more than just sexy, but that's the general idea.'

'And . . . you wouldn't like me to feel sexy?'

My heart took that trip again – straight up into my throat. 'Not . . . *unduly*, Leoni. I mean, I wouldn't want to be accused of . . .'

'But I *do* feel sexy,' she insisted, disarmingly casual, matter-of-fact. 'I am always feeling sexy – it is natural. Don't you always feel sexy?'

I coughed.

'Well, don't you?' she pursued, ready to be dismayed if I answered negatively.

'Yes,' I grinned.

'Ah.' She sounded relieved.

As we strolled across the park, she disengaged her hand and instead, looped her arm through mine, drawing us closer together, as though settling in to get to grips with the subject.

'It is nice to feel sexy – no?'

'It's lovely,' I agreed, amused yet excited by her frankness, her total lack of self-consciousness. 'With the right person,' I added, 'it's always lovely.'

'Ah, yes, with the right person.' She looked at me, her eyes soft and amused, enjoying the same bubbling feeling I was experiencing. 'There should be as much pleasure *after* making love as during it, don't you agree?'

'I agree entirely – otherwise the word love doesn't come into it. Then it's purely physical release.'

'Yes. But . . . are there not times when that is all that is required?'

'Oh, sure – that's why prostitutes do such a roaring trade. That's thinking from the male point of view, of course. But it also applies to women.' I grinned at her. 'Is there a woman who hasn't at some time or other "fancied a bit of rough", as they say? – who hasn't at least once in her life lost herself in fantasy about the big, good-looking milkman or – as you saw in the first film – a brawny physical instructor? There's no denying the need – or the benefit – of a bit of rough. Clears out the system a treat.'

She giggled at the phraseology. 'A "bit of rough" . . . . I will remember that, it describes it beautifully.'

Now we entered the fringe of denser vegetation bordering the shore, found a narrow path and disengaged each other, Leoni taking the lead, leaving me the pleasure of her gracefully undulating chassis as she padded cat-like along the beaten earth.

Emerging on to the sand, she once more turned and caught my arm, hugging it affectionately and indicating with a little laugh how much she was enjoying herself.

'Would you like to walk in the shallows of the water?' she asked.

'Paddle? Sure . . .'

I kicked off my beach shoes and removed my socks, Leoni merely having to step out of her thonged sandals.

'To paddle . . . that is what you call it? I thought that was to move a boat.'

'Both. Paddling is a great British tradition. In summertime our beaches are lined to capacity with elderly people standing ankle-deep in the sea, dresses hoisted and trousers rolled to the knee, handkerchiefs on their heads to protect them from the cruel English sun, and licking a sixpenny icecream cornet as they reflect on the wonders of the deep.'

She laughed gaily. 'They sound so funny . . . show me how they do it.'

'Well . . .' I bent down and rolled up my trousers, took out my handkerchief, knotted it at four corners and placed it on my head, waded into the shallows, stuck out my stomach to resemble a paunch, and used my thumb as an icecream.

She was in pleats. 'And that is all they do? They don't swim?'

'Good heavens, no, that's not the done thing. Besides, the water's so cold they'd drop like flies with heart attacks. No, but they do "stroll" . . . like this.' Stomach out, chin in, shoulders drooped, I turned and sauntered slowly along the water's edge, licking my imaginary icecream and inhaling deeply of the Blackpool ozone . . . then I turned and strolled back. 'There.'

'Is that all?'

'In British water, that's plenty, believe me. Even now their feet would be so blue you'd think they'd been painted.'

She joined me, laughing, this time throwing an arm around my waist and nestling against me, the pliant warmth of her body deliciously stirring. I slipped my arm around her and hugged her close, holding her at last.

For a moment we stood and gazed out over the lagoon, lit like day by the blazing moon, the island of Moorea plainly visible as a jagged, mystical silhouette against the star-riven sky.

'Leoni . . .' I sighed, 'I'm going to miss all this tomorrow.'

She gave a start. 'You are leaving Tahiti?'

'Yes, tomorrow afternoon. I'm flying on to Australia . . . to Sydney.'

'Oh . . . I am sorry. Have you been here long?'

'No, only a few days. It wasn't a holiday – just a stop-over on our way from America to Sydney. You remember the man who came into the film room with me . . . ?'

'Yes – the handsome, blond one.'

'That's him,' I laughed. 'I'll tell him you said so. Well, he's an Australian tennis player and he must get back for a tournament. I'm travelling with him.'

'Oh, you play tennis, too?'

'No, I'm going to work there for a while at something else.'

'At what?'

I shrugged. 'I don't know. He's going to find me a job. Would you like to "stroll"?'

'Like an English lady?' she laughed, trying hopelessly to push out the tiny, natural mound of her stomach into a paunch. 'How is that?'

'Somehow you're not quite making it, honey . . . I don't know, there's just something wrong somewhere. Ah, I know what it is . . . you're not wearing your hanky!'

I took the knotted handkerchief from my pocket and placed it on her head. 'There . . .! That's much better. Now you're the perfect English seaside lady paddler . . . well, almost. What you've got to do now to complete the picture is shout at your children, ten yards out in the sea, in a raucous Lancashire accent.'

'Show me how . . . show me how!' she giggled, enjoying the game.

I cupped my hands to my mouth. 'Persephon . . . eee! Stop chuckin' sand in ya brother's face! Peregrin . . . give yer sister back 'er rubber duck or I'll cum out there an' belt yer one!'

Leoni roared with laughter. 'Is that how they speak in England?'

'Some of them. We have a lot of different dialects in the British Isles – some even *I* don't understand.'

'Where were you born . . . Russ?'

It was the first time she'd tried my name.

'Near a big city called Liverpool. It's a big port . . . lots of docks and big ships.'

'Like Papeete?'

I grinned. 'Just a *little* bigger.'

'And how do they speak in Liverpool?'

'In all sorts of ways . . . some with a very pronounced accent, others with very little. The ones who speak with a broad Liverpudlian accent sound as if they've got acute adenoid trouble . . . and they say things like, "Eh, da, our kid's just 'ad a scuffle up a jigger wid a rozzer." '

Both the gutteral pronunciation and the meaningless sentence sent her into pleats of laughter. *'What . . .?'*

'I said – eh, da, our kid's just 'ad a scuffle up a jigger wid a rozzer! Can't yus understand a fella wen 'e speaks de Queen's Inglish, gerl?'

She was in danger of falling to her knees in the shallows. 'It sounds so *funny*! What does it mean?'

'Well, "our kid" means my brother or sister, and "a scuffle up a jigger with a rozzer" means he's had a bit of a fight in an alleyway with a policeman. A "jigger" is a sort of cobbled lane that separates the backs of two rows of houses. They call them "back entries", too.'

'Oh,' she said, probably not understanding at all, but letting it pass.

'So there you are,' I said, 'tonight you've learned a foreign language. When you get back home, burst through the door breathlessly and announce to your father, "Eh, da, our kid's just 'ad a scuffle up a jigger wid a rozzer!" And I'll bet you anything you like he'll answer, "Lissen 'ere, our Leoni – don' chew cum runnin' in 'ere clat-tail-tittin' on our Ronnie – gerrin the back kitchen an' 'elp yer muther wid de scouse!" '

Her laughter tinkled across the lagoon and in an attitude of helplessness she fell heavily against me, her face buried in my shoulder, shaking. 'You are so funny.'

'Well, you'll see.'

She raised her face, her tears of laughter catching the moonlight, such a perfectly beautiful face.

I took it in my hands and kissed her, stopping her laughter.

'Sweet bird,' I whispered.

'You see me as a bird?' she asked, very quietly.

'A bird of paradise . . . fragile and exquisite.'

'I like you very much, man from Liverpool.'

'And I like you, little pigeon.'

'Would you . . . come with me? I know a place where we can be all alone. We could swim . . . and I have food.'

The word food triggered off a sudden realization that I hadn't eaten for what seemed like days.

'You are hungry?' she asked eagerly, sensing my reaction.

'Leoni, I am starved!'

'Good! Come – I will take you.'

Like a couple of kids we raced hand in hand back to our belongings, quickly slipped on our shoes, then took off along the beach towards the wharf. Here she turned inland, taking a path that followed the bank of the inlet, walking beside me when the path allowed then taking the lead when it became too narrow.

Gradually the bushy vegetation became more dense, often, now, obscuring the narrowing inlet on our right and often joining with the tall bushes on our left to form a leafy arch high above our heads.

A few minutes more and a splash of tumbling water came to me distinctly, and I guessed we'd left the house and formal gardens far behind and were quite deep in uncultivated bushland.

'No tigers around here, are there?' I called to her, peering into the dark undergrowth.

She turned and grinned. 'No tigers.'

'Good.'

'Lions . . . leopards . . . and poisonous snakes – yes! But no tigers.'

'Eh?'

'Ha!' she laughed. 'You should see your face!'

As she turned away from me, I slipped up behind her and let out a fierce growl. 'WwmmmmAAAHHHHHH!'

She leapt a foot in the air and let go a shriek that echoed through the bush. 'You . . .!'

'Now you should see *your* face!'

I tucked her under my arm and marched with her, step for step.

'Where are you taking me?'

'To drown you in the waterfall for frightening me.'

'And I deserve it. How come you know your way around here so well?'

'Because I live near here – in a village not far away. As a child I used to come and play at the waterfall . . . before Monsieur D'Urville bought the land.'

'I see. And now the children aren't allowed to play here?'

'Oh, yes, they can come, Monsieur D'Urville is very kind. But now the children prefer to play at another waterfall on the other side of the village.'

'I see.'

With every passing moment the water noise grew louder, then suddenly we broke from the tunnel of tropical growth and emerged into the moonlight, into a setting so exquisitely beautiful it caught my breath and brought me to a halt.

No Hollywood art director could have designed a set more perfectly representative of Polynesian paradise than this nature-sculpted miracle. It had everything . . . a gently plummeting fall of sparkling water, a catchment lagoon reflecting the softly rippling moon and, on its far side, a quaint, thatched native summerhouse set in a little garden of cultivated flowers and an apron of close-cropped lawn.

It was the perfect summer-day retreat, cooled by the sight and sound of the waterfall, quiet, beautiful, serene.

'You like it?' Leoni asked brightly, pleased by my reaction.

'It's perfect. But . . . doesn't anybody come here?'

She shrugged. 'Sometimes . . . not often. But I do. It's my favourite place of all. Come – I will show you the house.'

'Who built it?' I asked, as we walked towards it.

'Monsieur D'Urville. He made the lawn and planted the flowers, but that is all. The rest has always been here.'

'How deep is the lagoon? Deep enough to swim?'

'Oh, yes . . . there, you see that flat rock at the side. You can dive from there. The water is more than three metres deep.'

'Any rocks under the water?'

She shook her head. 'Nothing. Monsieur D'Urville took them all out. It is beautifully clear. That is why you can swim and dive at night.'

'Wonderful.'

As we crossed the lawn, Leoni kicked off her sandals, luxuriating in the feel of the cool grass under her feet.

'Try it,' she grinned. 'It is very sexy.'

I shed my shoes and socks, agreeing with her.

'Come . . . see the house.'

'It's not locked?'

She looked at me as though I was mad. 'Of course not . . . no one here would steal anything.'

'Sorry, I keep forgetting where I am.'

She unlatched the door and entered, turned to her right and found matches on a wall shelf, struck one and lit a wall-mounted oil-lamp.

As the flame grew and my eyes adjusted, a room of comfortable rustic simplicity appeared . . . a stone fireplace, a settee, two armchairs, a small dining table and four chairs, a sideboard . . . all the basic requirements for a summer home.

'There is a kitchen through there . . .' she pointed. 'And through there is the bathroom.'

I nodded. 'What else could one possibly wish for?'

She cocked a cute brow. 'For . . . food, maybe?'

She did not mean food.

'For . . . food, definitely. What have we got in the larder?'

'Let's go and see.'

The kitchen, designed in rustic keeping with the rest of the little house, held few surprises and few luxuries – a modest bottle-gas, three-ring cooker constituting the only real concession to luxury living – discounting, of course, the tinned food.

'You like soup?' asked Leoni, crouched at a cupboard.

'Love it.'

'Turtle . . . asparagus . . . onion . . . tomato?'

'Asparagus – if you like it.'

'I like it. And do you like ravioli?'

'*Adore* ravioli.'

'I'm glad – there is nothing else.'

She picked out the tins and came to her feet, smiling at me apologetically. 'It's not very much, I'm afraid.'

'Leoni, it's a banquet. Who cares what we eat as long as you're here? I shall be so busy looking at you, I won't know what I'm eating.'

Her dark eyes twinkled. 'You say such pretty things.'

'You inspire them. Well, we're going to need a couple of pans, hm?'

'In that cupboard – there.'

I got out a couple and put them on the stove.

'Can opener?'

She was already doing it.

I went behind her and wrapped my arms around her, stopping her. 'Leoni . . .'

'Yes . . . Russ?'

'Before we eat, would you like a swim?'

'Would you?'

'I'd love one. I'd never forgive myself if I left here without a swim in that lagoon in that moonlight.'

She turned into me, eyes dancing. 'All right.'

'But if we're going to swim, shouldn't we make a fire first? Is it possible?'

'Oh, yes . . . there is wood in a box by the fireplace.'
'Then shall we?'
'Of course! It will be lovely. Then we can eat by the fire.'
I winked at her. 'You're on.' And then I kissed her.
Passion erupted within her, rose swiftly and fiercely, bringing her arms around my neck and her mouth hard against mine.
For many heated seconds we let it ride, then slowly broke away, staring at each other in breathless amazement.
'Wow . . .' I gasped. 'I . . . think I'd better go stoke that *other* fire.'
'Yes,' she laughed, 'perhaps you had better.'
Trembling from the encounter, I went into the other room, found wood and paper and got a blaze going, thinking all the time that I'd never enjoyed playing 'house' so much in my life. She was wonderful . . . enchanting . . . a delight to the eye, ear, heart, mind and body.
'Leoni . . .' I called, suddenly missing the sight of her.
She appeared in the doorway, her expression comically querying. 'Yes?'
'What are you doing in there?'
'Thinking about you.'
I laughed. 'Well . . . come in here and do it.'
She came, knelt at my side. 'Why?'
'Because I was missing you. You have no right to be out of my sight.'
In response she moved quickly and pecked me on the cheek. 'Then I will not be . . . not until you leave Tahiti . . .' then she added, uncertainly, 'If that is what you wish.'
I looked at her, the gentleness of her eyes, her expression, squeezing my heart. 'Hey . . .'
'What is the matter?'
'I . . .' I touched her cheek, stirred by its velvet softness.
A frown furrowed her brow. 'You do not wish that? You already have a girl?'
I smiled and shook my head. 'No, love, I haven't got another girl . . . and I certainly do wish it. It's just you . . . and the way you said what you just said. It was . . . very beautiful.'
'Oh, then I *may* stay with you until you leave?'
'Leoni, *I* should be asking *you*.'
'But of course you may!' she said, surprised. 'I like you very

much – so you may stay with me as long as you wish . . .' My smile baffled her. 'What is wrong?'

I shook my head. 'Nothing at all. It's just that you make it sound so beautifully simple . . . so wonderously uncomplicated. At home it's rarely as uncomplicated as this.' I gave a contented sigh. 'However, the subject is too deep for discussion – and I doubt if you'd fully understand anyway. So, let's . . . just enjoy it, hm?'

'Of course.'

'There! How's that for a fire? I'll have you know that Tobin is one of the best fire starters going.'

'Tobin?' she frowned.

'Oh . . . that's me, too – as well as the "Russ" part. Russ Tobin is the whole thing.'

'Russ . . . Tobin,' she repeated. 'I shall remember all my life.'

'Leoni . . . you are a love. Come on, let's go for that swim.'

It was, believe it or not, not until we were crossing the lawn, under the full, flooding moon, that I realized I had no swim trunks.

'Oh . . .' I grunted, slowing to a halt.

'What's the matter?'

'Erm . . . just occurred to me, I, er, haven't anything to swim in.'

She hesitated, puzzled. 'But you have the lagoon!'

'No,' I laughed. 'I mean . . . you know, swim trunks . . . shorts.'

Her eyes crinkled mischievously. 'So? Swimming was invented before shorts.'

'You . . . haven't got a costume either?'

'Of course not! Come!'

She took my hand and raced me across the lawn, along a little path, down to the area of flat rocks surrounding the diving rock. Here she released me and went forward to the platform, stood for a moment in provocative pose, the moon her key-light, then her hands went to the securing fold of her flowered pareu.

My heart stood still.

'Voila!' she proclaimed, and with a defiant flourish, ripped the skirt wide and dropped it behind her. 'C'est moi, monsieur!' she declared triumphantly, offering me sight of her glorious body, then, with an impish laugh, arc-ed into the air and cleaved the water with scarcely a splash.

Trousers off, shirt off, shorts abandoned, I was on the rock before she could surface – or so I thought. But as I balanced for the dive she rose like a mermaid from the depths and yahoo-ed 'Bravo!', throwing my dive awry and producing a belly-flop that had her shrieking with laughter.

I rose, spluttering, to the surface, to find her on her back, kicking up a frothy wake, laughing like a loon. 'A *superb* dive, mon cher – you must teach me how to do it!'

'Very funny,' I grinned, palming a stream of water at her.

I swam to her, conscious as hell of her nakedness – of our nakedness. 'You looked very beautiful standing there in the moonlight, Leoni . . . a goddess in bronze.'

'You, too, Russ Tobin.'

'A godd*ess*?' I frowned.

Her laughter echoed around the rocks. 'One could not make *that* mistake – even in moonlight!' She swam to meet me, caught my shoulders and wound her legs around my thighs, kissed me extravagantly, then broke away and struck out across the lagoon. '*Nor* under water!'

I went after her. With a squeal she dived, disappeared . . . reappeared moments later many yards away, taunted me with a wave, and as I crashed after her, disappeared again. The game was afoot.

She swam like a seal, covering distances at unbelievable speed, out-pacing me with ease, allowing me only fleeting glimpses of her nakedness before twisting away and disappearing into the dim reaches of the moonlit water.

I tried subterfuge – attempted to guess her intended direction and cut her off, but she always fooled me, doubling back in her track or turning the opposite way, and at last I surfaced, conceding defeat.

It was then that she came up behind me, capturing me at the waist with her strong legs.

'Ah, at last you have caught me,' she chuckled, hugging me.

'You're no woman,' I gasped, 'you're a penguin!'

'*Un pingouin*,' she repeated, liking the idea. 'And you . . . you are a . . .' she deepened her voice, impersonating a gruff old man, 'you are a big *morse* with long tusks and a moustache.'

'A walrus – yeh, that's about the size of it. Leoni . . . come round the front where I can see you.'

'Just . . . see?' she teased, breaking away.

I turned to face her, her breasts plainly visible beneath the water and far too close for comfort.

'Isn't the water wonderful?' she remarked innocently.

'I . . . wasn't thinking about the water just then.'

'I know. Neither was I.'

'Oh? What were you thinking of, Leoni?'

She tipped her head, coquettishly. 'About . . . our lovely fire . . . and how nice it would be to sit before it and . . .'

I grinned. 'And?'

'And . . . eat our soup and ravioli.'

I laughed. 'You know, that's *exactly* what I was thinking of,' I lied. 'Come on, let's eat.'

She gestured towards our exit rock. 'Après vous, monsieur.'

'Oh, *no* – ladies first, mademoiselle!'

She shook her head. 'Not on Tahiti. Here the gentleman *always* goes first – to protect his lady.'

'From what?'

'From dangerous tigers.'

'You minx,' I laughed. 'All right . . . see if I care!'

I struck out for the rock, swimming as fast as I could, knowing I *had* to have a five-yard start on her, but as I hauled myself out and turned to see how she was progressing, stap me, she was right underneath me.

'Bravo!' she cheered again.

I gave up then, reached down for her hand and brought her out of the water to stand dripping in front of me. For a moment we stood motionless, smiling, searching each other's eyes, then in mutual need we fell into each other's arms and held on tightly.

Her body against mine sent shock-waves of excitement through me – together with wonderment (and gratitude) that nature had endowed me with an apparently limitless capacity to appreciate this miracle, no matter how often it occurred.

'What are you thinking about?' she murmured, sensing the thought.

'Of how wonderful you feel.'

'You like my body?'

'I adore your body.'

'You, too, are very good to hold.'

She eased away from me and looked down, a teasing smile breaking on her lips. 'I excite you, yes?'

I laughed, shakily. 'I'm sure you don't expect an answer.'

She released a playful chuckle. 'You are very much man . . .' then she touched me, very gently. 'Very *much* man.'

'Leoni . . . I think we'd better go in.'

'Oh, yes,' she answered lightly. 'We will go in. We will dry ourselves by the fire and I shall cook for you.'

She left me, gathered up our clothes, then returned, slipped her arm around my waist and we started for the house.

'I am very happy here with you,' she said, tilting her head to my shoulder. 'I am very glad you have no other girl tonight.'

'So am I. I'm very surprised you hadn't a boyfriend, though. I'd have thought you'd be inundated with them at the party.'

'They tried – but I didn't like them.'

'Oh, why was that?'

'Because their eyes saw only my body.'

I grinned at her. 'Well, I must confess mine kind of strayed in that direction once or twice, too.'

She shook her head. 'No . . . your eyes were not like theirs. I knew it would be nice like this with you.'

I kissed the top of her head. 'You're a doll, you know that? *Une belle poupée*. And instead of ravioli – I shall eat you.'

'I would be a little tough,' she laughed. 'Though perhaps not quite so hard as you!'

'That is naughty.'

'But then I have good strong teeth . . .' She gnashed them together and I winced.

'Leoni, please . . .'

'Nnnnyyyooowwww!' she growled, making a dive with a pretended bite.

'Commonly known as biting off my nose to spite your face,' I said.

'Yes,' she grinned. 'I would certainly be the loser.'

We entered the house, finding the fire blazing beautifully.

'I will get some towels,' she said, crossing the room to a wall cupboard.

I knelt by the fire, welcoming its warmth, and threw on more logs. Leoni came back to me, dropped a towel at my feet and held another out to me.

'You would like to dry me, monsieur?' she asked softly.

I looked up at her, a glistening, satin-skinned Aphrodite, slender and graceful, so breathtakingly naked, the large dark-brown nipples of her breasts standing high and hard like the twin peaks of her native island, Orohena and Aorai.

Wordlessly, I accepted the towel and came to my knees, my face close to her breasts, then wrapped my arms around her thighs and drew her to me, placing a kiss, a gentle, christening caress on each brown button, dubbing them in turn, 'Orohena . . . and Aorai.'

Her laughter rang out and she clasped my face to her belly. 'How lovely . . .'

I held her tightly, the perfume of her skin in my head and on my lips, relishing every morsel of her, then in a sudden fever of desire she was down beside me, now lying down, holding me as I was holding her and looking up at me with eyes of misty fire.

'Make love to me,' she whispered urgently. 'I desire to know you . . . *now*.'

And so I entered paradise . . . and when we finally returned to earth the fire was almost out.

CHAPTER EIGHT

'I AM curious,' she said, stirring the soup, 'as to what you have in that bottle.'

Girded to the waist, only, in our towels, we were of course in the kitchen, Leoni at the stove and I sitting at a little table, smoking a cigarette, watched her, delightedly, perform her culinary chores . . . well, heating up the soup and ravioli.

'Why?' I asked her, glancing at the bottle on the table.

'Because I am. I would like to know what it's made of.'

'I told you – the leaves from a certain bush.'

'But which bush?'

'I don't know.'

'Perhaps I could tell from the smell . . . or the taste.'

'Smell, you may – taste, you may not.'

'Why?'

'I've already told you – it's a drug.'

'Huh,' she shrugged. 'If you can drink it, why can't I?'

'Because . . . because tomorrow I'm leaving Tahiti and will never drink it again. You live here and you might get hooked on it.'

'Oh . . .' Her eyes lit up mischievously. 'It is so . . . delicious? . . . so exciting?'

'It's a devil. Sends you way out into space . . . your arms and legs seem fifty metres long . . ., then, when things come back to normal, it makes you *terribly* sexy.'

'So now I know,' she grinned. 'I think perhaps you drank three bottles before I met you.'

'Huh – and if I didn't know better, I'd say *you'd* drunk a caseful!'

She giggled and came to me, plonked a kiss on my mouth and simultaneously grabbed for the bottle.

'Hey . . .' I protested.

'I just want to smell it!'

'You don't, you're going to drink it.'

'Would I do that when you have forbidden it?'

'Yes.'

She lifted her chin, affronted. 'In Tahiti a woman does not disobey her man!'

'Oh . . .' I resumed my seat. 'I'm sorry, I didn't know. Well, go ahead, then – have a sniff.'

Aloofly, as though still hurt by my ignorance of their custom, she uncorked the bottle and held it to her nose, sniffed it, at first tentatively then more deeply, a glint of recognition lighting her eyes. 'Aha!' she said, turning away across the kitchen, as deep in thought.'

'You know what it is?'

'Hm, hm,' she nodded, then suddenly changed character, dropped her assumed pose of indignation and tipped the bottle to her mouth.

I was out of the chair like a shot. 'Stop that . . .!'

By the time I reached her she'd taken six or seven damn good gulps.

'Leoni, you're mad . . .! Give me that!'

Laughing uproariously, she surrendered the bottle, spilling the liquid down her chin.

'God, girl, you'll be . . . now that was downright sneaky! You said Tahitian women didn't disobey their men!'

'Nor do they . . . when it suits them,' she laughed.

'You devil . . .'

'Hey, that is good – let me have some more.'

'Over my dead body. I think I'd better pour the rest down the sink.'

Her eyes flew wide. 'Oh, no . . . aren't you going to have some?'

'I've had some. It's supposed to last for twenty-four hours.'

'Ha!' she scoffed.

'What d'you mean – ha! What do you know about it?'

She smiled, enigmatically. 'Everything.'

I glanced at the bottle. 'You know what it is?'

'Of course.'

'You've . . . had it before?'

She shrugged. 'Of course.'

'Well, I'll be . . . well, what is it?'

'I will tell you if you have another drink.'

'Now, Leoni, I've already had *two*. I'm flying to Sydney tomorrow and I'd prefer to do it in a Qantas jet – not under my own steam.'

She was shaking her head. 'It won't harm you – and it does not last for twenty-four hours.'

'It . . . doesn't?'

'No – your lady lied.'

I frowned. 'I wonder why?'

Her eyes took on that infuriating all-knowing female look. 'Perhaps . . .'

'Go on – perhaps what?'

'Perhaps . . . she thought you needed an extra big dose of . . . of . . .' she struggled for the word.

'Dutch courage?' I hated suggesting.

'Oui – what you said.'

I gasped. 'I did not! I . . . well, never mind. Anyway, what is this stuff? Is is a drug?'

She nodded. 'Yes. It is called *kava* and is made from the root of the pepper plant. But it is not strong . . . it only makes you feel nice and . . .' she gave a light-hearted twirl, arms outstretched, head on one side.

'I know exactly how it makes you feel, Leoni, I've had some.'

She stopped and stared at me. 'And you did not like the feeling?'

I grinned at her. 'I didn't say that.'

'So – you will have some more? Please – just a drop, so you can be . . .' she executed the twirl again, '. . . like me.'

'Yes, well, it's not the . . .' I did the twirl, '. . . part that worries me. It's the . . . other part.'

'Oh? Which part is that?'

'The . . . Leoni, this stuff is a roaring aphrodisiac! And the way we go at it even *without* the stuff, we'll probably kill each other before morning!'

'But what a beautiful way to die . . .' she laughed. 'Oops . . . the soup!'

She made a dive for the pan as it boiled over, then, her hand to her forehead, took a couple of faltering steps backwards. 'Wheeeeee . . . !'

She was away!

I caught her and she collapsed against me, laughing. 'Whee-eeee *heeeeee*!'

'See – I told you. You better lie down on the couch for a minute.'

I helped her through the door and laid her down, having to laugh at her antics and the faces she was pulling. 'You have grown so *tall* . . . ! You are a giant . . . ten metres high!'

'And you are magnificently cock-eyed.'

'Come,' she slapped the couch at her side, 'lie down with me and drink some . . . then, in a few moments, we will dine on ravioli up there among the stars.'

'If I take another slug of this, love, we'll eat nothing for a week!'

'So . . .' she giggled, 'who wants to eat when they can make love instead? Come . . . I insist.'

'You do?'

'When a girl wishes her man to lie down and drink *kava* with her, he must do it – under penalty of death. It is an old Tahitian custom.'

'You know, I've got the sneakiest feeling you make these customs up as you go along.'

'Never! This one is true. I can call the police and have you shot, here in this room, for not doing it.'

'Oh. Well, in that case . . .'

She wriggled over to make room for me and I lay down beside her. 'Are you absolutely sure this doesn't last for twenty-four hours? I wouldn't want to rape the first girl I set eyes on in Sydney.'

'Absolutely sure.'

'All right, then . . . well, here goes.' I tipped the bottle to my mouth, took three or four glugs and stopped. The bottle was empty. 'Hey, how much did you drink, for heaven's sake?'

She snuggled into me, pressing her naked breast against my arm. 'Enough.'

'Enough for what?'

'Wait and see!'

I did not have to wait long. Within a minute or two that incipient glow began its devilish work, spreading north, south, east and west and straight down the middle to me vitals, and before you could ask 'what's for tea?' old Herc was not only building a Big Top out of my towel but was also laying the groundwork for a three-ring performance!

I felt more than heard the chuckle from the lady at my side. 'Russ . . .' she cooed softly in whimsical cadence, '. . . something very strange has just happened to your towel.'

'Really.'

'Where did you learn it?' she enquired guilessly.

'Where did I learn what, Leoni?'

'The Indian Rope Trick.'

'Very humorous.'

She sighed wistfully. 'Men are very fortunate – being able to do tricks like that. It is very clever.'

'Leoni, remove your hand from there or I shall not be answerable for the con . . .' flick! the towel was open, '. . . sequences. Now, what did you go and do that for?'

'So I could see him, of course. He's *very* beautiful.'

'He thinks very highly of you, too.'

'I have a secret.'

'Mm . . .? What is it?'

'This couch . . . it folds down . . . into a *very* comfortable bed.'

We had the couch folded down into a *very* comfortable bed in about three seconds, then resumed our positions almost identically – the only slight difference being that Leoni's towel was now keeping mine company on the floor.

'Where were we?' I asked.

'Discussing him,' she reminded me, with the tip of her forefinger.

'How's the *kava* treating you?'

'Delightfully,' she chuckled. 'I am floating one inch above the couch like a hovercraft. It is a truly beautiful feeling.'

'That's the word, Leoni. Hey, who discovered *kava*, do you know?'

'Oh, yes, I know – but no one has ever seen him. He drank too much of his own discovery and went into orbit round the sun. One day perhaps a spaceship will find him and bring him back.'

'I hope so – he deserves our thanks. Leoni, *that* . . . is utterly delightful.'

'You like what I do?'

'The utmost.'

'I will think of other things to do, just as nice.'

'I've already got some things in mind for you.'

'Everything you do is nice – especially letting me do nice things to you.'

I sighed. 'Leoni . . . you will make someone a perfect wife one day, you know that?'

'One day, perhaps.'

'But not just yet, I know how you feel . . .' I chuckled. 'Do I know how you *feel*!' I drew a deep, contented sigh. 'Well, I reckon I must have died sometime tonight without knowing it and entered heaven. This can't be any other place.'

'You say such nice things, Russ Tobin . . . and for a reward I am going to do something extra specially nice for you.'

'What's that?'

She made to get up. 'Spread the towels across the bed, I won't be a moment.'

'Where're you going?'

'To the kitchen.'

She sprang off the bed and disappeared.

I arranged the towels and lay down again, wondering what the little monkey was up to and finding myself smiling with pleasure at the thought of her, concocting some mischief in the other room. I didn't care what it was . . . I didn't care what she did. In truth I didn't care about anything, for I did not have a care in the world.

Was it the island? Was it the *kava*? Was it Leoni? that caused this feeling of supreme well-being in which I floated, as on a white cloud in a warm, blue summer sky? No doubt all three. I only knew I'd never been happier in my life and would never be, could never be happier than this again.

She returned, carrying a small dark bottle. 'Turn on your front,' she commanded.

I turned. 'What is that?'

'Wait and see.'

She knelt beside me. I heard the gurgle of liquid and felt its coolness on my shoulders . . . then the heavenly scent of flowers was all around me, invading my mind.

Leoni's hands, delicate as butterflies, found my flesh and

began their magic . . . across my shoulders and down my spine, each moment of her caress shooting tingles of sensual delight from my curling toes straight through to my brain, raising moans and groans and all manner of strange vocal manifestations of ecstasy from me en route.

'Perhaps it is foolish to ask if it pleases you?' she smiled.

I nodded into the pillow. 'It's foolish. Leoni, where *did* you learn to massage?'

'From my mother – who learned it from her mother.'

'My compliments to your mum and her mum, they did a great job.'

She chuckled softly. 'Wait till I do your front!'

Well, I reckon, conservatively, I was three quarters of the way to Mars by the time she'd finished my back. She'd covered every inch of me from neck to toe and I felt as though I'd been stripped to the bone and repacked with new, dynamic muscle, then re-upholstered with the finest satin. Unbelievable!

But if I thought *that* was something, I had a shock coming.

'Turn over,' she instructed, slapping my bottom.

I turned to face her, discovering an impish grin as she poured a fresh supply of oil into the palm of her hand. She was up to something.

Ignoring my nether regions, she leaned forward and began on my chest and shoulders, smoothing the exotic oil into my flesh with the lightest touch, even taking the spur line down each arm to my very finger-tips.

'You have such nice hands,' she remarked, inspecting one closely. 'Big, man's hands.'

'All the better to caress you with, my dear,' I leered wolfishly.

'*Comment?*' she frowned, detecting the characterization.

'Have you never heard of Little Red Riding Hood and the wicked wolf?'

She shook her head. 'No.'

'It's an English fairy story. The wicked wolf gobbles up Red Riding Hood's granny, disguises himself in her nightie and climbs into her bed to await Little Red Riding Hood. When Red Riding Hood arrives at the house, she says . . .'

I had to stop there because she was no longer working on my hand but had switched suddenly to my stomach, circuiting Herc in ever-decreasing circles, purposely missing him by mere fractions of an inch and finding erogenous zones I never knew existed.

'Yes ... go on,' she prompted softly. 'What did Red Riding Hood say?'

'She, hm, said ... "Granny, what big ... ears you've got" and ... oh, boy ...'

She looked up, smiling. 'You like that?'

'Leoni ...'

'And?'

'And the wolf said, "All the better to ... h ... hear you with, my dear." And then Red Riding Hood said ...'

Round ... and round, close ... and closer, now a fleeting, almost accidental touch, both of us marvelling at the extent of Herc's arousal taking place before our very eyes.

'How strong he grows,' she whispered in breathless awe, now taking him in her oil-smooth hand and sending me through the roof.

'All the better to ...'

'Yes,' she laughed. 'But what else did *Red Riding Hood* say?'

'Sh ... she said, "And, Granny, what big *eyes* you've got." And the wolf said ...' My voice tailed away in an ecstatic gasp as down she went, her mouth an *ahimaa* of molten magic, her tongue a devil's device.

'Mmm ... ?' she prompted me.

'And the wolf said, Leoni, I think I'm going to die of pleasure ... oh, God, that's fantastic ...'

She raised her head and kissed my stomach. 'Just an old Tahitian custom.'

'By gum, girl, you've got some great customs ... and I don't care if you *are* making them up as you go along.'

'We have another you would also like very much, I think.'

I nodded, sweating. 'Go on, I'll buy it.'

She raised herself up high, still kneeling, and stretched out one leg and knelt astride me, maintaining her height, smiling down at me teasingly. 'And what did the wicked wolf say to Red Riding Hood?'

I gulped. 'He said ... "All the better to s ... *see* you with, my dear ..." '

Slowly, barely moving, she began to descend. 'Yes ... go on.'

'And then Red Riding Hood said, "But, Granny, what big *teeth* you've got" ... and the wolf roared, "All the better to ..." '

She was there, all but touching me, a millimetre away.

She raised an arched brow. 'To ... ?'

And now she was there, sliding down on to me ... down ... down ... finally coming to rest on my thighs. 'To *eat* you with, my dear?'

I nodded, dumbly, heart thudding. 'You've heard it before?'

She smiled and nodded. 'But never told so beautifully. And now I shall tell you a Polynesian story ... about a Tahitian maiden who, one moonlight night, while bathing alone in a lagoon, chanced to meet a handsome prince from a far-off land. He was tired and weary from his travels and asked to share her couch ... and it being an old Tahitian custom never to refuse such a request from a strong, sexy, handsome young prince, she readily agreed. And so they went to bed.'

I grinned up at her. 'And ... ?'

'This is a *very* long story ... it may take all night.'

'Take you time, Tahitian maiden, miss not a single word.'

We never did get around to eating the soup and ravioli – nor anything else for that matter – unless you count each other. That story of hers had more twists and turns, unexpected developments and downright high-jinks than a Whitehall farce.

What an imagination – and what stamina!

We slept awhile – had to, exquisite exhaustion bringing a temporary intermission to our play. But then, with the coming of the sun, we woke refreshed and entered Act Two spiritedly, as though we'd just begun.

When the sun was warm we swam, cavorted like kids in the clear lagoon, splashed and chased each other, showed our prowess from the diving rock (she a cleaving knife-blade – me a two-ton boulder), contested for underwater duration (she a clear winner by thirty seconds), and clowned the morning away.

Then, sadly, the ogre of passing time loomed over our gaiety like a huge dark cloud, blocking out the sun.

I swam to her, troubled for the first time since the moment we'd met. 'Leoni ...'

She became still, knowing. 'Yes ... you must go.'

We returned to the hut in silence, dried ourselves and dressed. 'I must find my friend,' I said. 'Lord knows where he is and what he's been up to. I should think he's still over at the house.'

She nodded but wasn't really listening. 'You can find your own way there?'

'Yes.'

'I won't come with you . . . I would like to stay here.'

'Yes, of course. Leoni . . .'

I held out my arms and she came into them quickly, hard against me, her arms tightly around me. 'You will come back to Tahiti one day?'

'I should think it highly likely,' I smiled, stroking her hair.

'And you will look for Leoni?'

'That will be the very first thing I do, I promise.' I raised her lovely face from my shoulder and kissed her softly. 'Thank you, Angel Eyes . . . for showing me the real Tahiti.'

'And I thank you . . .' she said, her voice a whisper, '. . . for you.' Then, unexpectedly, a teasing little smile dispelled the sadness in her eyes. 'I have a farewell present for you . . . something I know you will like.'

'Oh, Leoni, you shouldn't . . .'

She was shaking her head. 'No, it is not a *thing*, it is . . . knowledge.'

I frowned. 'Oh?'

'About the *kava*.'

'Oh?'

'You believed it to be a powerful aphrodisiac – yes?'

I laughed. 'Well, sure, I mean, wow . . .'

Now her smile unfolded into a full-blooded grin and she was shaking her head again. 'It is not.'

My laughter died. 'Hm . . . ?'

'It is no such thing. It is a mild narcotic, nothing more. All your . . . man strength was your own.'

I gaped at her, then burst into laughter. 'Well, I'll be . . . Truly?'

'Yes,' she said softly, 'truly. Now go quickly . . . and think a little of Leoni – as I will think of you.'

CHAPTER NINE

Nobody will ever convince me that Old Nick didn't have a big hand in setting down the rules of life – otherwise there'd be a much better way of ending a moment of wonderous pleasure than with a penalty of pure bloody misery.

I walked back along that path feeling so damned down I could've chucked meself in the stream and finished it all.

Nothing looked good right then – not the sun, not the water, not D'Urville's garden nor any damn thing else . . . and for two pins I'd have cancelled my onward trip with Buzz and rushed back to Leoni.

But, as always, common sense prevailed, worst luck, and the nearer I got to the house and to the problem of locating Buzz, the further the thought of turning beachcomber receded from my mind. I had to find him in a hurry or he'd miss his plane and the tennis tournament – but where was he likely to be?

Retracing my path along the beach, I broke through the fringe of denser bush and entered the park-garden, finding it completely deserted, an eerie sight, as though the entire complement of guests, staff and musicians had been mysteriously spirited away. There wasn't so much as a gardener in sight.

Well, now . . .

I tried to reason what Buzz would do after leaving the film lounge – if indeed he *had* left it! Maybe he was still in there – watching 'Raped By A Redskin' or 'Doodled By A Donkey' or something – or maybe he'd simply fallen asleep from crushing boredom.

Well, that was as good a place as any to start.

I crossed the garden and took a path between two thatched bungalows, circuited the house and found the rear door, amazed that so far I hadn't encountered a living soul. As I entered the corridor I checked my watch, getting worried about the time. Granted it was still only ten thirty, but I had to find Buzz, find transport, get back to the hotel, pack, and get out to the airport by one thirty for the two o'clock flight, and I reckoned we were going to need all of the three hours.

I reached the film room door and listened at it, heard nothing, so eased it open and popped my head in, finding it deserted. At least it looked it, but as I was about to reclose the door a naked female arm suddenly rose above the back of a distant couch like a weaving boa constrictor and waved a floppy hello.

'Hey, there . . .' drawled a voice, heavy with sleep or booze or both or maybe something else entirely. 'Anybody there gotta cigarette?'

Well, I just *had* to take a look at this one.

I entered the room and crossed to the couch, fearing the sight that would soon be revealed to me. I approached gingerly, ready for speedy retreat if necessary. You never can tell at this kind of party.

'Hey . . . anybody *there*?'

A head and shoulders struggled into view and hung over the back of the couch, trying to get me in focus. Boy, she was a mess – an explosion of blonde bouffant and streaked make-up, like one of those abstract masterpieces done with six cans of multi-coloured paint and an old tractor tyre.

'Hi . . .' she frowned. 'Who're you?'

'Saint George . . . I'm looking for a dragon.'

'Reckon yuh found one. Gimme a cigarette, hm, I'm dyin'.'

I walked round the couch and wished I hadn't. She had a dress on – just, but it was both up and down around her waist and what I couldn't see of her body wasn't worth looking for. She'd obviously had him right there on the couch . . . him or them.

I fished out my fags and offered her one, and in its acceptance she became aware of her state of virtual nakedness, muttered, 'Pardon me,' stuffed her breasts back inside her dress and made a showing of tugging the hemline down an inch or two. Being silky material, however, it shot back up again, leaving me a right old eyeful, but she didn't seem to notice.

She placed the cigarette between her lips with a shaking hand and accepted a light without comment. 'Jeezus, I feel awful.' She looked up at me, wincing. 'Say, you wouldn't happen to have a li-l hair-a-the-dog on yuh, would you?'

'I'm sorry, no.'

'What time is it?'

'Just after ten thirty.'

'Just after ten thirty what?'

'In the morning. It's a brand new day out there.'

She restrained me. 'Please – spare me all bad news, I'm on vacation.' Then with a groan she fell back, covering her eyes with an arm in dread of the ceiling light. 'Oh, *God,* I wanna die. Tell me it's all bin a bad dream . . . that I'm really back home in LA.'

'I was, er, looking for a pal of mine . . . big blond fella, Australian. I don't suppose you've seen him?'

'Who knows . . . who knows,' she groaned. 'Does he speak Australian with a French accent?'

'Not normally, no.'

'Then I ain't had him . . . seen him.'

'Oh . . . Yes, well, I'd . . . better get on and try and find him, we've got a plane to catch at two.'

'Well, bully for you . . . mine left an hour ago. Oh, God, my *head* . . .'

'Yes, well . . .'

Silently I backed away, made ten feet then tiptoed out on the run.

Phew! It was great to be out in the fresh air again.

Right . . . now, Malone, where the hell *are* you?

The line of bungalows caught my eye. Could he? Would he? Was he? It was as good a place as any.

With a furtive glance in all directions, I slid into the bushes, then proceeded to repeat the ludicrous skulking performance of the night before, pausing at each of the bungalow windows.

I reached the first window, raised myself up and peered in. Two beautiful human beings lay naked in each other's arms, dead to the world, smiles of rapturous repletion softening their countenances. The only mildly surprising detail about the tableau being that they were both female. Ah, well . . .

I moved on to the second window. Here *three* beautiful human beings were strewn ditto, the one in the middle smiling most benignly of all. He was the fella. Sleep well, kiddies.

Third window. And a scene of domestic contentment – not without its humour. On the left – a well-stacked redhead (natural), sprawled in enviable oblivion. And on her right – her muscular Tahitian stud, a tiny Stars and Stripes flag adorning his pendulous, flaccid manhood. A singular honour for a great multiple performance, no doubt.

Fourth window. My God, they were still at it!

Fifth window. Yeh, it was Buzz, all right – I could hear him snoring from outside. He was lying flat on his back, mouth open, one knee raised beneath a single sheet covering. No, on second thoughts, it wasn't his knee, randy swine.

He was, however, alone. Maybe that's why his knee was up. Buzz? No, never . . . whoever she'd been had scarpered.

I nipped round the bungalow and entered the little hall, knocked on the bedroom door. 'Buzz!'

Nothing.

I thumped on it. 'BUZZ!'

'Aaahhgggmmmnnnphtt.'

'Malone, wake up . . . it's me!'

'Phhttnnnmmmggghhaaaa.'

'Malone – wake up!'

'Who is it?'

'Your father!'

'Oh, Christ . . . hang on. OK, come in . . .'

I entered, looked around, sniffed critically at her lingering perfume and dazzled him with a radiant smile. '*Good* morning, sunshine, I *do* hope you slept . . .'

'Aaawww . . . NO!' he howled, and buried his head under the pillow.

'Never . . .' I declared, 'in the length and breadth of my considerable boudoir experience have I occasioned upon a room so randily redolent with the rancid remains of a bawdy, tawdry, biff-bang orgy. Malone, I'm ashamed of you.'

I got a muffled reply far too indelicate to repeat.

'Aha!' I cried, removing a tiny black lace bra from the floor and holding it aloft between finger and thumb. 'So – my worst fears about you are realized at last . . . you *are* a secret transvestite!'

One bleary, bloodshot eye, reminiscent of a squid's blow-hole, peered out from under the pillow. 'It's not my size,' he croaked, as through gravel. 'I take a forty-four B.'

Now he emerged fully, spoiling my beautiful morning, a tangle of hair and creased skin, lipstick on the end of his nose and four distinct nail scratches down one arm.

'Oh, boy . . .' I sighed.

'Oh, mother . . .' he groaned. 'Tobin, come back tomorrow.' He gazed about him, brow puckering with recollection of the night's debachery, then with a groan slowly sank down on his face and pulled the pillow back over his head. 'Awwwww . . .'

'Anything I can get you, Buzz – an aspirin . . . Alka Seltzer . . . a length of rope?'

'How hum hor fo huhin heerful?' he demanded.

'Buzz, I'm sorry, I didn't quite get that.'

He came roaring out of his pillow. *'I said how come you're so fucking cheerful!'*

I settled on the edge of the bed and studied the bra. 'Because I live a good, clean, celibate life, Malone. I'll have you know that while you were waist-deep in vile fornication last night – *I* was swimming in a spartan lagoon. I also had another swim this morning – at sunrise. Most bracing.'

'I'll bloody bet . . .' He struggled to sitting position and gave a nasty cough. 'Aw . . . got a fag, mate, I'm out.'

'For the count, by the look of you. Here . . .'

I lit it for him and waiting until he's stopped hacking. 'Malone, you are truly in great shape. God help those fellas in the tournament when they face you across the net – and I do mean God help 'em. Galloping consumption is not nice to behold when you're playing tennis.'

He fell back against the headboard one arm behind his head, and managed his first smile of the day, heaved an exhausted sigh and gasped, 'Wow . . .'

I grinned at him. 'What happened?'

'Uh uh, you first.'

'Me?' I shrugged. 'I told you – I spent most of my time swimming.'

'Cock!'

'Hardly any at all.'

'Tobin, I *saw* you leaving the funny house with that gorgeous Tahitian doll who served the drinks!'

'Oh.'

'Yes, oh . . . and I was not at all happy with the development.'

'Ah – your concern for me.'

'No. I fancied her myself but she wouldn't have any.'

'You know, that was one of the first things I noticed about her – her sense of good taste.'

He repeated the rude word. 'So – how did it go?'

'Charmingly. She took me home to meet her mother. We had a quiet family meal of asparagus soup and ravioli, a game of Ludo, and . . . but my evening was of no consequence, Buzz, let's get to yours.'

He shook his head, gazed before him blankly as in stupor. 'Unbelievable . . . I mean, I do *not* believe it happened.'

I held up the bra. 'Who was she?'

'Mm . . . ?' He did a funny sort of double-take. 'Oh, she was later . . . much later.'

'My God . . .'

'Lovely girl . . . French . . . works for D'Urville.'

'I'll bet! So – what transpired before her?'

He shook his head. 'I think I was drugged.'

'Eh? Not the stuff I gave you?'

'No, that seemed to wear off pretty quickly.'

'So I discovered. Proceed.'

'Well, after you left with . . .'

'Leoni.'

'That her name? Smashing piece.'

'I know.'

'Well, after you left with her, they showed a couple more films. The first was the usual kind of thing – "The Rent Collector" – bird can't pay her rent so she invites the bloke in to talk the problem over and he very quickly arrives at a solution – all over her stomach . . .'

I nodded. 'I do believe I've seen it – or was that "The Hire Purchase Collector"? No matter – carry on.'

'Well, half-way through this film I am suddenly not alone any more. Sitting there on the couch with me is a wild-looking piece of grumble with eighty six-inch tits and a look in her eye that says I'm just the bloke she's been looking for for the last couple of months. Strange bird – sort of gypsy-looking, dark flashing eyes, savage-looking . . .'

'I know the type – our vicar married one at home.'

'You're kiddin'!'

'Yes. Go on.'

'Well, one thing this chick did not believe in was wasting time. She came on with all the subtlety of a boarding party, whispering sweet somethings in my ear and sticking her tongue down it, then she fished a hip-flask out of her handbag and gave me a drink – which I thought was scotch.'

'And what was it?'

'Scotch.'

'Hm?'

'But I reckon scotch-and-something-else . . . like scotch-and-Spanish Fly, for instance, because inside a couple of minutes I was, well, need I say more?'

'No, you need not, Malone. The only thing that puzzles me is how you can blame the drink for your excessive sexual excitation when it appears, from my own observation, to be your normal and permanent condition.'

'Be that as it may, Tobin, this was something altogether different. Mind you, on reflection, it *might* have had something to do with the fact that by now she had her hand on it and did not once remove it during the entirety of the next film.'

'Which was?'

'A weirdo. A Black Magic get-together in a clearing in the woods.'

'Aha – wondered if that one would pop up. Beautiful blonde sacrifice laid out on an altar and a dozen prancing mop-heads having their lusty way with her?'

'No.'

'Oh.'

'A complete reversal – the prancing mop-heads were birds! The human sacrifice was a lad named Colossal O'Toole and, by the twitch, if ever a bloke deserved the name it was him. I reckon if he'd entered it in a marrow contest he'd have been disqualified for force-feeding.'

I shrugged. 'Well, Buzz, some of us have it and some of us don't . . .'

'Ha! Tobin, I have never regarded myself as being exactly *puny* in that department, but compared to this kid, mine was in-grown! However, Delores did not appear to be too dismayed at what she'd been lumbered with and . . .'

'Delores? This was the gypsy, I take it?'

'This was the gypsy and *she* was taking it – because the things that were going on up there on the screen were beginning to have a profound effect on her and at one point I got the distinct impression she'd come in not so much to the films as for late supper!'

'Point taken.'

'Ho! not just the point, lad. I've seen "Deep Throat" but this was ridiculous!'

'And what *was* going on up there on the screen – as if I can't guess?'

'Every damn thing. Those birds cavorted naked around old Colossal, sprinkling him with rose petals and tattooing him with cabalistic signs – even his old man – Jeezus, I just hope they weren't using oil paints . . .'

'Sore,' I winced.

'They worked themselves up into a fine old sexual frenzy, dancing like whirling dervishes until they were out of their skulls . . . and then they attacked him.'

'Attacked him?'

'Came in out of the sun, son, and systematically raped him! Twelve of 'em!'

'My God. And what was he doing while all this was going on?'

'Laughing himself sick, having a ball. And that's when Delores whispered in my ear, "And how would *you* like to be in his position?" ' He laughed. 'Well, what could I say?'

'Yes?'

'Hell, no! I didn't fancy being lashed to an altar and raped by twelve crazy women. Six, maybe . . . but a blinkin' dozen!'

I nodded. 'I agree – one *can* get too much of a good thing – or so I've been told. So – how did she take it?'

' "Oh," she said, "well, in which film would you have liked to have been?" Well, I had to think about that one – and I was just about to tell her I wouldn't have minded being Jack the Giant in the gymnasium, when she asked me how many films I'd seen. I told her four and she tutted and said, "Oh, then you haven't seen them all. How can you possibly choose when you haven't seen them all?" '

'Blimey, how many were there altogether?'

'Ten!'

'Good God. Well, go on, what happened then?'

' "There's only one thing to do," she said, "Come with me," and she led me out of the room. Russ, have you any idea how big that house really *is*? It's bloody en*orm*ous! And it looks single-storeyed, doesn't it? Well, it isn't – not really, because there's a hell of a lot more up in that roof than cobwebs and a rusty old water tank! Hey, you remember the tour we took of that hotel in Las Vegas . . . the Mint Hotel?'

'Yes, sure.'

'And being taken up into that room above the casino and looking down on the tables through those huge one-way mirrors . . . and the guide telling us that was the way they kept the croupiers honest . . . ?'

'Yes, of course.'

'Well, it was like that – a wooden walk-way stretching from one end of the house to the other so you could look down into every room in the place!'

'No kidding.'

'I swear it. Well, we climbed a flight of stairs into the roof, got on this walk-way, and Delores looked down and said, "How d'you fancy this one, Big Boy?" I joined her and hung over the rail and . . .' he broke off for a chuckle, 'mate, you'll never believe it . . . the room below was built like a movie set of a bathroom – you know, a big, square bath and a wall-flat with a window in it . . .'

'Yeh, I know.'

'Well, *outside* the window, as it were, was a bloke with a ladder, a bucket of water and a window-leather, preparing to start work. And in the bath, which really was filled with water, was a stupendous-looking brunette, built like you'd never believe, soaping herself all over and bringing up a lather on more than the loofah . . .!'

'Meaning you.'

'Who else? You should get yourself an overhead shot of a bird in a bath sometime, it'll add ten years to your life. So, anyway, there she is, loofahing away, quite unconcerned, thinking about jam-making and what she's going to crochet for Christmas, when suddenly Dan Dan the window-cleaner man appears at the window to start earning his money. But does she let out a scream and sink beneath the suds?'

'I've got a feeling the answer is no.'

'Right on. The crafty minx takes one look at his brawny shoulders, his muscle-knotted arms and promptly sticks her right toe up the cold-water tap! "Help!" she screams. Dan is so taken aback by this apparition of naked loveliness in distress he nearly falls off his ladder. "I'll go and fetch the fire-brigade!" he shouts. "Not on your life!" she replies. "*You* nip in and remove it!"'

'I am beginning to get the picture,' I said sinisterly. 'This is a frustrated housewife's fantasy!'

Buzz grinned. 'Near – but not quite.'

'But she's making the running.'

'True – but as Dan climbs through the window and starts wrestling her toe out of the tap a transformation overcomes him. His embarrassment and shyness disappear like suds down the plug hole, and having rescued the toe he turns his lust upon her – only to find she's five times hotter than he is! Frenziedly he rips off his clothes and leaps into the bath with her and then, by God, they really go at it – like a couple of frantic ferrets – in the bath, out of the bath, over the side of it and on the floor. I tell you, mate, they made Jack the Giant and his bird look like a couple of senile tortoises!'

'Blimey! So what d'you reckon – that it was the window-cleaner's fantasy?'

'Both. She was satisfying her wildest dreams of being raped by a big, butch window-cleaner – and the bloke was satisfying his life-long ambition to play the classic window-cleaner-who-finds bird-in-bath-with-toe-stuck-in-tap role.'

'Aha!' I exclaimed. 'And D'Urville had set the whole thing up for them ... first the films to excite the imagination, then identical props to provide authenticity. Well, by God, it's no wonder his parties are held in such high esteem. He's running a fantasy farm! And what was Delores doing while all this was going on?'

He shrugged. 'Nothing – just watching me watching the scene.'

'And then what?'

'She asked me if I fancied being the window-cleaner and I

said not particularly, so she said, "Well, let's see what we *can* interest you in" and we moved on down the walk-way.'

I glanced at my watch. 'Buzz, I want to hear it all, but you'd better whistle and ride – it's gone eleven. We've got two and a half hours to get back to the hotel, pack, pay the bill and get out to the airport . . .'

'Christ, why didn't you say . . . !' He shot out of bed and 'streaked' to the bathroom. 'Try and find my clobber, mate, I think it's under the bed.'

I got down on my hands and knees and hauled out his trousers – plus a dainty pair of black-lace panties to match the bra.

'Hey, Buzz . . . what colour shorts were you wearing?'

'Tiger stripes!'

'A fine story. Wait till this gets round the tennis club!'

He popped his head out of the door, gaped at the black lace flimsies I was dangling and shrugged. 'So – we all got hang-ups. But you tell on me and I'll *swear* I borrowed them from you!'

I tutted. 'Malone, you know I *never* wear black – it's so frightfully *démodé*.'

'With you, mate, wearing *anything* is frightfully *démodé*.'

I gathered together his crumpled clothes and took them into the bathroom. 'Here – tiger stripes and all. What did she do when she saw those – reach for her gun?'

'Reached for something,' he splutter/chuckled, head in the basin. 'By the way, which bird are we currently referring to?'

'Let's stick to Delores – I can't cope with that sort of confusion on top of everything else. So – after the window-cleaning episode, what next?'

He came out of the towel with a grin. 'Yoiks and tallyho! Apparently we'd missed a film called "Bareback Rider" . . .'

I winced. 'Yeh, I know. It should've been called "Never Mind The Fox – Let's Get On With The Chase". The set was a barn, complete with belting-looking blonde in a riding habit, lying exhausted in the hay – looked like she'd just cantered in from South America or somewhere. Then, suddenly, in storms Simon Legree – moustache, top-hat, riding boots and leather crop . . .'

'Nothing else?'

'Not a stick. "Aha!" he snarls, espying the comely wench in the hay. "At last I have you in my power! You must pay the penalty for trespassing in my barn – take your clothes off." '

'The *swine*! And did she?'

'*In* a wink – never seen anything faster – all except her riding boots, of course. And *very* stylish they were, too . . . tooled leather in diamond-shaped panels with clocks of overlaid multi-coloured stitching up the . . .'

'Malone . . .'

'Oh – you're not interested, Russell? I just thought in passing I'd . . . well, anyway . . .'

He grabbed his clothes from me and stepped into the tiger stripes, continuing as he tucked home his meat and veg. 'Well, the bastard really lays into the poor kid with his crop, cracking her a dozen or so across her bare ass, and you can tell from the agonized contortion of her face and the tears welling in her big blue eyes she's loving every minute of it. But, then, as Legree raises his crop for another crack, he accidentally on purpose let's go if it and he has to turn round and bend down to pick it up. Tallyho! She's over there quicker than Trigger, fetching him such a delicious thwack across the botty he falls face-down over a bale of hay and is completely at the she devil's mercy.'

'Well, good for her. What happened then?'

'I don't know. I think Delores detected from my yawn the scene was not quite rivetting my complete attention, so we moved on . . . got a comb, mate?'

Now fully dressed, he turned to the mirror to put the final touches to, at best, a lousy job. He looked as though he'd been run over by a herd of stampeding Longhorns.

'And in the next set?' I prompted him.

'Ah – Jack the Giant and his jumping gymnasium . . .' he turned, grinning, handed me back the comb. 'Son, *that* was a riot – wish you'd been there. The bloke playing Jack, a little bald, fat guy, had just got started on the old vibrator, giving it stick to a well-stacked redhead, when the belt flew off one side of the machine! He went flying back across the room and landed with a hell of a thump on his arse. Then he got up, ran back to the machine to try and catch the whirling belt, mistimed it completely and the leather end caught him smack in the balls! Boy, you should have heard him – bellowed like a castrated bull, then passed out. They had to carry him out on a stretcher.'

'What happened to the redhead?' I laughed.

'She carried on by herself until a replacement arrived . . . had a lovely time.'

'Great . . . are you ready?'

He nodded . . . then paused, the thought suddenly striking home. 'Hey – how do we get back to Papeete?'

'God knows. Buzz, there isn't a living soul out there – the place is absolutely deserted – or was when I came in. I reckon everyone's still asleep.'

'Well, let's take a look.'

We took a look, finding the situation unchanged.

'Blimey,' said Buzz, 'it's like a graveyard.' Then, thoughtfully, he rubbed his chin. 'I wonder . . .'

'About what?'

'About Paul Martin . . . come on.'

He was off.

'Where to?'

'The car park.'

'Good thinking. If Martin's car's still there . . . but, hey, Buzz, he might not be driving back to Papeete early enough for us.'

'True,' he nodded, striding on, undeterred.

'In which case, we phone for a taxi,' I said, answering my own objection.

We hurried through the formal gardens and emerged into the car park, finding it still well-occupied.

'Looks as though that bloke was right about D'Urville's parties,' I commented. 'Maybe they never do end.'

'Could be . . .' muttered Buzz, preoccupied, scanning the cars. 'There's Martin's Citroen, he's still here.'

'Great. Now all we've got to do is find him and hope he's leaving for Papeete like right now. Buzz, time is getting mighty short . . . don't you think we'd better phone for a taxi?'

He answered me as he started off across the car park. 'Russ, how long did it take us to drive out here?'

'Mm . . . half an hour, maybe a bit more.'

'Right – so at the very least a taxi would take forty minutes to get here and the same back again – say an hour and a half for the round trip. What's the time now?'

'It's . . . good God, it's a quarter to twelve!'

'Right – so that means a quarter past one back at the hotel at the earliest. Only a quarter of an hour to pack, pay the bill and get out to the airport. We'd never do it.'

I gaped at him. 'So what do we do?'

He didn't answer until we reached the Citroen, then he stooped to look through the driver's window and rose to regard me with a foxy grin. 'The keys are here, Russell.'

I shrugged. 'Fine – but where's Paul Martin? Hell, he could be . . . anywhere . . .'

My voice tailed away as the motivation for his leer struck home, the audacity of his intention startling me. 'Hey, Buzz, we can't . . .!'

'D'you want to miss the plane, Tobin?'

'No, of course I don't . . .'

'And can you think of alternative transport that will get us to the airport in time . . . ?'

'Well, no . . .'

'And would you not agree that Paul Martin owes me a *little* something for pinching my bird last night . . . ?'

'But, Buzz, he's a pilot . . . I mean, he may need to . . .'

'Get to the airport? Russ, he can't be flying today or he wouldn't have been boozing last night. Tell you what we'll do – we'll phone D'Urville from the airport and let Martin know it's there. D'Urville can probably arrange to have someone drive it back here. Martin'll have it back by three. Russ, time is flying!'

'I know, I know . . .'

'So?'

I grinned at him. 'So – who drives, you or me?'

He had the engine roaring before I'd closed my door.

'OK – continue with your naughty narrative,' I said, handing him a cigarette.

We'd just turned out on to the main Papeete road and the seemingly endless D'Urville grounds were at last behind us. I began breathing a bit easier. Anyway, what could Martin do to us? – charge us for the petrol we'd used? Call us a few choice names? And Buzz was right – Martin did owe him something for seducing Carol. Marvellous the excuses you can come up with to clear your conscience, isn't it?

'Where was I?' frowned Buzz.

'Jack the Giant had just been carted off on a stretcher and the redhead was playing vibro-solitaire.'

'Oh, yes ... well, we moved on to the next set and came upon a study in unsurpassed kink – a mediaeval torture-chamber, complete with thumb-screws, branding irons and a rack. There was a bloke stretched out starkers on the rack, being tortured by four birds wearing nothing but German helmets and jackboots.'

'My God ...'

'Oh, he was having a ball – because there was a fifth bird sitting astride him, taking notes as they tortured the information out of him. I've never seen a fella look so painfully happy.'

'Boy,' I laughed, 'we must have missed some beautiful films.'

'Dandies. Delores said, "How about this for a turn-on?" and I told her no, I fancied the stenographer bit but not the rack, I was tall enough, so we moved on. I reckon she was getting a bit worried by now that she'd landed a eunuch.'

'Ridiculous. What came next?'

'A baker's shop.'

'Eh?'

'No kidding,' he laughed. 'This guy walks into a baker's shop, stocked with bread and cream cakes and things. Behind the counter there's a honey of a blonde wearing a baker's hat and a big welcoming smile ...'

'Nothing else?'

'Need you ask? She's putting the final touches to a big cream cake – squirting whipped cream on it from a giant aerosol can. This guy says he'd like to have a go, so she invites him round the counter and hands him the can. But does he squirt in on the cake? No, sir – he lets her have it straight on the left boob and then ...'

'He sucks it off.'

He laughed and nodded. 'He sucks it off. She's tickled pink with this, loves it, and invites him to have a go on her right one, and before you can say cherry, he's got her on the counter, spraying the stuff in the most incredible places and ...'

'Sucking it off,' I laughed.

'Sucking it off. Then *she* wants a go, so ...'

'Off comes his clobber . . .'

'And on goes the whipped cream, and . . .'

'Off comes the whipped cream, and . . .'

'Off comes the bloke . . . and we moved on to the next set.'

'Incredible. Buzz, d'you reckon people really have fantasies about doing those things?'

'Well, I certainly don't,' he said. 'I can't *stand* whipped cream.'

I laughed. 'What happened then?'

'Oh, then it was the "Castaway" thing – a bird tied to a post in the village compound – only there was only one bloke there – the Chief. I told Delores I didn't fancy getting blacked-up so we scrubbed that one – and I reckon she was getting very fed up with me by then because we were fast running out of film sets.'

'What about the "Rent Collector" thing?'

'That came next – very draggy. The guy playing the collector was so pissed he couldn't get it up. The bird gave him the money instead.'

'And the "Rape By The Witches"?' I laughed.

'Ah . . . well, that's where I nearly passed out.'

'Eh?'

'Yeh – I told you I thought Delores had slipped me something in that drink . . .'

'Yes.'

'Well, things started to go mighty peculiar right then . . . a bit like the effect of the Cum-Cum Juice you gave me, but more so. I knew what was going on, all right, but I didn't give a damn, know what I mean? Everything was weird and floaty. Delores saw it had happened to me and I knew this was what she'd been waiting for.

'She moved fast, then – caught hold of my hand and hurried along the walk-way and down a flight of stairs. I asked where we were going in such a rush and she said, "Come on, they're waiting for you!" I asked her who and she just laughed and said, "Your fans!"

'We got to the bottom of the stairs and went along a corridor, then through a door into a room full of . . .' he glanced sideways at me, grinning, '. . . witches?'

'Oh, blimey . . .'

'Yeh,' he nodded. 'That Delores was sort of talent scout for the coven – she'd been doing the rounds looking for a suitable male sacrifice – and I was it! Well, I tell you, mate, as bombed as I was, I wanted to turn and run! Like I said, I can enjoy fun and games with the best of them, but when it comes to being strapped to an altar and mounted by a procession of twelve cock-eyed female jockeys . . . well, my name's Malone – not Hyperion the Second! A joke's a joke but balls to a pantomime!'

'So what did you do?' I gasped, vividly picturing the scene.

'Right then – nothing. I didn't get a chance to. As soon as I appeared through the door, they were on me like a pack of wolves – every one of them completely starkers and wearing a pointed hat and a gruesome witch-mask. Frightened the hell out of me. But what could I do? I mean you can't fight them, can you – you can't hit women! Next thing I knew I was on the floor and they were ripping my clothes off – that's why they're in such a bloody state. Then they picked me up and dumped me on the table and . . .'

'You reckon they were all hyped up on something?'

'Christ, yes . . .! Mate, that's what made it so frightening! This was a love-in in a loony-bin! They were out of their skulls!'

'So, go on . . .'

'Well, I reckon they thought I'd volunteered as the sacrifice and was just putting up a token struggle as part of the game, because they didn't bother to tie me down properly – just slung a couple of straps across my legs and chest and left my arms free – thank God! Then they started dancing round and round me, prelude to getting me properly worked up, and the lights went out except for a couple of dim, flickering red ones in a corner, representing a fire or something. Jeezus, it was creepy . . . all those gruesome faces and naked bodies in the flickering fire-light, Malone, I thought, what are you *doing* here, you silly bugger? This is not your scene. You should be tucked up in a nice, normal bed with a nice, normal, good-looking chick who needs nothing more for kicks than a nice, normal, good-look . . . well, fella! I mean, who *needs* to pretend he's a bleeding window-cleaner!'

'Quite.'

'Right, I thought, I'm off out of this lot . . . so – one, two – I slipped the buckles on the straps and was off the table like a rocket, grabbed my clothes and was out of the door before they knew what had hit 'em. But, by God, I didn't know what I'd let myself in for or I'd have probably stayed right there on the table and taken my licks . . . pun intended! You should have heard them! Screaming like banshees! Madder than hell! Then out they came – after me.'

'Oh, Christ . . .'

'Too bleeding right. And you know why?'

'Well . . .'

'Because it was all part of the *game*, mate! It was a contrived, full-blooded man-hunt – and I'd fallen for it! They *wanted* me to escape!'

'But . . . how did you find that out?'

'The little French bird told me later.'

'Oh, the . . . black lace panties . . .'

'Yeh,' he grinned. 'Saved my life, that little chicken.'

'And I'm sure she was well-rewarded.'

He shrugged. 'Well . . .'

'And meanwhile – back at the chase?'

He shook his head woefully. 'Russ . . .' he broke off with a wry laugh. 'Can you imagine the *scene*, man . . . me – stark bollock-naked – being chased hell-for-leather out of the house and round and round that bloody garden by twelve naked birds in masks and witches hats . . .' He exploded with laughter, bringing me on, our laughter building until tears were running down our cheeks.

'Godalmighty . . .' he gasped, 'if someone had had a movie camera right then, they'd have got the slapstick comedy of the year . . . all those bare asses and boobs wobbling and bouncing around and me tearing across that park, clutching my clothes like I'd just been caught in the ladies' lav . . . man, what a scene.'

'How did you finally escape?' I asked, wiping my eyes.

He tapped his head. 'Genius. Those kinky buggers chased me clean down to the beach and thought they'd cornered me, but . . . well, in a way *you* saved my life – at least at first.'

'*I* did?'

'Well, not so much you as your boat – the one you landed in

from the cruiser. I knew it was warmed up and operative, so I made a bee line for it and made it just in time. By God, it was close, though . . . those devils were haring down the wharf as I got the engine going and a couple of them actually dived in the bloody water as I was pulling away!'

'Wow! And what did they do then?'

'Hurled abuse like you've never heard! Screamed at me . . . chucked a couple of stones . . . and then one of them spotted another fella in the bushes – I guess he'd seen the chase and followed us down to the beach – and they took off after that poor sod. And that, thank God, was the last I saw of them.'

'Blimey,' I gasped. 'What a night!'

'Too right. Well, I thought my troubles were over then, and I decided to take a little putter out to sea, clear my brain of the gunk Delores had poured into me, then start all over again on a fresh tack.'

'Oh – then you weren't *entirely* put off the prospect of a little sensual dalliance by what had happened.'

'Hm?' he frowned.

'Daft question. Go on.'

'Well, there I was – puttering around the lagoon all by myself, about a mile offshore, I should think, really enjoying the moonlight on the water and the stars huge in the heavens above . . .'

I winced. 'Get on with it.'

'Then, suddenly . . . I wasn't.'

Silence.

I jerked a look at him. 'Then suddenly you wasn't . . . weren't what?'

'Puttering.'

'Why not?'

'Because I'd run out of gas, you bum! You hadn't left me enough to fill my lighter!'

'Well, it wasn't *my* fault! How did *I* know you . . . so what happened?'

'What d'you think happened – I just sat there! For hours! There was nothing to paddle with and I wasn't going over the side into that water – Christ knows what was lurking down there. So I just sat and waited.'

'For what?'

'The first thing that came along – like a war canoe . . . or dawn or something.'

'Rotten, that.'

'Not at all pleasant, Tobin – especially when all I had to think about was you having a flamin' marvellous time on shore with that gorgeous Tahitian piece!'

'How right you were. And how very disconcerting for you, Buzz. So – then what happened.'

'I fell asleep.'

'Eh?'

'Dropped right off . . . and the next thing I knew, there was this cracking little French piece hanging over the side, flicking water at me.'

'A mile offshore!'

He nodded, shamefacedly. 'Yeh – she'd seen the whole thing, the chase, my escape in the boat, and had heard it run out of juice . . . and she'd swum all the way out to rescue me. Made me feel a right berk, I can tell you.'

'No, fair's fair – you didn't know the water, mate. So you . . . sort of . . .'

'Yeh,' he grinned, 'we sort of . . . By *heck*, what a night – I think I might have been safer with the witches!'

'So,' I sighed, stretching extravagantly, 'all in all *quite* a party . . . and quite a little sojourn in old Tahiti. Tell me, Malone, do you, er, consider your personal contribution to the island's love-kitty sufficient to have satisfied all previous expectations?'

'Hell, no.'

'Eh?'

'Of course not,' he grinned. 'But then I've been saving myself for Sydney, haven't I?'

CHAPTER TEN

'QANTAS AIRLINES announce the departure of their 747 flight to Sydney. Will passengers kindly proceed through Gate Number Two to Passport Control.'

'Now!' I told Buzz.

He plopped the money in the box and dialled.

'It's ringing.' He turned to me with a grin. 'Hell, I'd love to see Martin's face when D'Urville tells him . . . hello . . . hello, may I speak to Monsieur D'Urville, please? My name's Malone, miss . . . well, it's kind of personal. Oh, he is? Well, could you possibly transfer me?' He turned to me, hand over the mouth-piece. 'He's down at the pool, she's putting me through.'

'We'd better hurry up, there aren't many passengers to go through.'

'The finer we cut it the better – then there can't be any repercussions before we take off . . . hello . . . hello, Monsieur D'Urville? This is Buzz Malone. I don't expect you'll remember me but I was at your party last night . . . I came with Russ Tobin . . . Paul Martin introduced us. He . . . oh, you do? I'm surprised – there were so many people there. Well, first of all, Russ and I want to thank you very much for a fabulous time. We're sorry we couldn't say goodbye this morning but we were in a terrible hurry to get to the airport . . . yes, we're here now, our flight leaves in a few minutes. Anyway, thank you *very* much . . . but there's something we have to tell you . . . it's about Paul Martin's car. We were in a bit of a fix this morning . . . the house and grounds all seemed deserted and . . . well, we had no time to try and find Paul *or* wait for a taxi to come out from Papeete, so I'm afraid we . . . well, we *borrowed* Paul's car. We're sorry if it causes him any inconvenience and . . . hm? . . . yes, it's here at the airport – in the parking lot, keys under the mat. Oh, you will . . . well, thanks very . . . hm? yes, the two o'clock Qantas flight to Sydney, we're going through right now.

We thought maybe you might know someone at the airport who could drive it out to you . . . ah, you do, good. Well, thanks very much again – the party was really terrific. Hope to meet you again sometime. Goodbye . . .'

Buzz hung up and turned to me with a shoulder hunch. 'No trouble at all – nice as pie. He says he'll relay the message to Martin and get someone to drive it out there. So . . .' he slung an arm round my shoulder. 'Let's get went to Sydney!'

Minutes later we were climbing the forward steps of the giant Boeing to be greeted by a couple of smiling Aussie airstews who passed us on to another smiling Aussie airstew who took us way down the plane to our seats – a window and a middle on the starboard side, looking out on the terminal building.

We took our time settling in, getting comfortable for the long 4,000-mile haul to Sydney, then had a little time for reflection.

Gazing past Buzz through the window, I shook my head and heaved a sigh – of nostalgia, incredulity and downright exhaustion.

'Can you believe it's only forty-eight hours since we touched down here, Buzz?'

'Nope,' he grinned. 'Seems like we've been here for ever. No wonder – we've packed a lifetime of living into those forty-eight hours, cock. I was just trying to remember if we've slept at all.'

'Sure, we have, it was . . . was it the day *before* yesterday? Yeh . . . quite a place Tahiti. Mind you, I don't reckon I could live here permanently, do you – all kidding aside?'

'Nah, I reckon I've had enough. Tell you the truth, I'm really looking forward to getting home now. Haven't seen old Sydney in quite a while. Just think – in . . . what? – eight hours we'll be touching down there . . . we'll be at the flat by, oh, say, nine o'clock – knocking off the time lag . . . we'll have a quick sluice to freshen up, then I'll take you out on the town – meet some of the lads for a jar or two. How does that sound?'

'Fabulous. I'm really looking forward to it myself, Buzz . . . new city, new faces – and a new *job*. Think you *can* get me fixed up with something?'

He grinned a grin of particular sneakiness. 'Sure, I can. Matter of fact I've been giving it a bit of thought lately . . . and I reckon I've come up with *just* the right thing for you, Tobin.'

My heart quickened. 'You have?'

'Yeh.'

'Malone . . . it is possible that I'm being overly suspicious, but somehow I don't like that grin. I think you're up to something!'

'No, I'm not . . .'

'Malone, the last time I saw that grin was in Toronto when you also fixed me up with a job – as Father Bloody Christmas in Simpsons!'

'Hell, man, this is nothing like that.'

'Well, what is it?'

'Trust me – this one's right up your street.'

I shrugged. 'So – tell me.'

He chuckled, most suspiciously. 'Nah, you'll be impossible to live with until we get there. I'd get no peace.'

'God's honour, I won't mention it . . . won't breathe a word . . .!'

'You will, Tobin, it's so terrific you won't be able to help yourself . . . hello.' Something out on the tarmac had caught his attention – or so he was pretending.

'What?'

'Couple of cops walking towards the plane.' He gave a laugh. 'Coming to arrest you for over-screwing your quota.'

'Never mind the cops, Malone, come on – what's this job?'

He turned to me, his expression now doubtful. 'On second thoughts, I'm not at all sure you could cope, Tobin. I've told you about Australian women . . . it takes a real man to handle them.'

My eyes lit up. 'Women? The job's got something to do with . . .'

'Not something, son – everything,' he said, infuriatingly casual as he idly watched the cops – one a European, the other a Tahitian – mount the steps and enter the aircraft.

'Malone . . .' I muttered threateningly, 'if you don't . . . Buzz, *please* . . .!'

'OK,' he grinned, 'I'll put you out of your misery. I've got a pal who's just started up an . . .' he paused, eyes twinkling, dragging out the revelation to the bitter end '. . . an escort agency?'

I gasped.

'*And* he's always on the look-out for tall, dark, handsome, personable-looking blokes who've got a working conversation on one or two subects other than birds, booze and Bondi . . .'

'Buzz . . . now, you're joking!'

He laughed. 'I'm not! Honest Injun, he's just formed this . . .'

'And you can get me *in*?'

He shrugged. 'Like a shot. I think you'd be terrific . . . charm the little sheilas clean out of their panties.'

'Aw, mate . . . mate! How long does this thing take to get there – eight hours? I'll have a word with the skipper, see if he can't push it along a bit . . .'

'Oh, Christ, I knew I'd get no peace.'

'Aw, but Buzz . . . an *escort* agency! You know, that's the one job I've always wanted to have a crack at! Think of the human interest value . . . a different bird every night . . . from all walks of life. The conversation will be exhilarating . . .'

'Ha!'

'No, I mean it! Buzz, I can't believe it . . . it's terrific! Thanks a million! Now, come on, skip, get this crate in the air . . .' I checked my watch and frowned. It was after two. We should have been off by now. 'Buzz . . . what's going on out there? What's the hold up? What's . . .'

But Buzz, I suddenly realized, was not listening. He was gazing straight ahead, wearing a most peculiar expression – a sort of innate disbelief slowly surrendering to an appalled, dawning horror.

I jerked round, following his eyeline, and received a jolt under the heart at the purposeful approach of the two cops, now only a few feet away, the objects of their visit plainly apparent from the focused direction of their hard, unsmiling eyes.

My heart exploded. I heard Buzz murmur, 'Oh, Jeezus . . .' and then they were upon us, the European officer bending forward towards me, his arm coming to rest on the seat in front.

'Monsieur Tobin . . .'

'Y . . . yes.' My voice was a thin, choked croak.

'. . . and Monsieur Malone?'

Buzz nodded dumbly.

'I regret, gentlemen, that it will be necessary for you to

accompany me to police headquarters. There are some questions we would like you to answer regarding ... a stolen car.'

I gaped at him ... at Buzz ... back to the cop. 'B ... but we explained ... we telephoned ... we only *borrowed* it ...'

'Without the owner's permission?'

'Well ... in a *way* ...'

'In what way, monsieur? It could have been borrowed either *with* or *without* the owner's permission – there is no other way ... and since he is claiming it was without his permission, he is therefore claiming it was stolen. I am sorry, but this matter will have to be cleared up before you can leave Tahiti.'

Again I gaped at Buzz. 'B ... but our *flight* ...! We're flying to *Sydney*! Our luggage ...'

I got a perfect French shrug – apology well-laced with monumental indifference. 'I regret, monsieur. If the matter can be cleared up quickly, you can perhaps catch the next flight to Sydney ... in three days' time.'

My chin dropped. 'Three days!'

'And if the matter *cannot* be cleared up quickly, your baggage will be returned to you from Sydney, also in three days' time. Now, Messieurs, if you please ...'

He stepped back, giving me room to rise, which I did on rubber legs, gasping at Buzz. 'Three days ...!'

'That bloody bastard!' he seethed. 'That low-down, bird-seducing son-of-a-bitch!'

'My job, Buzz, my job ...!'

'And my bloody tennis tournament! Christ, we could be here for months!'

'Messieurs, *if* you please! You are holding up the flight!'

We hauled out our hand-luggage from under our seats and trudged in disgrace down the long ... long aisle to the forward door, our ears filled with the whisper of passenger gossip ... bank robbers ... haven't paid their hotel bill ... criminals – you can tell by their earlobes.

Out of the door, avoiding the eyes of the non-smiling air-stews, and down the steps, conscious of a hundred hungry eyes boring holes in our backs as we crossed the endless stretch of tarmac.

How different now Tahiti seemed ... I couldn't bear to look at it. The sparkling turquoise sea ... the towering, majestic heights of Orohena and Aorai . . . I'd swap the bleeding lot for one cramped seat on that taxiing jet.

For taxiing it was.

As we reached the terminal entrance, the roar of its mighty engines, prelude to take-off, caused us to pause and turn. There she went . . . cantering down the straight . . . now into full gallop . . . faster . . . faster . . . and lift off!

I heard Buzz gulp.

'Never mind, mate,' I said consolingly, 'they can't hang us . . . they use the guillotine in France.'

An authoritative hand fell upon my arm. 'Monsieur – inside, if you please . . .'

Disconsolately we marched through the hall, through Customs . . . and, stap me, if two Tahitian lovelies didn't come waltzing up to sling flower leis around our necks and wish us, 'Iaora! Welcome to Tahiti!'

'Thanks a million,' muttered Buzz, then turned to me. 'What's Polynesian for "get stuffed"?'

I still don't know whether Paul Martin meant it as a punishment or a favour.

For four excruciating hours we sweltered and sweated in a tiny, airless box-room at police headquarters, contemplating our fate and convincing ourselves that the very least we'd get was seven-to-ten on Devil's Island, manacled by the ankles and forced to break rocks under a pitiless tropical sun.

'You seen "Papillon"?' I asked Buzz.

'Shut up,' he said.

'Worth remembering – that escape trick with the bag of floating coconuts.'

'What are you, Tobin – a masochist or something?'

'Just preparing for the worst, Buzz, that's all. Hey, you don't think they'd punish us Polynesian-style, do you – like tying our legs to two bent palm trees and cutting the rope . . . ssqqqqiii-kkkk! – split us straight up the middle?'

At least I got him laughing.

The door opened then – and in came the French cop, looking stern as hell.

My heart sank. I could hear his voice before he spoke . . . 'You will be taken from here to a place of execution and severed at the neck until dead.'

He didn't say that.

What he said was, 'All right, you can go.'

Silence.

Stunned, disbelieving nothingness.

'Hm?' we muttered.

'I said you may go . . . leave . . . depart. The charge has been dropped.'

'Hm?'

He regarded us, each in turn, *very* sternly. 'Messieurs, you are now obliged to remain on this island for a further three days. During that time you will comport yourselves in exemplary manner. We will be keeping a very close eye on you. My advice to you is . . .' the merest hint of amusement softened the severity of his compressed lips. 'Oh . . . get out!'

We got.

Three more terrible days on this wretched island – by order of the police. I mean, how much luckier can a couple of guys get!

And we've got it all nicely worked out for the third day. *I* hire a car and Buzz borrows it – without my permission, see – then, just as we're about to take off, on come the police and . . . well, I'm sure you've got the picture.

Listen – if we *ever* get to Sydney and I ever take that job with the escort agency, I'll drop you a line and let you know how I got on . . . if you'll pardon the expression.

All right?

Got to fly now, my ravioli's getting cold.

Tarra.